WAGES OF CINN

Praise for INHERIT THE STARS:

"Debut novelist Peak goes old school in this slam-bang SF quest novel." *Publishers Weekly*
"This ultra-cool retro story combines the best of old-school sci-fi with modern-day storytelling, resulting in a book perfect for fans of fantastical SF." Barnes & Noble.com
"This is another old-fashioned space adventure, something we always need more of." io9

BOOKS BY TONY PEAK

Inherit the Stars (2015)
Prophet of Pathways (2017)
Signal (2018)

Wages of Cinn

Tony Peak

To all the phoenixes that rise from their ashes to fly again. To anyone who has ever failed, but dared to try again.

Acknowledgements

I'd like to thank my agent Ethan Ellenberg for not giving up on this novel—he helped it to finally find a home. Then there are my beta readers: Ian Welke, Scott Jessup, Josh Vogt, and Jason Lairamoore, each of whom provided the sort of constructive criticism that helped transform an extended brainstorm session into an actual story. I appreciate all of the helpful feedback the original short stories received from the Online Writing Workshop (A Heroine by Any Other Name, All Cinns Forgiven, Cydonian Cinns) and to Ian Welke and Meredith Morgenstern Lopez for their thoughts on Tomorrow's Pyre—this novel was built upon those works. Finally I'd like to thank my family, who understand that if I didn't write this stuff I would go (even more) insane.

CHAPTER 1

Roxie followed the black smoke around Pyramid Twelve in a crouched run, revolver held in both hands. With a throat raw from breathing the gritty, unfiltered air, she mouthed hoarse whispers.

"Please don't be dead. Don't be dead."

Someone screamed. She ran faster.

"Bloody hell, just hang on …"

Turning the corner, she stiffened.

An invisible force yanked the pilot from the smoking gravjet and flung him against Pyramid Twelve. The impact snapped his torso at an odd angle, and the corpse thudded into the red sand twenty meters away. So much for saving him. Unless she ate a tab right now, she'd not see the phantom in time to defend herself.

Roxie thumbed through her belt pouch. Only one tab left.

"Shite."

She hunkered down behind a grid generator and cocked her revolver.

Dust stirred as something moved behind the pyramid.

Windborne sand forced Roxie to tug her goggles back down while aiming her gun. Just what she needed. Almost blinded while trying to get a bead on her target.

She tapped her earbud, but no sound came. The phantom's presence had already shorted out her 'tronics, then. No way to call for help now. Gripping the gun in both hands, she crept from the generator to a dish array.

A gurgling noise made her halt.

One of the forms inside the gravjet stirred, moaned, and went limp.

Roxie glimpsed the man's scorched uniform, the melted flesh sliding off his skull. The stench of charbroiled meat and burnt plastic took her breath. The phantom had burned him quick. It had to be a Class B, one of the stronger types.

They'd been lurking around Cydonia in greater numbers. In the last week alone, eighteen fossil prospectors had been killed, plus two sentries. And now the personnel on that gravjet. At least she'd still get the creds if she shot the phantom.

But she should have saved them. She clenched her teeth and moved on.

Pacing alongside Pyramid Twelve, she scanned the area. Centuries of rust and dirt caked the colonial structure, standing a hundred meters tall. The rest of Cydonia was dotted with pyramids cordoned off for research.

She rolled her eyes. Stupid archaeologists, stirring up phantoms. All those excavation pits just made her job harder; keeping an eye out while not falling into one.

Phantoms often hid inside the ancient ruins. They were invisible to human eyes, showing up only in the electromagnetic spectrum, in ultraviolet. Their natural radiation ruined all 'tronics in the vicinity, leaving hunters few options with which to see them.

Roxie's left hand drifted toward her belt and stopped. She had only one tab left.

Best wait until the phantom got close.

If her partner Doggie Boy was doing what the he was supposed to be doing, she might have it cornered behind this pyramid. Roxie drew a thermo grenade from her duster. Last one she had, and it might not even work. But nothing else distracted those things except for technology—and living flesh.

"Here you go, love."

Roxie pulled the pin and tossed the grenade around the corner. Drawing her duster over her head, she crouched and counted to ten.

A dull thud vibrated the ground. Rusty flakes slid off the pyramid wall.

She counted to five then slowly approached the corner.

Fifty meters ahead, something tossed sand and tools against the pyramid. The grenade's explosion of infrared light had angered it. Dirty Cool claimed the grenades blinded the phantoms, but whatever. All she cared about was that it was headed for her comrade near Pyramid Thirteen.

She hoped Doggie Boy would be ready.

As Roxie headed between the two pyramids, the plain blurred with blown dust. Unless the things had learned to fly, the phantom had only one way to go: straight into the excavation pits. If she ate a Cinn tab, she'd see it. Then shooting it would be easy.

Her gloved fingers flexed over the belt pouch. Her mouth watered.

Not yet.

She crept through the narrow alley between Pyramids Twelve and Thirteen. Another muted thud sounded ahead on her left. A crackle rippled through the air.

Static electricity made her hair stand on end.

Roxie broke into a run.

Maybe Doggie Boy set off his own thermo grenade. The phantom might double back and—

A tool crate sailed toward her.

Roxie ducked and fell onto her stomach. The crate slammed into Pyramid Twelve. Drills, forcehammers, and laser picks toppled down the walls and struck the ground around her. She moved right before a forcehammer landed where she'd been lying.

The air popped with more electricity. Her skin tingled.

Roxie yanked out her last Cinn tab and crushed it between shaking gums. The phantom was almost on top of her, she had nowhere to run, and she was in no mood to die. Swishing the tab's remnants in her mouth, she willed the drug to work.

"I'm not coming yet, Mum. Not yet."

She sighted down the gun barrel. Ten rounds in the chamber, but shooting blind, she'd waste them all.

A sweet, spicy taste filled her mouth. Roxie's legs squirmed in anticipation. The Cinn was finally maturing, entering her bloodstream. She smiled as fear melded into excitement. Body prickling with eager desperation, she rose to her knees. Pushed the goggles back into her spiky black hair.

"Here I am, love."

With each second Roxie's pleasure grew, sucking in air through her nose, nibbling her lip, rubbing her inner thighs together.

As the drug took hold, the pyramids on either side of her glowed with a gray etherealness. Giant hieroglyphics shown through centuries of dirt, and lion-headed designs appeared on the bricks. The sky overhead turned from dull pink to a vibrant orange as her eyesight surrendered to the grandeur of the electromagnetic spectrum.

Laughing, she rushed back up the alley after the phantom. Around the corner she caught sight of a tall blue humanoid. Its glowing, transparent form drew wisps of smoke from whatever it touched.

Roxie swallowed thick saliva. A hot wetness spread in her crotch.

A gunshot echoed over the plain. She ran.

Turning another corner, she was out in the open again. She skidded to a halt in the red soil and blinked. While on Cinn, her eyes burned from all the colors her brain was unaccustomed to processing. Her skull throbbed with the effort, but the pain was a long caressing lick on her consciousness.

Twenty meters on her right, the phantom snatched up a hoverbike and started to throw it at a figure taking cover inside an excavation pit.

"Come get some!" she yelled.

As the phantom turned, it flung the hoverbike at her. Roxie fired. In her heightened eyesight, the EM bullet streaked through the air like a tiny supernova. It struck the phantom, which disintegrated into a cloud of azure debris. Wherever it dusted the ground, sand fused together. Pyramid Thirteen's wall blackened from the heat.

Snickering, Roxie didn't even duck as the hoverbike crunched into the ground nearby. One of the handlebars flew off and smacked into her left side. A flaming piece of metal scorched through her left glove. Both registers of pain spiked her endorphins, fired her adrenaline, and forced her to wail as an orgasm ripped through her body.

Cinn always made the pain delicious.

"Rox? You okay?"

The voice swam in her pleasure-soaked consciousness. She chuckled and stepped forward, but the ache in her left side forced her to her knees. A swelling heat grew behind her. Her hair stood on end. Cinn fueled her laughter as she turned.

"One behind me!"

Another shot fired. Something exploded in brilliant blue clouds meters away.

"That was too close." The voice laughed. "Bastard almost got you."

"Doggie Boy?" She blinked as her vision swayed. The pyramids still glowed.

"Who else is going to rescue you, Rox?"

A figure walked through the fading blue cloud, a revolver in each hand. Tinted shades and a jumpsuit covered in bounty patches blurred in and out of sight.

"Nobody but you."

Roxie grinned as a blue shape hovered behind Doggie Boy. His smile dropped a little. Maybe he spotted it in the reflection of her goggles as she lifted her gun and squeezed the trigger.

The round blew right past Doggie Boy's shoulder and struck the phantom woman in the head. Its leonine features dissipated into nothingness. Hot dampness trickled down Roxie's leg and she laughed again, though the pyramids glowed less. The sky gave way to a duller pink. The pain in her side and burned hand provided less pleasure and more of an irritable throbbing.

Doggie Boy stumbled into the pyramid wall and chuckled.

"Wow, good shot, Rox. Very good shot…"

Roxie leaned over and heaved up a steaming puddle. The Cinn was wearing off. Already she couldn't see the ancient designs underneath the pyramids' dirt, and none of her wounds felt good anymore. Dropping the gun, she fumbled on her belt for the detoxer. One little shot and the crash wouldn't be as bad.

"F…fuck, where is it?"

Groaning, Doggie Buy clutched his right shoulder. A large scorch mark covered it as he patted out burning fibers.

"You almost winged me. This mean I get sick pay?"

Brows furrowed, Roxie dug through her belt pouches as her wounds ached even more. Shivers tore across her body. Phobos appeared from behind a cloud, blinding her. The Martian landscape around Cydonia stopped shimmering as her senses returned to normal. She bit back a gasp as the pain in her side increased.

Doggie Boy raised his shades and shook dust from his brown ponytail.

"We barely bagged them. And they destroyed a lot of shit this time."

She tried to stand, then grunted and held her left side. He offered a hand but she glared up at him and shoved her gun into its holster.

"Just bloody wait, I brought it with me."

He rubbed his stubbled jaw.

"If you're using the detoxer after the Cinn has already worn off, you got it bad. Hell, I'm not preaching here. You want to keep hunting though, you need to stop taking them while off-duty."

Roxie finally snatched his hand and pulled herself up. Her left side throbbed again, but she stood straight and tried to glower at him. He grinned.

"You need something, Rox, you know where my apartment is. I mean, goddamn. I never thought you'd pick a little orange tablet over the Boy."

She looked away, then glanced at him and laughed.

"Fucking berk. Can't I ever stay mad at you for long?"

"Not if I want to keep my reputation." His grin melted as static popped from her earbud. He touched his own and stared over the plain.

"Trent, Doggie, this is Spotter Control," the voice said in her ear. "SATSCAN detects no more phantom activity at Cydonia."

She gazed over the horizon where smoke still drifted from the gravjet.

Those people would be alive if she'd have acted faster.

"Trent, you eliminated two Class B's. Doggie, you shot a Class C. Coming around Pyramid Eleven's courtyard for evac. Acknowledge."

"Okay, ac-know-ledge that." He glanced at the smoke, then her. "What?"

Roxie took a cig from his chest pocket.

"One Class C? Thought I showed you how to fire that thing, love."

He grabbed the cig back and lit it.

"Don't change the subject. I distracted that other one long enough for you to shoot it. You going to buy me a drink with all those creds you're about to get?"

Before he could take a second puff, she pulled the cig from his lips and shoved it through her own. Its metacaffeine smoke made her side throb less.

"Maybe." She smoked the cig down to a stub and flicked it away.

"Or maybe I'll buy you a new box of those."

"I thought you'd quit?"

Doggie Boy reached into his pocket for another, but the pack was empty.

"My last one? Thanks."

She laughed, but it was hoarse from where the Cinn had dehydrated her.

"Let's shove off before another prospector gravjet gets downed."

Together they walked the paths crisscrossing Cydonia. Centuries old, each had been excavated and cordoned off with electrical grids. At night the place glowed like a miniature city. Dozens of tool crates lay here and there, the work of their owners interrupted once again by phantoms. When she'd first come here, Roxie didn't believe the ghost stories. So many crazy rumors, she'd discovered, were lies.

The truth was far worse.

Doggie Boy dug half of a slim, stone disc from a belt pouch.

"Look at what I found back there. Found it after I bagged my phantom."

Roxie took it and ran a finger over the etched hieroglyphics. Sunlight caught the remains of a leonine visage on it. She'd seen such objects before, had even taken a few contracts to retrieve them from ancient ruins. Collectors, fossil prospectors—any who were interested in Mars's original colonists—paid good creds for them.

"You think it's as old as they say this place is? The first to live on this fucking rock, building all this weird shit. Maybe they were aliens? We come along hundreds of years later, and their ghosts haunt us."

"Then some of us bollocks up in society, get sentenced to this dustbowl, and have to shoot them for the UGPD. I'm missing the significance here."

Roxie grunted again, her side reminding her that the handlebar had smacked her but good. Dizziness made her vision swirl. She dug for the detoxer again.

As they neared Pyramid Eleven's courtyard, he tucked the disc into his pouch.

"You've never acted the same since that guard found you asleep outside Pyramid Eight three months ago. You know, when you'd claimed to have quit Cinn?"

Though his smile didn't mock her, his words gnawed on her guilt. Sure, she'd almost weaned herself from using the drug on downtime. Little good it had done her. As a criminal sentenced to ten years' service on Mars, she'd not been able to find legitimate work. Without Cinn, there was no way she could see the phantoms to shoot them—and thus earn her keep with the UGPD. If she ever planned on leaving Mars, either by buying out her sentence or surviving it, she needed Cinn.

She was only twenty-three. She could still have a future someday.

"You want to talk about it?" he asked.

Roxie gave him an annoyed look.

"You can't save every dumbass that crosses a phantom." He pointed at the smoke.

She kept walking, her steps buried in the sand. Just like she mentally buried the faces of those she could have saved.

A low hum filled the air. Soon a gravjet flew toward them from the southeast, the direction of New Paris. Hoverbikes and carry-alls glided back into the Cydonian complex. Roxie eyed them as they got closer. Fossil prospectors in brown fatigues, archaeologists, UG soldiers. Ever since the United Government had declared Mars subject to Earth law, a mad rush for land had sent an already beleaguered planet into turmoil.

She nudged Doggie Boy. "Maybe you should sell that disc to these blokes."

"*La Rèsistance* pays more. Or one of those New Jovian weirdos. You find a money termite, and this stuff will sell."

"For now. The UG will raze this place too, build a new city. Have to make room for all those buggers on the Caravans."

Doggie Boy winked at a woman prospector.

"Who cares? The UG will always need someone like us to clean up things. Shoot terrorist gunfighters. Kill ghosts. You know, all that bullshit that makes the feeds these days, gives the UG brass a hard-on."

The gravjet touched down, scattering dust. Roxie cinched her duster and tugged down the goggles. Feeling light-headed, she checked the g-ballasts on her wrists. Both still functioned, balancing her weight in Mars's lower gravity. Born and raised on Luna, she had dwelled under artificial Earth gravity for most of her life. Her first year on Mars had been filled with discomfort as her body adjusted to the weaker g.

That had been easy. Criminals didn't get just ten years of servitude. It wasn't until the gravjet hatch opened that she realized she'd been clasping her stomach.

She couldn't think about that right now. They'd not taken everything from her.

They walked onto the gravjet's ramp. Though Doggie Boy spouted cheerful banter at the prospectors, Roxie stomped inside and sat. The attendant ran a handheld scanner over her until it beeped twice. He shot her an irritated look.

She shrugged. "Those fuckers were close. My irradiation shots are up to date."

"Maybe I should scan you again," the attendant said. "Class B's leave a lot of ionized radioactive residue. Besides, can't have you contaminating the rest of us."

They had her records right there on the network. She and the other hunters always had to prove themselves. Never good enough for these UG assholes, fresh from the Caravans and full of attitude.

Propping her leg up, Roxie scratched at her right boot. Her fingers brushed the detoxer inside. Finally. She'd left her flat in a hurry, stuffing equipment wherever.

She popped off the cap, rolled up a glove, and stuck the needle into her wrist—right below her ConRec tattoo. Her tremors lessened. The dizziness faded.

The attendant stared with contempt. Roxie gave him the bird.

In the cockpit, the pilot shook his head. His voice came over her earbud.

"Come on, Doggie Dick, let's get this one logged and done."

Doggie Boy entered and sat opposite Roxie.

"Never disappoint the fans."

"Must be nice." Roxie jerked the glove back over the tattoo.

"Oh, I have plenty. But I'm your number one fan. Relax, we'll save the next group of dipshits that run into phantoms. You hear me?"

Roxie stared out the ramp hatch until it slid shut.

"I hear you."

He'd never asked what she'd done to get sentenced to Mars, nor she him.

It was best that way.

He dug a cig from his belt, feigned surprise, then tossed it to her. "Fooled you."

She laughed. "Wanker."

Chapter 2

The gravjet flew over the crop fields and ranches surrounding New Paris, the largest metropolis on Mars. It was a massive cylindrical structure flanked by native homes and spaceports. Hectares of solar power arrays encircled the sprawl in concentric rings. Kilometers of hovertram track snaked around the towering city, founded when the Tellurics tried to overwhelm the original colonists centuries ago.

Now the UG assumed that role, even though it'd crushed the Tellurics to 'free' Mars: hiring mercenaries to clear away phantoms, kill bots, and rebels as more settlers arrived from the Caravans.

Doggie Boy tapped his window and whistled.

"Looks like they're walling off the grain silos again."

"They must be expecting another food shortage," Roxie said.

"And there are more residential blocks to the north. Bet they relocated them like the last bunch of natives."

She sighed. "Either way, it means more sods for us to shoot."

He leaned back, smiled, and stretched.

"Job security, right?"

When she'd grown up on Luna, she'd only seen Earth from orbit: blue oceans, expansive continents swathed in brown and olive, but never the bright greens she'd seen in archival vids. Mum had claimed it was too polluted. Even then, millions had already boarded the Caravans, a large fleet making the trip from Earth to the Outer Systems around Jupiter, Saturn, and Neptune. Mars was in the middle, the only planet to be successfully terraformed, the only one to grow plants in its soil.

The world everyone wanted to live on now.

Roxie adjusted the cold press pack the attendant had strapped over her left side. The gel on her bandaged left hand burned, but at least she didn't feel like throwing up now. The view outside still churned her stomach enough, and not from fear of flying.

More starships than usual clogged New Paris's spaceports. All those rich people waking from Caravan stasis and coming here. They didn't know what life was like here.

And the more that came, the more phantoms the UGPD had to deal with.

The gravjet veered to port, making its final approach. The city's thousands of windows lit up the plain, reflecting the sunset. Level upon level, each wealthier than the previous one, until the richest lived at the top. The bottom levels, Roxie knew all too well, housed the homeless, the poor, and indentured servants.

Doggie Boy grinned down at the city.

"She's beautiful. Though not as gorgeous as you, Street Angel. You ready for this bullshit?"

"You know I hate that fucking name. Besides, what can those buggers say? We finished the mission."

He gave her a knowing look. The UGPD had wanted them to kill the phantoms before Cydonia's power grid had been disabled. That meant they wouldn't get a bonus.

After the gravjet landed, Roxie and Doggie Boy entered the UGPD dock on Level 18. The wind slapped against her duster and tossed his ponytail until the door hissed shut behind them. They waited until the scanner terminal beeped three times and her ConRec tattoo pulsed. Serving as badge and identification, the tattoo's nanites contained all of her records. Coded with her DNA, she could be tracked anywhere on Mars.

Roxie gasped with relief as she deactivated the g-ballasts on her wrists and ankles. Now back under false gravity, she could relax. The things always made her joints ache.

"Yay, I sound like a real man now," Doggie Boy said, his voice a little deeper in the city's heavier atmosphere. Roxie snorted and smiled.

They entered a white-tiled lobby lined with med stations and gurneys for wounded hunters. An anti-septic stench wrinkled Roxie's nose. A paramedic wheelcd a body bag away while an officer trashed the dead hunter's belongings. One hunter, burned by a phantom, screamed and kicked on a gurney until medics tranquilized him.

"Always a jolly homecoming," she said.

The next corridor branched off into offices, arsenals, gravjet docks, and other facilities. Hunters came and went, criminals from across Colonized Space like her. Day or night, there was always a hunt going down.

"What's with the smell?" Doggie Boy asked a passing hunter.

"Moloch brought a dingo back from a contract near Ophir Chasma," the hunter said. "Little shit kept puking in our gravity."

"Where's the poor thing now?" Roxie asked.

"You know how Harmon is." The hunter moved on.

She bristled. Ever since Governor Harmon started running the UGPD directly, native life was even more expendable. The animal hadn't asked to be brought here.

Like her.

UG soldiers in blue uniforms patrolled the next area, though few fights erupted between hunters—only the crazy ones risked adding years to their sentences. They passed a service bot washing graffiti off the wall outside a restroom.

"*Souvenir…?*" Doggie Boy squinted at the smeared text.

"*Souvenir de la Bastille,*" Roxie said. "More of that *La Rèsistance* twaddle."

"These locals are getting braver, writing shit like that right under the UGPD's nose," a passing soldier said. "You assholes need to do your job and kill them."

"Yes, sir!" Doggie Boy gave the soldier a mock salute, but the man kept walking.

Roxie shook her head.

"Next they'll be painting Fleurant's picture in the loos again. Stupid sods want us to shoot them, it seems."

Doggie Boy cocked an eyebrow.

"I need a drink first. Heading to the *Salon*?"

"Where else?"

Roxie cut across the wide corridor to *Fantôme Salon*, the most exclusive hunter bar in New Paris. Probably the whole Solar System, since the phantoms only appeared on Mars. Windows fifteen meters high took up the western wall, offering a panoramic view of Lunae Plain's irrigated farmland. Farther out west, the triple peaks of the Tharsis Mountains jutted from the landscape like overgrown warts.

Hunters sat at tables drinking, eating, and above all boasting about their exploits. A few made out with male or female Mannequins, android prostitutes as beautiful as an Astro Bunny centerfold. Several sat alone, nursing a drink while studying everyone else.

Large vidscreens showed current events: the power outage at Cydonia, a riot in Icaria to the south. Offworld, the New Jovian Covenant was protesting the Caravans' encroachment into the Outer Systems, while another screen displayed updates on Titan's murdered governor. A ship bearing Daedala, ambassador of the New Jovian Covenant, was due to arrive at New Paris the next morning. Few of the gathered hunters paid these any mind. Most eyed the obituary vids or gauged the current bounty rankings.

As Roxie walked in, all eyes flicked her way. Most expressions weren't cordial.

"Well, if it ain't Street Angel herself. Come on in honey, you sure look tired."

The voice made her turn to where Legs sat alone near the windows. The sunset gleamed off his red lipstick, painted nails, and tight plasti skirt. A long blonde wig framed a rugged face that needed a shave. He ogled her while puffing on a cig.

Doggie Boy elbowed her. "Go on, get some. I'm after a few cans of Drown."

She removed her duster and laid it over a chair opposite Legs.

"What's the deal, love? Every bloke in here just gave me the fucking stink eye."

A muscular, swarthy man rose from a nearby table.

"Wouldn't give you any shit if you hadn't left so much work for the rest of us."

Roxie eyed Dirty Cool and unzipped her synthskin shirt. The material kept dust and cold out, but it was like wearing a full-body condom.

"How's that? We took out all three phantoms."

Dirty Cool tugged at the red bandana around his neck.

"Bunch of necrostructs showed up afterwards. Now the UGPD has selected some of us to return and clear them off. With no extra pay."

Necrostructs were one of the various kill bots the Tellurics had placed all over Mars centuries ago. The bots were attracted to the phantoms' electromagnetic signature, and were programmed to destroy them, but now the things attacked anyone.

"Not my fault that hunting phantoms brings kill bots like flies to buffalo shite." Roxie motioned at a server. "Lunar whiskey on the rocks, with a pomi-berry chaser."

"You're slipping," Dirty Cool said in a low voice. "The Roxie I knew, she would have taken all three down herself, with Cydonia's power still up and running."

Roxie indicated the bounty ranking screen.

"I'm still ranked number three."

Legs pushed a chair out for Roxie with a fishnet-clad leg.

"Which means you get a discount. We need a lil' rush every now and then, right?"

Dirty Cool leaned closer to Roxie.

"Right now you're the number one dumbass. I saw that graze burn on Doggie's shoulder, and I smell detoxer stink on you. There's a lot of dead people out there. You and Doggie Dick need to get your shit together."

Roxie stared back, though he towered at least twenty centimeters over her and was built like a boosted wrestler who'd grown up in a high-G weight room.

"Or what?"

"I mean it. You're upping the risks for all of us."

Dirty Cool tugged on a black synthskin mask, then collected a quad shotgun at the *Salon*'s door. Ranked number two, he was one of the most experienced hunters—and he didn't use Cinn to find phantoms.

He'd never threatened her before, either.

"Sit down sweetie, let that asshole go," Legs said. "Delivery guaranteed, like I told you before you left."

Roxie sat as the server brought her whiskey and chaser. "I told you …"

"Told me what? Street Angel, you're climbing out of that hole you put yourself in a few months back. I got whatcha need to get back on top."

Legs drew a small packet from his bra: plasti-wrapped orange tabs.

Cinnamon was its street name. Though highly illegal, the UGPD looked the other way while its hunters utilized the drug to see their targets.

She downed the whiskey and chased it with the juice. The alcohol burned a sweet torrent all the way down her throat, and the tart juice scoured any nerves remaining along her esophagus. She eyed the shot glass, painted with the UGPD's blue skull and crossed pistols. Just like her ConRec tattoo.

"I just got back."

"If you plan on ever going back, you'll need this. Thirty percent discount. I know you ain't eating enough. Still in that apartment on Level Seven?"

Legs slid the packet across the table while studying the vidscreens. The reflections played over his painted visage. He was ranked fourth, right below her. He'd taken her under his wing when she first arrived. Taught her all of his hunting tricks.

Introduced her to Cinn.

She slid back a cred voucher and tried to flex her left hand. The skin still burned.

"What do you care?"

"We do what we gotta do," Legs murmured, still gazing at the screens. Ashes fell off his cig, smoldering on the tabletop. "Ain't nobody on this world gives a damn about people like us. We play their lil' games and survive. That's how we stay high in the rankings, honey. That's why we ain't the phantoms out there."

She shoved the tabs into her pouch.

"They keep changing the rules."

"Like you did on *Jubilee*?"

Roxie twitched, knocking over the empty shot glass.

Legs set the glass upright and met her eyes.

"Those terrorists are dead, even if it made you a convict. You ain't a real criminal like the rest of us. You made your own rules then, sugar. Make 'em now."

"You still haven't told me why you got sentenced to Mars," she said.

"One day, Street Angel. One day."

Legs got up and left, high-heels clacking on the floor.

Twirling the empty shot glass on her trigger finger, Roxie wished Legs hadn't mentioned her past. He'd helped her survive, saved her in gunfights. Now he just hung around to sell her tomorrow's fix.

But she needed it tonight.

Doggie Boy slammed a can of the offworld beer before Roxie.

"Who needs a round of Drown?"

"Me!"

With her face painted white like a Geisha, Amai Shi was one of the newer hunters. Dressed in tight synthskin, she wore a stockless SMG slung over her back, along with an assortment of blades at her belt. Short, slight, with the face of an Astro Bunny, she was a former rival-turned friend.

"Come here, you." Roxie grinned up at her. "You've got man stink all over you."

"Always mix business and pleasure. Next time you're coming with me, *tenshi*."

It'd taken Roxie a month to learn that Amai Shi's little name for her meant 'angel.' Dirty Cool's mocking nickname for her had stuck, even among friends.

Doggie Boy broke the can's seal and slurped from it.

"Hey, I saw Dirty Cool over here. Bitching as usual? He's just pissed because he always has to go out and clean up."

"He does hate necrostructs," Roxie said.

Amai Shi tossed her straight black hair and gulped from her own can.

"Dirty Cool can eat my *manjuu*; you kicked ass today. Go on, drink up!"

Roxie opened her can and took a long swig. The sweet, gritty drink made her throat even rawer, its thick sugariness difficult to swallow. She belched, drank again, then laughed as Doggie Boy shook a second can and opened it, spraying her and Amai Shi.

"Ha, eat my cherry, then!"

Amai Shi flicked a red olive at Doggie Boy, who caught it in his mouth. Roxie guffawed as he tried to steal her Drown, eager to douse the olive's fiery taste. After a few laughs, they settled down and studied the vidscreens.

Using a magknife, Amai Shi sliced her empty can into the shape of a smiley face.

"So why'd you two take so long? You finally get some Doggie Dick, Roxie?"

Roxie grinned and took another drink.

"Not without you, love. The phantoms were all over the sodding place. Doggie here almost busted his big fat knackers trying to get ahead so we could corner one."

"It was probably *La Rèsistance,* summoning more with an emitter again."

She swiped Roxie's empty can in half and balanced it on the tip of her blade.

Doggie Boy rolled his eyes. "Holy shit, not that again."

"They've done it before," Roxie said.

"For the right reasons. You should know, after that shit at Amazonis Town."

Roxie shuddered. "Maybe."

Amai Shi nudged Doggie Boy.

"You must be drunk already. Always barking crazy shit like a *kusobaba.*"

He winked at her. "I might come barking at your door later."

Amai Shi cocked her head to one side and grinned. "Doggie style?"

Roxie chuckled.

"Rule number one, you twats: never shag another hunter."

They all laughed, drank more Drown, and talked louder than everyone else. Other hunters eyed them with jealous indifference. For a few blissful minutes, Roxie felt as carefree as her friends. Until she spotted one of the vidscreens.

It showed another riot in the Amazonis Basin, site of Mars's richest farmland. Years ago, before Roxie had gotten hooked on Cinn, she'd helped the UG clear out squatters from the Basin. Corporations always drove natives off arable territory, then built commercial farms on them. She had befriended a few rebels during the operation, helping them save some of the natives.

She'd refused to escort the children, though. It'd been too hard, too soon.

A million years was too bloody soon.

"Wake up!"

Amai Shi flicked a metacaffeine popper at Roxie as she danced with a Mannequin. Raising a can of Drown in each hand, Doggie Boy posed near the plaque of Moloch at the bar, the only hunter to stay with the UGPD after his sentence was up.

Roxie's hand neared the Cinn packet in her pocket, then she retracted it. She couldn't let them see how much she needed it right now.

Though Doggie Boy and Amai Shi bought another round, Roxie didn't open her can. She kept staring at the vids. Mars was a battlefield now, like those ancient ones on Earth. There were even gang wars on the Caravans.

Mum forbid her to venture away from Luna, but Roxie had wanted to be a pilot. Wanted so many things. Maybe that's what

Legs had been looking at while staring into space; things he'd never have. Just a fucking Cinn tab.

Roxie rose and laid her duster over her left arm. The contact with her bandaged hand made her wince.

"I'll see you both later."

Amai Shi smirked. "Not so fast."

As she stabbed at Roxie's unopened Drown can, Roxie snatched it off the table, thumbed the tab back, and sprayed beer all over Amai Shi in one motion. Doggie Boy scooted back, eyes wide, then laughed along with Amai Shi. Even a few other hunters whooped in appreciation of Roxie's skill.

"Small wonder you bungled the Cydonian operation if you're that slow."

She turned and frowned at Styra, who walked across the *Salon*. Everyone stopped and watched. One guy even turned down the vid-screen volume.

"I wanted to make sure you could see it, love. Any faster and those boosted eyes of yours would have missed it."

"I have been ranked number one for six years. Don't even."

Though Styra was as tall as Dirty Cool and almost as muscular, her short blonde hair and grey eyes were her last claims to humanity. Her limbs whirred with internal motors, and the left side of her face was molded into a chrome skull. It had been blasted away years ago in a firefight. Covered in armor, she never boozed, never laughed.

"You still here?" Roxie asked.

"Over thirty necrostructs have been detected near Cydonia," Styra said. "More than has ever come that close to the pyramids."

Roxie forced down a yawn. She'd only gotten two hours of sleep before the previous mission.

"And?"

Styra stepped closer. "Some say you used an emitter to draw the phantoms. Pieces of one were found, along with crushed artifacts. Theft is a serious crime."

"We're all criminals here. Even you."

"Things will change soon," Styra said. "Fucking count on it."

Roxie glanced at the bounty vidscreen and grinned.

"Well, I'll be buggered, you're right. You're on the list to take out those necrostructs. Happy hunting, love."

Styra's chrome jaw clenched, then she turned and left.

"The hell?" Amai Shi asked. "Were you going to draw on her?"

Only then did Roxie realize her right hand rested above her holstered revolver. She loosed a shaking breath and swallowed hard. Maybe Dirty Cool was right—she was losing her edge, if Styra could get her worked up that easily.

Doggie Boy grabbed Roxie's half-empty can from the table.

"Styra's just fucking jealous, like the rest. They're getting old."

"So old that she has to upgrade her asshole just to fart." Amai Shi laughed and sipped from Doggie Boy's can.

Roxie ran a hand through her hair. "I'm sodding off. Need some sleep."

Amai Shi stiffened her finger and licked it.

"You need some cock, *tenshi*. Lighten up, will you? You used to tell me that when I first came here."

"I can't spare the creds—"

"Yeah, whatever. Just like last time. If you need us, give a call. Somebody has to keep an eye on you."

"Thanks, love." Roxie smiled at them and left.

Once outside the *Salon*, she found the elevator and keyed in her access code. Several hunters went with her, getting off after a few levels, but the elevator kept taking her down.

All the way down to Level 7, as Legs had reminded her.

Each level she passed, Roxie glimpsed clean hallways, locked doors, and patrolled balustrades she wasn't allowed to enter. The further down she went, the worse the smell was, the more the paint peeled. By the time the doors slid open to Level 7, she kept a hand near her gun, eyes darting to every corner and shadow.

The Drown had given her a buzz, but not enough to deaden the throb in her left side. Few hunters lived so low in New Paris since the UGPD paid well. Free to live anywhere below Level 12, hunters were restricted from leaving New Paris on their own. Yet they could spend creds on all the ass, booze, dope, and gambling they wanted. Doggie Boy and Amai Shi loved the lifestyle. Roxie had, too. Before it got this bad.

She walked through aisles packed with ranch hands, farmers, and maintenance workers. The stench of burnt metal, sweat, and piss stung her nose. Flashing signs and holographic ads urged her to join the UG military, drink Drown Ultra, or eat the new Ares beef sirloin while riding the hovertram to Valles Marineris.

"Get your hands off me!" a female voice cried out from an alley on her left.

A fierce shiver traveled up Roxie's spine. As sounds of a scuffle and several male chuckles came from the alley, she strode up to it.

Two miners held down a Martian woman, her coveralls ripped open. Another miner licked his lips while gouging his fingers into her breasts.

"Looks like we got us a nice one this time," one miner said.

The woman's Neo-French accent was marred by her busted lip.

"Please … please don't hurt me …"

"Leave her alone," Roxie said.

The men turned. The woman stared wide-eyed, quivering in their grasp.

"Get the fuck outta here, or you're next," a miner said.

Roxie removed her glove and showed her ConRec tattoo.

The miners' leers turned into frowns.

"You got no contract down here, bitch," another miner said. "Go hunt ghosts."

She rested a hand on her holstered gun. Maintained her unflinching stare.

If she killed these men, she'd be thrown into the brig and have her sentence lengthened. No more hunts, no more Cinn.

She kept staring at them.

"Fuck it. Ain't worth it, anyway."

The miner nudged his friends, who dropped the woman and hurried out the other end of the alley. They kept throwing hateful looks over their shoulder, but Roxie remained still until they were all gone.

As the woman stood, clutching her ruined coveralls, Roxie offered a hand.

"You okay, love?"

Face scrunched up with hate, the woman spat in Roxie's face.

"The Flame take you offworlders! You're the reason this happened!" She fled.

Roxie flung the spittle away and stared at the alley wall. An old Caravans poster showed a starship descending from the sky while smiling families waited below. The figures were tall, Earth-types. Not Martians.

Leaving the alley, she hurried through the crowds, duster collar pulled up, goggles down. She kept wanting to wipe her face but walked faster instead.

Finally at her apartment door, Roxie kept an eye out as she keyed in the code. Two men fondled a Mannequin across the aisle, her plasti skin reflecting their leers. A gang cornered a farmer and robbed him. A UG magistrate passed without even looking.

Roxie wasn't accepted by them, even though she lived down here. She wasn't anyone's Street Angel.

Once her door slid aside, Roxie backed in and made sure the lock slid into place. As soon as the door shut, she drew her gun and scoped out the apartment before allowing herself to relax. She swiped her computer off as a late payment message blinked on it.

"Oh, bollocks."

So much for her rankings. Down here, she was nothing.

Roxie tossed her duster onto the stained, sunken couch and unbuckled her gunbelt. It weighed down her good hand, and her left stung when she used it to unfasten the last button. The gun hit the floor.

"Damn it."

She snatched the revolver back up. She used to take better care of her guns. Girl's best friend out here. Her only friend.

A Draco EMB-47, the gun was standard issue for UGPD hunters. The cylinder held ten .48 caliber rounds. This one was her best piece; two more lay under her bed, in need of repair. The phantoms shorted out the UG's newer, 'tronic guns, and frack rounds didn't even stun them. The Draco's EM rounds spread a radioactive burst, destroying a phantom's energy field. An old weapon for an old war.

Bit by bit she removed her boots, pouches, and the g-ballasts from her wrists and ankles. They needed recharging or she'd be puking on her next mission. She took one look at the shower, sniffed her pits, and grimaced. Water was expensive, but if she didn't bathe now, they'd have to send her to Necro Row just to burn off the stink.

Inside the shower, Roxie pushed the chemical dispenser. Gritty delouser squirted her. Lukewarm water tinkled over her body. She lathered up her face first, eager to scour off all trace of the woman's spit.

They hated people like her. Coming to Mars, killing their heroes and freedom fighters. Killing the ghosts of their ancestors. Roxie kept scrubbing but she still felt dirty.

The hair on her legs had lengthened, her armpits were a shaggy jungle, but she at least skimmed off her pubic growth with a razor. Never know, maybe she would shag Doggie Boy anyway. He was handsome enough. Stupid, but handsome.

She glanced at the unmade cot where her dildo lay under the mattress. She left the shower, grabbed the knobby-ended member, and stepped back under the water.

Roxie stood there, the cold sex toy in her hands. Trembling, she tried to fantasize—about Doggie Boy, anyone—but nothing happened. No warmth spread down her loins, no tingles of excitement.

Slamming off the water lever, she glared at the dildo. It'd never been so difficult before. She was young, she loved a good shag. Roxie thought about the last guy she'd invited over, how he'd smelled, how hard she'd rode him…

Breathing heavy, her gaze darted over the apartment until it fell on the Cinn packet she'd bought from Legs. Yes, there it was. That would make this plastic cock do something. Make her squeal and squirm. Only with Cinn.

"Fuck," she mumbled in a thick voice.

Her wringing grasp activated the dildo's internal vibrator by accident. Startled, she flung the pulsating member. It shattered on the wall.

Covering her face with both hands, Roxie slumped against the shower wall.

Doggie Boy was right. She did use too much.

Not even drying off, she tugged on an old shirt and got into bed. Old food crumbs in the sheets and a sticky beer stain clung to her damp skin. She clasped the Cinn packet and rolled onto her right side as the left one throbbed again. Nestled both hands, still holding the Cinn between her legs. Shivering in the cold apartment, nothing could keep her warm but those orange tabs. Nothing.

She hated it.

For a while she watched a few piloting feeds on her vidscreen. One more year, and she'd have gotten her license. If not for those terrorists…

Quaking on the bed, Roxie shut her eyes as she recalled pulling the trigger on *Jubilee*. They'd ran right at her, she'd no other choice, she wished they had listened—

She sucked too much air down her throat, then coughed and sat up. The computer terminal blinked with new messages. She started to roll over but noticed the clock.

She'd slept five hours. Leaning from the cot, she thumbed the terminal button.

"For fuck's sake," she mumbled in a hoarse voice, then coughed again.

A New Jovian ship had crashed on Syrtis Plain—the other side of Mars. The one carrying Daedala, the ambassador from the news vid. At last report, many phantoms had surrounded the crash site.

They wanted her to go.

Chapter 3

"Thought you were cleaning up my fuckups from yesterday?" Roxie asked Dirty Cool as they boarded the gravjet ramp. Early morning dew, tainted gray from overworked atmospheric cyclers, glistened on the dock.

Dirty Cool laid his shotgun over his shoulder. "Styra, Wallaby, and me took them out. Nothing beats a load of concussives."

"You're my hero."

Roxie flicked a spent cig over the dock's edge. Darkness still hugged the horizon, and the night shift farmhands were just now coming back on the hovertrams far below.

He barred her entrance into the gravjet.

"You bring enough EM rounds in that silly duster? Don't make me regret this."

Roxie gave him a flat stare. "Regret what?"

"I asked the UGPD to include you on this mission." He entered the gravjet.

She wasn't sure whether to laugh or curse. So he admitted that she had the skills. No use in gloating over it. It'd taken a fair share of her bounty pay from yesterday to buy enough EM rounds, plus a layered armor vest. If the Covenant's ambassador was in danger, and the military couldn't handle it, that meant a lot of phantoms were out there.

As Roxie boarded the gravjet, she glanced over the other passengers. Doggie Boy and Amai Shi sat on one side, with Legs, Dirty Cool, and three others she wasn't familiar with. Legs lifted his pinky and waggled it at her. Doggie Boy patted his lap and smiled.

"Yeah, right."

She sat beside Doggie Boy instead and sniffed his musky *Viril Poussée* cologne, an expensive brand. He never saved his earnings.

"Get enough sleep?"

"Sleep can kiss my ass." Doggie Boy popped open a metacaffeine stick and squeezed the gel into his mouth. "Just makes me groggy this early, anyway."

Amai Shi smacked a clip into her SMG.

"They've called out all hunters of Grade 3 and above. Time to earn a promotion."

Dirty Cool grunted. "Or a body bag."

Doggie Boy snickered.

"You're so cheap, they'll bury you in plasti wrap."

"What are you saving up for?" Roxie nudged Dirty Cool's boot with her own.

Dirty Cool simply adjusted the red bandana around his neck, staring out the hatch.

The craft lifted from the dock. Legs chuckled to himself while oiling his double-barreled Draco. The other hunters said nothing but their eyes shifted here and there. More than a few times they stared at Roxie.

"Get a good look," she said. "This is what Mars does to you."

After a few minutes Roxie relaxed as she listened to the engines, felt the craft ascending beneath her feet. Gravjets were among the first things she'd learned to fly at the United Government Naval Academy. She could almost feel the manuals in her hands.

The ride was a bumpy one, with turbulence tossing her against Doggie Boy every few seconds. Their pilot maintained constant communication with other UGPD gravjets. Roxie guessed there were four others. With at least eight hunters to each craft, that meant over thirty bounty hunters were heading to Syrtis Plain. They'd be so close together, they would be shooting each other.

"I heard your old gang made the news vids again, sugar," Legs said to Amai Shi. "Another Caravan starship quarantined?"

Amai Shi ran a waterstone along her magblade. "The Geishas protect people. The UG only closes off a vessel when they plan to exterminate passengers."

Legs snapped the dual cylinder into his modified Draco.

"You'd sure know all 'bout that, wouldn't you?"

"So the fuck what? I killed that other gang to save my family. It was honorable *nawabari-arasoi.*"

Amai Shi shoved the waterstone into her belt pouch. In the process, her shirt sleeve drew back, revealing her Ronin tattoos. Only Geisha who'd sworn loyalty to a powerful gangster had them. The images of swords and dragons shimmered.

Roxie rubbed her left hand. Numb from painkillers, it wouldn't do her much service in the coming action. She'd lied to the medic who asked the usual health questions before each mission.

"Why you bringing that up, Legs?"

Legs sighted down the Draco's twin barrels.

"The UGPD has brought out all the best, along with the rookies. It gets hot out there, I wanna know who's covering my ass."

Amai Shi slammed her magblade into its sheath.

"Oh, don't worry, *dameman.* 'cause I won't be."

"Come on, you two," Roxie said. "At least pretend we're on the same team."

Doggie Boy elbowed her. "Shh. It's getting good."

"I know you can shoot," Legs said. "While you're on Cinn, though—"

"I'm awesome. 'cause I have a future. One day I'm leaving this bloody marble. I doubt you ever will." Amai Shi laid a bag of powered amphetaline on her knee.

Legs shook his head.

"That's gonna get you off Mars? Please."

Amai Shi whipped out her magknife. "Listen, asshole—"

"Shut up." Dirty Cool nodded at the cockpit. "Messages coming in."

Roxie leaned forward and caught a few snippets from the radio speakers. The pilot and attendant turned pale. As she listened her heart beat quicker. Legs stopped smirking. Even Doggie's Boy's smile waned.

"HQ, we have visual of the ambassador's ship, *Phaethon*," a voice said over the speaker. "Hull is intact, but we have two confirmed casualties outside. We have no contact with Daedala or her staff. Phantom Alert Level is Red."

Everyone fidgeted or frowned. Red was the worst alert level.

"Well, have a cig, Rox." Doggie Boy drew one from his chest pocket. "My cred account's about to get pregnant. Let's celebrate!"

Dirty Cool tugged down his mask, then tied a knot in his bandana.

"If we don't find the ambassador alive, no one gets a single goddamn cred."

"You're such a buzz kill." Doggie Boy lit the cig, puffed, then passed it to Roxie. "Besides, with this many of the best, how can we lose? They might as well dump creds on me like a baby with rust diarrhea."

Roxie took a draw and handed the cig back.

"Since when have phantoms attacked a starship? I mean, how the bloody hell did they bring *Phaethon* down?"

Dirty Cool thumbed a few EM shells into his shotgun.

"Mars is a magnet for trouble. Always has been."

"But you, Rox, you're a magnet for crotch heat." Doggie Boy sucked his cig all the way down and flicked the butt at her. "Bombs away!"

She flicked it back at him before it landed. They shared a grin.

"Hunters, equip your earbuds," the attendant said as the gravjet descended from cloud cover. "Place your thumb on the scanner for final contract agreement. The UGPD is not liable for any—"

"Get stuffed, we've heard it all before."

Roxie removed her glove, mashed her thumb on the scanner bot as it rolled by, then put the glove back on.

The other hunters followed suit. One even kissed his Telluric crucifix before doing so, while another whispered a prayer afterward. Mum had given her old crucifix to Roxie when she'd left Luna to train in the UG fleet. Just likes her previous one, the other hunter's crucifix featured a nude woman crucified to a Luna T-antenna. The old story went that Mother Mary had been executed for sending her son into space to save all who braved the cosmic darkness. Roxie stopped believing that long ago. Seeing a crucifix, though, still made her shudder.

Mum had wanted grandchildren so bad. Roxie had never told her the truth about her conviction, or her sentence to Mars. Even when Mum died three years ago, she still believed Roxie was a pilot—and married. She'd had to pay that cute guy in New Paris to take a picture with her for Mum's holo feed.

The gravjet touched down, jolting Roxie from her thoughts. She pressed her harness's quick release, shoved her goggles down, and drew her gun. Dirty Cool was the first out, quad shotgun aimed at everything. Next went Doggie Boy, revolver in each hand, followed by Legs, Amai Shi, and the rest.

Roxie exited last, the wind pelting her with tiny basalt pebbles.

With a clang, the ramp shut and the gravjet lifted away.

"Fuck." Doggie Boy whistled. "Rub my feet when we're done here, Rox?"

"I'm sure Dirty Cool will."

She studied Syrtis Plain's basalt horrorscape. As far as the eye could see, the area was nothing but blackened dirt, being the caldera of an inactive volcano. None had settled the harsh region, even though the volcano was declared dead by scientists. But everything looked dead out here.

As she walked around, sharp basalt scraped her boots. One hunter stumbled and scratched his knee on a jagged outcropping.

"You blokes need someone to hold your hand?" Roxie called. "Pay attention."

"Screw this." Amai Shi coughed and donned a filter mask. Her flesh-bonded Geisha makeup wasn't marred by the contact.

Roxie slipped on her own mask and took a deep, filtered breath. It tasted like ass, but at least she didn't cough. Doggie Boy put his on, but Legs and Dirty Cool eschewed theirs and continued across the plain. Everyone wobbled on the loose surface. Roxie thought about deactivating her g-ballasts so she would lighten a little.

Amai Shi caught her studying the ballast and snorted.

"Give it up, *tenshi*. Your ass is too big to float."

"And too little for you to shoot." Roxie grinned.

When they'd been rivals, Amai Shi had almost gunned Roxie down so she could bag a phantom. Like most new hunters, she'd been frightened and desperate to prove herself. Now Roxie trusted her, and Doggie Boy, more than she'd ever trusted anyone.

"My parents were on that quarantined Caravan ship," Amai Shi said. "Even though I'm here…I'd kill all those *sujimon* assholes again."

"That why you joined the Geishas?" Roxie asked. "How you got that tattoo?"

A hardness entered Amai Shi's voice. "Life on the Caravans isn't what everyone thinks. We're not all rich, we're not all in stasis. But we all want to live."

Roxie trailed her friend a short distance from the others until Amai Shi continued. "My *katana* saved my family, my face paint frightened the other gangs. They were eating people on that goddamn ship, *tenshi*. Just to survive while waiting to get a home here."

"No wonder the UG is quaranti—fuck, I'm sorry love."

"It's okay." Amai Shi squeezed Roxie's arm. "I know my parents are dead now. But I still have a future. That's why my father urged me to kill the other *sujimon*—he knew it was the only way I'd make it to Mars. As a *hanzai-sha*: a criminal."

They walked in silence. Roxie checked her bullets, then tapped her earbud. Anything to occupy her besides her friend's pain.

"So what comes after?" Roxie finally asked.

Amai Shi smirked. "Once I'm off this rock, I'm going to make it big in the vids. I've already had contract offers, if I can buy out my sentence within two years."

Legs snickered as he walked past them.

"Two years? Not gonna happen for you, honey. You blow creds faster than a Mannequin blows—"

"Sod off, Legs," Roxie said. "I don't see you leaving Mars."

"I like it here," Legs said. "Ain't nobody can tell us what—"

"Look sharp, assholes," Dirty Cool called. "Trent, Shi? Stay with the group."

Amai Shi opened the amphetaline bag, pushed her mask back, and sniffed the powder in one go. Only addicts could handle so much at once. With all that synthetic adrenaline in her system, the girl would think she could fly.

Syrtis Plain went on forever in each direction, a shithole of tumulus and basalt jaggies just waiting to shear through Roxie's boots. Streaks of dust hundreds of meters long stretched from the lips of craters, pushed there by constant winds.

"I don't get it," Roxie said. "No cyclers for dozens of kilometers, no towns, not even a bloody Sykes Corp strip mine."

"Honey, whatcha getting at?" Legs asked.

"Phantoms usually prowl inhabited areas. Places they can bollocks up, right? There's nothing out here. No reason for phantoms to appear, take out a Jovian cruiser, and then wait around. It took us a flipping hour to fly out here."

"Two seconds to die out here, so shut up." Dirty Cool tapped his earbud. "Okay nanny wagon, tell us how it is."

"Dirty, this is Spotter Control," the pilot's voice came through Roxie's earbud. "Sensors show eight Class C phantoms a kilometer northeast of your position. *Phaethon* lies half a kilometer east."

"Nice of those shitheads to set us down that far away," Amai Shi said.

"Wait," Spotter Control said. "Possibly several Class Cs and Bs south of you."

"Possibly? Fuck me." Doggie Boy kicked a basalt chunk from his path.

"Distance?" Roxie asked, touching her earbud.

Doggie Boy was right to be concerned. Unless used in the presence of strong electromagnetic radiation, SATSCAN detected a weak Class C bogey to its exact coordinates. Something was wrong.

"Less than half a kilometer, but we're getting interference," Spotter Control said.

"Let's move."

Dirty Cool jogged over the land, not looking back. Roxie followed close behind and the rest trailed after. Amai Shi soon passed her, not even winded, though her limbs shook. Doggie Boy caught up to Roxie and grinned.

"Dirty Cool's manliness is so fucking awesome," Doggie Boy muttered. "Remind me again why the UGPD lumped us with this jack-off?"

"You've teamed up with Dirty Cool before." Roxie jumped over a tiny crater, then ran around a large one. "You should be used to him."

"One never gets accustomed to having the shits," he said.

Amai Shi overtook them all. Dirty Cool called after her, but she continued until they lost her in a field of tree-like basalt protrusions and craters.

"Dammit, Shi!" Doggie Boy stumbled atop a basalt formation pushed up into slag by a meteor. His voice echoed in the crater below.

Roxie caught his arm. "What if we go around, maybe we can catch her?"

"Stick together!" Dirty Cool ran to their position.

Legs neared the crater's edge.

"To hell with her. We gotta get the job done, not make names for ourselves."

Roxie tapped Dirty Cool's arm. "You asked for us, love. Deal with it."

He faced her, those merciless dark eyes centered on the hunt as always. She'd never met a more dedicated killer, more determined mercenary.

"No. I asked for you."

Before she replied, Dirty Cool hurried around the crater. "Nanny wagon? Talk."

"You are nearing the crash site," the voice in her earbud said. "We're still tracking the phantoms. Numbers have not changed."

They rushed over the plain, their footsteps creating a commotion of snapped basalt and pebbles sliding into craters. Sweat dappled Roxie's forehead. She grew hot in the synthskin and duster. After a few minutes, a dark shape spread into the sky.

Roxie jerked her goggles up and glimpsed smoke rising in the distance.

"We're running blind. Those bloody phantoms could be all around us."

"Eat a tab then, sugar," Legs said.

"Ha! Time to rake in the creds. So long, fearless leader."

Doggie Boy saluted Dirty Cool, then ran on ahead.

"You stupid berk!" Roxie called. "Wait!"

"Let him go," Dirty Cool said. "We're gonna rescue that undusted Jovian, not line our pockets."

"I've got contact!" a voice cried over her earbud. "Sighted one at—"

Static popped over the connection.

"Copy that, Spotter Control?" Roxie asked, nearing another crater.

In the distance, a metallic hull reflected the rising sun in pink-orange fury.

"We lost contact with Wallaby," Spotter Control replied. "All hunters report in."

A collection of voices answered, but Roxie remained silent, intent on the wreck of *Phaethon*. Skimming over the basalt, she reached a stretch of sand leaks around shallow craters. The sand cushioned her steps and allowed for greater speed.

She didn't have time to answer Spotter Control or wait for what Dirty Cool would do. Her friends were out there. Eager for creds, hurrying to get ranked, maybe even wanting suicide—the reason didn't matter. Dirty Cool had nicknamed her Street Angel because she cared too much about others at the expense of her own welfare. So be it.

Her earbud crackled and she tapped it. Nothing. She slid down the flexible datapad from her belt. It was dead.

No 'tronics meant the phantoms were less than thirty meters away.

A rattling noise reverberated across Syrtis Plain. Roxie squinted at the horizon. Little bumps spread along her flesh. A suctioning noise in the mask made her realize she was breathing too fast.

The rattling rose in volume. Something blurred over *Phaethon*'s hull, then blew across the sand and basalt void around her.

"Rust wind!"

She yanked the full face mask from her duster and shoved it over her head. The cyclers, while making Mars breathable, had never tamed the planet's dust storms. She had seen them cover entire towns. The blown particles could shred skin.

Other sounds reached her ears as the wind whipped at her body. Pops, cracks. Wails. Roxie turned as a squad of UG soldiers fled from the east. Their dark blue armor was scorched. Melted flesh hung from one man's face while another clutched his smoking, handless arm. One fired her frack rifle, but the hail of slugs hit nothing.

As the rust wind thrashed the landscape ahead, Roxie yanked a Cinn tab from her pouch and ate it. Gun cocked and raised, she tried to circumvent the deadly gale. The thought of getting pummeled by rust wind while on a Cinn high made her lick her lips.

No, she had to focus.

The woman flew past Roxie and crunched into a basalt pillar, her armor smoking.

A sweetness filled Roxie's mouth, tickling her body. The sunrise went from dull orange to vivid pink in her eyesight. A phantom coalesced in her vision, a tall woman in a corrugated jumpsuit, supposedly an ancient colonist.

Roxie smiled and aimed.

A fierce blast resounded over the plain. The phantom exploded into cerulean nothingness. Roxie lowered her gun as Dirty Cool hurried toward her, cocking his shotgun. Further back, Legs fired at a phantom man. Another hunter yelled as blue arms ripped his legs off.

Laughing, Roxie blasted a phantom who leapt at Dirty Cool from behind a pillar. The gun's humming report filled her ears. The phantom's dissipation made him duck.

"I got you covered, love!"

She faced another phantom as the rust wind slammed into her back. Millions of tiny stones, dust particles, and iron chips struck her, borne on a squall long feared by colonists since terraforming began.

Roxie stumbled through the storm. Though the mask and goggles protected her, she shielded her face with one hand. She aimed at an azure glow and fired twice.

The rust wind screamed over the land. Buffeting her, blowing sand pits into giant clouds. She turned this way and that, aiming the gun, stumbling on basalt, sinking to her knees in a sand drift, then escaping and repeating the whole process. She giggled. Nothing mattered when she felt like this. No Mary of Sol to judge her, no Mum to lie to, and no guilt over the *Jubilee* passengers she'd killed.

Nothing but her and Cinn.

Roxie reached for another tab, willing to risk removing her mask to eat it in the metal flake storm, but her face collided with an unforgiving surface. She coughed as blood flowed from her busted nose into her filter mask, then she tripped over a thick form and smacked into the hard surface again.

Fumbling around, she realized she'd tripped over a dead body. Its face was burned off. The insignia on the tunic was unmistakable despite the storm: a large sphere with a red eye, surrounded by four smaller spheres.

It was a Jovian. Which meant the object she'd blooded herself on was *Phaethon*.

Laughing, Roxie spread her arms and let the rust wind pound her while Cinn could still make it feel like paradise.

CHAPTER 4

Roxie sucked down another breath as she braced herself against *Phaethon*'s hull. Minutes had passed since the Cinn had worn off, she'd lost the detoxer, and there wasn't any sign of her friends over the desolate plain.

"Doggie Boy?" Her dry throat made her cough. "Shi?"

Though the rust wind had passed, her duster hung in tatters. The armored vest remained serviceable, but the lacing guards on her boots were gone, and one lens in her goggles was cracked. Her synthskin pants was covered in tiny flecks and pebbles; unable to penetrate, but sticking to her like glue. She tossed the mask, filter, and goggles. All were useless now.

Holding the gun in her right hand, Roxie pecked the hull with her left.

"Anyone there?"

No one answered.

Roxie walked further along the hull until she reached a cargo hold that had been blasted open. Charred bodies lay in a crooked, smoldering heap. Brain matter still sizzled inside a split skull like eggs on a skillet. The ashy cruor stink stole her breath.

Whether from Cinn crash or the stench, she retched up grit-filled globs. "Fuck…"

Faint noises made her stop.

Gunfire ripped over the plain. An explosion, followed by a vibration. Possibly a thermo grenade. Voices, then more shots. Roxie tapped her earbud and scanned the skies.

"Spotter Control?"

Nothing but corpulent gray clouds. Sunshine stabbed through them at odd intervals, casting Syrtis into black gold veneer one moment, forlorn cragged wasteland the next.

"Hey you, nanny wagon." She tapped the earbud again, sighed, and peered through the damaged hull.

Something moved between dim bulkheads and smoking wires.

Roxie wormed past burning consoles until she reached a corridor. Bodies lay everywhere in various scorched states. Jovians, UG soldiers.

A soldier, half his face a blackened ruin, still moved. Both eyes had liquefied and dried on his cheeks. A blistered tongue waggled from a lipless maw.

Roxie drew her magknife and ended his suffering.

While she'd been out there soaking her underwear on Cinn, phantoms had killed these people. She was so stupid.

A murmur made Roxie stiffen. She followed it deeper into *Phaethon*.

Outside the bridge, a tawny woman in a white jumpsuit knelt beside more corpses. Reddish-blonde hair hung over her shoulders. She touched a dead body.

"From nova to dust, from oceans of void to oceans of thought, may you travel as dust again," the woman said in a lyrical Jovian accent.

Roxie's boot crunched over a piece of burned hull.

The woman jerked back. "Are you from the UG?"

"I'm here to keep the phantoms busy while the UG picks up any survivors. Are you it?"

"The rest are …" the woman glanced at the bodies.

"And the ambassador, Daedala? Bugger it all, have you—"

"I am the ambassador."

"Jolly good, then." Roxie reloaded her gun. "The rest bought it?"

"Excuse me?" Daedala rose, her brow creased.

"Are they dead, like this lot here?"

Roxie snapped the full cylinder back into place and touched the Cinn packet in her pocket. The rust wind hadn't taken the tabs.

Daedala took a loop from her pants pocket and tied her hair back.

"I am the lone survivor of *Phaethon*. And you are …?"

"Roxie Trent. Bounty hunter, United Government Paranormal Division."

"So you are one of those who murder the spirits."

"Whatever, love. We need to leave this cozy little shite bin and contact Spotter Control for evac."

Roxie exited the gutted vessel. Gunfire still echoed over the plain, along with a different sound. A clank, a whine.

She cocked the gun. "Come on, no fannying about."

As Daedala gingerly left the wreckage and tried to brush sand off her shoes, Roxie scanned the horizon. A basalt pillar here, a crater lip there, more sand streams … with deep footprints in them.

A whirring noise reached her ear, then a whoosh. A rumble traveled on the air.

"Move!"

She yanked Daedala by the arm and ran around *Phaethon*'s hull. The engine cores lay exposed, their massive black cones radiating so much heat Roxie had to squint and run faster. As they reached the other side of the vessel, she shoved Daedala to the ground and fired. The bullet blew an arm off the necrostruct.

The skeletal bot trudged toward her and raised its other arm: little more than a pylon fitted with a coilgun. Firing EM sabot rounds, a necrostruct could bring down a Class A phantom or an armored hovercar. Its face was a leathered monstrosity of gaping jaws and sunken eye sockets. Nanites held the thing together, same as when the Tellurics seeded the entire planet with them centuries ago to fight the phantoms.

"What is it?" Daedala rose to her elbows.

Roxie, not wanting to waste EM rounds, switched her gun to standard bullets. Before the necrostruct's coilgun recharged, she blasted its head apart.

After pulling Daedala to her feet, Roxie ran from *Phaethon*. A hissing blast rebounded through the air, making Roxie run faster.

Daedala grunted as the plain's sharp rocks shredded her white shoes.

"On my back!"

Roxie squatted as a second necrostruct walked up from a crater straight ahead. Its coilgun focused on her. She popped two rounds at its head, but it turned. The bullets only tore away its ancient face, exposing the rusted exoskeleton beneath.

The coilgun hummed louder.

"Get on my back, damn you!"

Roxie fired again, this time crumpling the necrostruct's metal cranium as the coilgun loosed its payload. Though astray, the shot still plowed through basalt on her left, pelting her with superheated nuggets. They sizzled through her synthskin, burning her left arm. She cried out. The ground beside her hardened into glass crystals.

"Let me help you." Daedala offered a hand.

"I'm here to save you, now move your ass!"

Daedala looped her arms around Roxie's shoulders and Roxie stood, then staggered and caught her breath. The pain in her left side pounded her body, and her burnt arm demanded something cool to sooth the irritated nerves.

"Hang on," she said while reloading. In her peripheral vision two more skeletal figures plodded closer. The burns hurt so much, her eyesight blurred with tears.

"Those things," Daedala whispered. "What are they?"

Roxie hauled her past a steep impact crater. "On any other day, my meal ticket."

Something heavy stomped behind them. More gunfire in the distance, maybe from the south. Roxie huffed and grunted, both arms under Daedala's thighs as she ran the best she could. Only a few meters later her ankle twisted into a crevice and they toppled into a sand stream. While Daedala rolled off her, Roxie drew her gun and shot a necrostruct straight thorough its black mechanical eye. Two more followed. One fired, the round dashing aside a basalt pillar in a cloud of onyx shrapnel. Roxie ducked into the sand, heart thumping against her chest.

"They're still coming!" Daedala cried.

Roxie tried to shoot, but ducked again as a coil round scorched past her.

She raised her head in time to see Amai Shi swipe a necrostruct's head off with her magblade. The sparkling cranium rolled away while Amai Shi laughed. The other necrostruct came close, but she enfiladed it with several SMG bursts until it blew apart.

"Oh fuck, mmm yeah," Amai Shi muttered, wild eyes darting everywhere. Looking for another target to kill so she could get off again.

Relief turned to loathing as Roxie studied her friend. The eager gaze, the face drawn into a sickly grin—she realized this is what she must look like while on Cinn.

"Can we—?"

Roxie clamped a hand over Daedala's mouth. In that state Amai Shi would shoot or stab anything that moved. She'd hunted with her, taught her a few tricks, but Amai Shi had never given in to Cinn this much. Legs was right: she wasn't dependable anymore.

Voices rose from *Phaethon*'s direction and Amai Shi headed that way. After counting to ten, Roxie dragged Daedala to another crater.

"Spotter Control?" Roxie tapped her earbud.

"The spirits shorted out all of our onboard systems. We are lost out here."

"Hey, you hear me up there? This is Trent." She wiggled the earbud in her ear.

Daedala lifted a handful of sand and allowed it to sift between her fingers.

"Perhaps it is time we return from whence we came."

"Sure thing, love. To New Paris." Roxie glanced back over the lip and shivered.

Over a dozen more necrostructs ambled across Syrtis Plain.

"Spotter Control!" She wanted to yank the earbud out and toss it, but she froze as Daedala regarded her quizzically.

"What is it?" Daedala asked. "Are they coming?"

"Must be another phantom nearby. That's what's drawing these fuckers."

Roxie dug out the Cinn packet and pried an orange tab loose. Daedala scowled.

"You would sully the sacrament? So you use our sacred chemicals to grant you the sight of the cosmos, only to use it for destruction?"

"You only talk in questions?"

Eating the tab, Roxie tried to keep the gun steady. Cinn trickled into her system as she stood, warming her body.

"Trent, you copy? Damn it, Trent, somebody down there, acknowledge!"

The earbud voice made her grin as Cinn's joy engorged her. "Give it to me."

"Trent, we can evac you in a zone two hundred meters to the northwest. You must get there now, because we have phantom signals all over the pace, plus kill bot encroachment. Copy?"

"Copy." Roxie blew apart a necrostruct with one EM shot. The rounds were expensive, but watching the bot scatter everywhere … she creamed herself.

"What's happening?" Daedala asked.

"Back from whence we came!" Roxie fired twice, one shot missing, the other clipping a necrostruct's coilgun—then she fled. Her boots scraped over basalt and she tumbled over a crater. Alive with Cinn, she used the momentum to propel herself forward. The burns along her arm throbbed with delicious agony.

Shimmering mirages filled her eyesight as the plain gleamed with yellow-spackled sunlight. The sky yawned above her as the clouds cleared, and a low whooshing sound made her run faster.

A voice shouted in her ear. Concussive blasts shook the ground behind her. Another whoosh and an angry shooting star flew over her head. A red-haired Mannequin ran alongside her, yelling something about spirits.

The yelling changed in pitch until it sounded like children screaming. Roxie aimed this way and that, the landscape a kaleidoscope of nightmare colors bleeding into her brain. Amid the warbling hues came two small shapes, running at her. Crying.

"Don't make me shoot you," Roxie murmured, her gun shaking.

Why wasn't Cinn making this feel good?

The shapes charged her. Two small boys, eyes filled with terror. Their bodies strapped with explosives.

"Don't make me fucking shoot you!" she yelled.

She blinked. The boys were gone, replaced by a phantom.

A blue energy wave roared up against her. Roxie dodged, landing on her bruised side. Laughing until she wept, she rolled over and fired twice. One shot went wide, but the second split apart a beautiful angel of azure death that clawed after her even as it disintegrated. The Mannequin beside her screamed and beat Roxie's back, but she stood just as a second blue wave hovered above her.

It waited, sporting leonine features and flowing robes. The gun wavered in Roxie's hand, the round hot and ready to pierce the ghost, pierce all this death, pierce the emptiness deep within her heart. She orgasmed again but the joy hurt her face, pressed the air from her lugs. The phantom came closer. Its steps dissolved sand and melted basalt back into magma waste. It was a primordial god come to take her away from all this, away from the ghosts of *Jubilee*, back to Mum on Luna, where she could dream a better reality than this one.

Her finger numbed on the trigger.

"Give it to me…"

The cerulean form faded. Roxie stared out over a plain filled with limping, lifeless killers bent on an ancient genocide. The Mannequin looked like Daedala again as Cinn waned in Roxie's consciousness.

"Roxie!" Daedala tapped her shoulder again. "The gravjet is here!"

One of the necrostructs lifted its coilgun. It was so close she glimpsed a reflection in its black glassy eyes.

A blue flame surrounded her, then vanished.

"No!"

Roxie blasted the necrostruct apart, then fired at each shape until the cylinder spun empty. Only when the gun clicked did she realize a light shone behind her and voices shouted her name.

"Get on the fucking gravjet!" someone yelled.

She turned and fled up the ramp with Daedala. The pilot lifted off before the hatch finished closing. A coilgun round blew it off. Sparks and shrapnel flew into the cabin, searing the attendant's face. A sliver of metal blew into the cockpit, puncturing the pilot's neck. Blood splashed the canopy.

The aircraft careened to port. Roxie leapt into the cockpit and grabbed the manuals. While the pilot convulsed and bled on her, she righted the gravjet's flight path. The pilot's neck wound spurted, painting the instruments crimson until Roxie unbuckled and shoved him from the cockpit.

"What are you doing, we'll die in here!" Daedala shouted.

Roxie settled into the messy seat and smudged steaming plasma from the instruments. Taking deep breaths, she flew the gravjet as if she'd done it yesterday. For a moment, the sunlight peeking through the blood-stained canopy reminded her of the stars she'd seen aboard *Jubilee*'s bridge.

The gravjet lost altitude.

Shuddering, Roxie forced herself to sit straight. With deliberate movements she increased thrust and gently pulled the manuals back. The aircraft climbed.

"May your blessed energy return to us," Daedala said to a burning bulkhead, then sprayed it with an extinguisher. The attendant screamed and writhed on the floor.

As the gravjet gained altitude, Roxie spotted more necrostructs just beyond the crater, as well as *Phaethon*'s burning hull. With Cinn departing her body, Roxie jerked with spasms. Her gut churned with hunger, then nausea. Her left hand hurt so bad she clutched it against her chest. The burns along her arm blazed into her nerves without mercy. Cold sweat ran down her face.

"Get him under control!" Roxie shouted back at Daedala as the agonized attendant thrashed, kicking her chair.

Daedala pressed sparkling crystals to his face. Calming, he gasped long and hard.

"He will sleep for a time." Daedala searched for a restraint while air blew over them through the missing hatch. "Why didn't you do it?"

Fumbling with the buckles, Roxie finally slammed one end into the quick release and lay her head back against the seat.

"Do what?"

Daedala buckled herself to a hook restraint on the ceiling, which allowed her to reach the cockpit.

"You did not destroy that lion spirit. You screamed at it. That you didn't want to shoot it."

"I…fuck, I don't want to talk right now."

She manipulated the manuals one-handed, knowing she might never get another chance to do this.

"Killing it would have earned you how much? A thousand creds? Perhaps triple that if it was a powerful spirit?"

"What do you bloody well care?"

"That's why I came here," Daedala said. "With your help, others might care, too."

Roxie laughed, then grunted as her left side throbbed again. "Spare me the platitudes. You're just another piece of crumpet trying to sell something."

"Except that what I offer is free." Daedala opened a med kit and aimed a syringe at Roxie's left arm.

"Are you daft?" Roxie asked. "You medicate me, I can't fly this thing!"

Daedala produced a damp sponge and wiped Roxie's face. "You are badly injured. Let me—"

"Those bloody phantoms almost did you in," Roxie said in a loud voice as more air flooded the cabin. "People like me, we save lives."

"People like you serve only one purpose," Daedala said. "You end lives."

They stared at each other until a flurry of voices crackled from the cockpit speakers. Roxie made out Dirty Cool's voice, a scream, some horrid feedback, then a UG military officer saying his unit was withdrawing due to heavy losses.

"Spotter Control, acknowledge," another pilot said. "Evac available on your coordinates now, Dirty Cool."

Roxie jerked up in her seat and tapped her mic.

"Hear anything from Doggie Boy, or Amai Shi?"

"Not all have reported in yet." The other pilot's voice became harder to hear as the rush of air flapped her restraints. Daedala watched her from the cabin, hair blowing.

Roxie wondered if her friends had survived. She'd never heard of so many phantoms and necrostructs appearing in the same location before. Especially a dead place like Syrtis Plain. How *Phaethon* had been grounded…she sighed. She needed food, sleep, something to drink. At least this time no one could accuse of her ruining the mission.

Even the UG military had been unable to rescue Daedala.

Maybe her cred account would finally get out of the negative. Back then, when hunters like Aparajita had been her rival, or when she'd gunned down Allard Salvaire, she'd never hurt for money.

Back then, though…she'd never cared.

Roxie wiped her nose. Right now she just hurt all over. But it'd be worth it to see the looks on everyone's faces when she landed this heap at New Paris.

Worth every bruise and scratch.

Chapter 5

The news vid cut to yet another scene of anxious mobs crowding the Jovian embassy inside New Paris. The screen provided the only light in Roxie's apartment as she got dressed.

A bonus. That's all the UGPD had given her. She had single-handedly saved Daedala, commandeered a gravjet after the pilot's death, delivered them to New Paris in once piece…

A goddamn bonus.

Moloch had once saved an empty hovertram from a terrorist bombing, and the UG had lessened his sentence by a full year.

And she had rescued one of the key leaders in the Solar System.

Roxie slid into her synthskin pants, though upon sealing the waistband, she had to inhale. She was due for her cycle again. What a cruel torment, considering her sterility. All that blood pouring from her, cramps, bloating—and she would never give birth.

She yanked her boots on. One didn't slip on fast enough, so she kicked the wall until her foot fit into the boot. A muffled shout came from the other side of the wall.

"Fuck off!" She leaned against the sink and covered her eyes with a shaking hand.

Every criminal sent to Mars was sterilized. A reminder that the future didn't belong to them anymore. The UG had removed her ovarian tubes, preventing pregnancy.

Each monthly jam rag mocked her.

She glared at herself in the mirror. Like she deserved to have children of her own.

Though she still saw those faces in her nightmares, Roxie had never seen the dead children during a hunt before, with Cinn in her system. Was she going looney? Was Dirty Cool right about her? She glowered at the mirror, willing the memories to remain buried.

They slid into her mind anyway, like razors through spider webs.

When the Titan Liberation Front hijacked the cruise starship *Jubilee*, she'd been head of security—and the only officer to survive their initial attack. She'd raced against time, trying to save passengers before the TLF tortured and murdered them. After Roxie had killed the terrorists one by one, a handful made a last stand on the bridge.

Breathing through clenched teeth, Roxie sunk to her knees before the sink as she recalled waiting in the corridor, pistol at the ready. She still smelled burnt metal as her torch bot cut through the bridge hatch. Still felt the sweat sliding down her neck, the bruises where she'd fought and killed a terrorist in the previous corridor.

She'd never forget those five faces when the hatch finally opened. Two girls and three boys, with explosives strapped to their waists. Frightened, they'd ran straight for Roxie, a familiar face. Just one blast would have destroyed the entire ship, and the hundreds of passengers still alive.

How well-trained she'd been. Gunning the children down. Racing into the bridge and butchering the last three terrorists. All of it caught on video, replayed at her trial.

Lying underneath the sink, Roxie wished she could at least cry. She couldn't recall the last time she'd wept for anything…or anyone.

Her gaze flicked to the Cinn packet beside the cot, and she rose in a huff.

A bonus. She'd preferred a lesser sentence.

Roxie's eyes settled on the packet again. Just one tab, it'd make her feel better…

The news feed changed, catching Roxie's attention. Crowds of Martians tried to get a peek at Daedala as she exited a hovercar and walked into the embassy. Floating camera bots captured every frame of desperation, anger, and hope in their faces. Resplendent in flowing white robes, Daedala waved, her smile perfect ivory. Martians waved back and sang ghost rhymes, popular among those who chafed under UG rule.

Roxie snorted and opened her small fridge. The message bar indicated that most of her food had spoiled. She pulled out the last bottle of Lunar whiskey. It was empty.

"Sod it all, then."

She kneed the fridge shut and wrapped her torso in a thermal brace. Its nanites bonded with her flesh, compressing her bruises to speed healing. Next she applied lotion to her left arm. Though the burns weren't bad, they'd scar for life.

A message beeped over the vidscreen and Doggie Boy's face appeared. "Hey Rox! Shit, you better not be asleep. We're waiting for you at the *Salon*. Remember, you owe me a foot massage. Plus you're buying the drinks!" The message ended.

Groaning, she donned a gray t-shirt, black leather jacket, and dark shades. No use dressing up just to get a drink, but she was glad Doggie Boy and Amai Shi were okay. As she neared the door, she switched off the terminal and grabbed her gunbelt. Strapping it on, she grunted as her bloated abdomen seemed to swell.

Her boots struck something just outside the apartment: a snuffed candle, smoke still rising from the wick. A circle of blood-smeared shell casings lay around it.

Hand on her revolver, Roxie scanned the narrow aisle, the connecting corridors.

All empty. Not even a beggar was present.

While she'd slept after returning from Syrtis, someone had left a calling card. Only a member of *La Rèsistance* left such a warning. A snuffed candle meant her life would soon be extinguished. Bloody shell casings meant she would be killed by a gun.

She ambled through Level 7, nearing the dispenser mart. None of the machines worked, having been gutted and pillaged long ago. A beggar lay in one, while a Mannequin dry-humped a prospective client's leg in another. Two Psycoids walked by carrying packages;

their eyes looked like milky pools. The reanimated servants always made her shiver.

A UG magistrate ogled her until Roxie showed her ConRec tattoo. The UGPD blue and silver skull glittered under her skin. The magistrate spat and moved on.

A figure in a red Mardi Gras mask and brown coat paced nearby.

Roxie strolled into a public latrine and took shallow breaths. Rank urine pools lay here and there, along with soiled panties and cig stubs. A cracked sink mirror still played decade-old music feeds, the artists' faces visible beside one's reflection.

Graffiti marked every stall door and wall with the usual phrases: 'Souvenir de la Bastille', 'Liberté Dans le Cul', and 'Révolte Mort Rouge', plus the typical loo vulgarities. One stall shook as two people moaned from within. A horrid stench wafted from one where a man chuckled inside. The last stall contained the body of a teenage boy, his throat slit. It was a slow day for Level 7.

Roxie pretended to examine herself in the mirror.

The masked figure in the brown coat entered the latrine.

She dug a lipstick paster from her jacket and pouted at her reflection.

The figure jiggled the first stall's door. "Fuck, you believe these janitors?"

The paster glided over Roxie's lips, coating them deep red.

Something gleamed in the mirror.

Ducking, Roxie turned and pressed the paster's button as a bullet whizzed past her cheek. It shattered the mirror. Her paster's shot smacked into an old man's neck. Red splattered the stall he'd been laughing in.

A man and woman burst from the other stall, guns raised.

The masked figure reached into his coat.

Roxie drew and fired three times. The man and woman both dropped, faces blown apart. The masked one stumbled into a stall. Clutching his neck, the old man tried to fire, but Roxie squeezed the trigger. The round pierced the man's heart and slammed him back onto a choad-stained seat.

Racing into the next stall, Roxie crammed her boot onto the masked figure's chest where a bullet hole smoked. The man cried out. She nudged the mask off with her boot. His tanned cheeks gave him away as a native. Hatred filled his eyes.

"Nobody takes my mickey in the loo," she said. "*La Rèsistance* want me dead?"

"We'll dance in your ashes, UG bitch."

The man drew a pistol, but Roxie blew his hand off at the wrist with an EM round. He shrieked as blood spurted from his stump.

"Why? You another cunt loyal to Salvaire's memory?" Roxie glanced at the exit.

No sign of a magistrate yet. She had maybe a minute, tops.

"You fucked her over," the man said. "The one who comes to burn us all."

Roxie frowned. "Daedala? That Jovian tart?"

"You're not good enough!"

The man grabbed at Roxie as a thin blade extended from his other wrist. An implanted magneedle. Like she'd never seen that before

Roxie fired. His head slammed against the toilet. Brains slid down the wall.

La Rèsistance assassins were sworn to succeed or die trying. If she hadn't killed them all, this lot would have followed her.

After digging in the dead man's coat, Roxie found a cig and lit it. The ruined mirror continued playing a slurred version of the same song. She puffed three times, tossed the butt into the toilet, and kicked the flusher.

Roxie hated the jam rag.

Swaggering, Roxie entered the *Fantôme Salon*. Confidence must be advertised, whether she felt it or not. The thermal brace eased her bruised left side, but she still needed a drink. *La Rèsistance* hadn't

gunned after her for a year, and they had a lot more friends in New Paris than she did.

She paused just inside the *Salon*'s doors. Conversation died. All the hunters and UGPD officials stared at her.

"There she is!" Doggie Boy raised a can of Drown Ultra to her.

A few hunters raised their glasses, a couple flipped her off, though all regarded her with new respect. Legs winked at her. Dirty Cool studied her over his glass of water, too cheap to buy a real drink. Even Styra watched her with detached interest.

Every vidscreen showed her exiting the gravjet with Daedala earlier that morning. The news vids displayed her profile, the style of duster she wore, even the type of holster she used. So much attention after killing four people was a jarring contrast. For a moment she experienced vertigo, the vidscreens all around her, displaying her face.

She really needed that drink.

"You're owning the feeds, *tenshi*." Amai Shi walked over to her. "I can't even piss without the mirrors replaying your return from Syrtis Plain."

Roxie forced a grin and nudged Amai Shi's arm. "Glad you made it. And you too, Doggie Dick."

She snatched a red olive from the bar and flung it at him. He caught it in his mouth and chewed.

"Where you been, Street Angel?" Legs sat an empty wine glass on the bar. "Been sending messages to your datapad. You spending those creds already?"

Roxie started to reply, then frowned as Legs tapped the little black packet between his cleavage. The vidscreens kept displaying her face after landing the gravjet at the dock: pale from the Cinn crash. Her throat became parched and the room heated up. She tugged off her jacket and tossed it onto a nearby table.

"You racked up nice," Doggie Boy said. "You should buy us a drink. Or three."

"Listen, I've no clue what's going down," Roxie said. "They gave me a pity-shag bonus. What's the big deal?"

"You did what the UG jarheads couldn't." Doggie Boy beckoned the bartender for a refill. "Lots of pretty UG boys and girls are lying dead out at Syrtis. Wallaby, Miss Corruption, The Captain—all killed, and three other hunters wounded. No Jovian survivors, save for that chocolate goddess you rescued. Think you can set me up with her? You know how big my dick is."

"But I don't know how it tastes, love. So I'm special now?" Roxie ordered Lunar whiskey on the rocks, no chaser. She made herself not glance at Legs or his packet.

"Daedala mentioned you to the vidpress." Amai Shi sat on a bar-stool beside her. "Roxie Trent, famed *barikeedo* and bounty hunter, saves the holiest piece of ass in the Solar System. You do her?"

"I got first dibs!" Doggie Boy pinched Amai Shi's rump, but with the flick of a wrist she drew her magblade and slapped his ass right back. They laughed.

"You over-sexed berks."

Roxie downed the shot and ordered another. It burned her guts, seared her throat. She breathed through her nose and tried ignoring the vidscreens plastered with her face.

Doggie Boy swiped away her next shot and downed it himself, then pointed at the hunter rankings screen.

"You really don't get it, do you? Look."

She was ranked number one.

The whoops and laughter of her friends faded as Roxie stared at her name beside that number. There was a time she would have celebrated such an achievement.

"Not bad." Styra shoved Doggie Boy aside. "For the UG's latest pistol bitch."

"Thought that was you." Roxie twirled the empty shot glass across her knuckles.

Styra scooted closer, her body stinking of oil and burnt plasti.

"I was. Once."

Everyone in the *Salon* watched with interest. Some whispered bets to each other. Dirty Cool slowly walked over, his face like unyielding iron. Legs puffed hard on a cig.

"Have a drink on me, then."

Roxie flicked the shot glass at her, but Styra caught and crushed it onto the bar, her metal fist denting the surface.

"A total fuckup like you doesn't deserve this attention," Styra said. "I never let Burners scorch an entire crop field in the Basin, or left a fellow hunter to phantoms like you did Aparajita. I never gunned down children just to kill terrorists on *Jubilee*."

The urge to draw and mow Styra down made Roxie grind her teeth. A fiery itch crawled down her shooting hand. But she was still tired, still healing. Worst of all, everyone watched with anticipation. Like all they expected from her was death.

Styra's hand waited above her holster. No one spoke or even puffed on a cig.

A voice spoke over the intercom. "Roxie Trent, your presence is required in Conference Room D, North Wing. Repeat, Roxie Trent, your..."

The intercom voice echoed in the room. Roxie didn't blink or move. Styra finally grunted and left the *Salon*.

Everyone loosed an audible breath. Dirty Cool shouldered his shotgun, glowered at Roxie, then walked away. Chuckling, Legs flicked his cig butt into another hunter's beer and sauntered off.

"Holy fucking shit," Doggie Boy said. "She backed down!"

Amai Shi sniffed a pinch of metacaffeine dust from the bar's popper bowl.

"You should have done it. You could have taken that *hamaguri*."

"Doesn't matter." Roxie slung her jacket over her shoulder. "I have to shove off."

As she exited the *Salon*, the vidscreens kept playing Daedala's comments:

"She rescued me from a threat that the United Government has tried to suppress with force. Roxie Trent did far more than her duty. She made me believe there is a chance we can have peace with the spirits of ancient Mars."

Roxie hurried to the nearest elevator before she puked.

❦ ❦ ❦

The North Wing bustled with a wave of blue uniforms discussing strategy over holo maps, interviewing phantom attack survivors, or filing a cost claim for yet another destroyed food processing center. A few people glanced at her with contemptuous respect. Only in the last two decades had the UG allowed bounty hunters to seek and destroy the phantoms. Before, the UGPD's officer branch had attempted it—with terrible results. With no 'tronics operating in a phantom's presence, and officers forbidden to partake narcotics, a unique workforce was created. One comprised of expendable off-world convicts who weren't afraid to kill.

As she strolled through the offices, virtual cubicles and holo screens hinted at the technology available on the Caravans. Roxie had grown up with some of it on Luna. Martian natives rarely caught a glimpse of it.

Judging from the symmetrical physiques around her, many officers were boosted. Cybernetic joints, nanite countermeasures in the blood, hormone-engorged muscles. Like having a crowd of Styras staring at her.

Her ConRec tattoo prickled.

A wall section slid aside. A holo attendant gestured for Roxie to enter. "You are expected, Roxie Trent. This way to Conference Room D."

After walking through, Roxie stilled herself as the wall slid back into place. Not wearing her G-ballasts, since New Paris enjoyed false gravity, Roxie floated a few centimeters off the floor. The lower gravity brought back memories: her academy training, the oaths she'd swore, the first time she'd stepped onto Mars…

No matter where Roxie went or what she did, she was never grounded in it. Just floating off somewhere else. Maybe Styra was right.

A wide window offered a grand view of the verdant Lunae Plain. Kilometer after kilometer of crop fields, pastures, fruit groves, and greenhouses testified to human ingenuity. Hydroponics stations rimmed a collection of solar domes. Hovertram tracks crossed the landscape like spider webs from a Telluric fairytale. Atmospheric cyclers, each over a hundred and fifty meters tall, pierced the horizon. Gravjet traffic sped to and fro in flourishes of rippled contrails.

"A wonderful view. One made possible by people like you, Trent."

She turned and tried limiting her disgust to a polite frown.

Lorne Harmon sat in a hoverchair, swiping his hands over a holoboard. Fingers passed over illusionary keys and buttons while the opposite wall acted as a vidscreen, displaying what he was working on: Roxie's datafile.

"You're welcome," she said.

Harmon glanced at her and raised his brows. He might be handsome if he didn't exude so much arrogance. Short blonde hair, cool blue eyes, a pressed UG uniform. The last time they'd met, he'd contracted her to find relics in Pyramid Eight. It had not been a successful mission, and she'd gotten no pay.

"You're making it possible for all those people on the Caravans to find a new home. Earth made Mars everything that it is."

"I've never seen a Caravan berk work a farm or build a cycler," Roxie said.

"It is our right to settle Mars," Harmon said. "I know about your rebel sympathies. But do you know how many colonists perished in preparing this planet for the rest of humanity?"

"You brought me here for a bloody lecture?"

Harmon's smile held less humor than Styra on a bad day.

"Two million colonists died to terraform Mars in the past three centuries. Six million, if you believe those Jovian revisionists. A small price to save Earth's billions. A price Earth has already paid with an even more ruined climate due to rapid shipbuilding."

Touching the window, Roxie studied kilometers of green fields outside.

"There's still not enough room on Mars. The gravity, the low-level radiation, the storms—"

"Exactly. The Second Earth movement is a failure. Before, the phantoms rarely appeared, much less attacked. Now the kill bots aren't enough, and they too have become a hazard. Yet people still keep coming here. We need another solution."

"You've been keeping the vidscreens busy with that shite," Roxie said.

Harmon swiped the holoboard and the vidscreen went dark. Orange sunlight filled the room as the window's tint filter lessened.

"We have both been busy. You are ranked number one on the Hunter Statistics Index. Impressive."

"And you were head of UG alien relics." Roxie pushed off the window, making herself float to him. "Now you're the Governor of Mars."

"We share a penchant for promotion. You look like you need it. I hear Cinn affects the sexual drive first. Then the appetite. Finally, the eyes."

"So what's your excuse, love?" She pushed her shades up.

"I am not interested in primitive mating displays." Harmon leered. "I do, however, like to fuck over my enemies."

"And your friends."

Harmon leaned over the arm of his chair.

"You've been fucked over since you came to Mars. Haven't you?"

Her trigger finger itched, but she gazed out the window. Tried to focus on one of the cyclers, those stupid gravjets. Anything to keep from punching him.

"You've taken everything in the ass—but not with a smile."

"Should I have?" she asked.

"No." Harmon chuckled. "You are too stubborn. I need a stubborn person right now. One who isn't afraid to get fucked over if the rewards are great enough."

Roxie shrugged. "Lay it out, then."

"Everyone in the Inner and Outer Systems knows your name now, your face. They know you saved Daedala single-handedly. Again, I'm impressed."

"I'm touched."

Swiping his holoboard, Harmon nodded at the vidscreen.

"Daedala's entourage was killed aboard *Phaethon,* including her bodyguards. The next Jovian vessel isn't due from Ganymede for three days."

The vidscreen displayed Valles Marineris, the huge canyon complex south of New Paris. Harmon tapped a button and the image zoomed to a section of the chasm.

"Daedala and I will be debating each other at Chasma City, in the Tithonium canyon," Harmon said. "To maintain the appearance of neutrality, the UG must provide an escort for her. Our troops would be too suspect, with the Covenant in an uproar. Instead, we have convinced her to select mercenaries as escort. She trusts you. Her speeches about you have been amusing. Pairing you together would provide great PR—"

"How much?"

"You still have, what, five years left in your sentence?" Harmon brought her profile up on the holoboard again. "Should everything go well … I will consider the remainder as time served."

Roxie gaped, then shut her mouth.

"Daedala will be departing New Paris an hour before noon tomorrow. You will be given access to Level 24. She will be provided with a private gravjet. You are to stay with her at all times until she leaves Mars."

All of that bloodshed on *Jubilee,* forgiven if she just babysat some Jovian priestess. Leave Mars, with no more red dust, no annoying gravity … no orange tabs …

Roxie slid the shades over her eyes. "I'm in."

Chapter 6

Roxie waited outside Amai Shi's apartment on Level 11 with her duffel bag. The corridors were clean, wall screens showed comforting scenes from old Earth, and people were more polite, but she remained anxious. It was after dark, she was a marked target, and now that she was number one, everyone would be gunning for her.

"Shi?" She stared into the tiny camera in the center of the door. "It's Roxie."

The door slid open and the strains of an electric koto teased Roxie's ears. Amai Shi appeared, wearing a red silk tunic that hid little of her tattooed figure. Her hair was tied back and up in a bow shape, the *nihongami* worn by the Geisha.

"*Kon'nichiwa, tenshi.*" Amai Shi glanced down the corridor. "You're alone?"

"Sure, love. Mind if I visit for a minute?"

Smiling, she motioned Roxie in. After the door slid shut, it locked automatically.

The apartment was larger than Roxie's, with an actual window overlooking Lunae Plain. Artificial plants and flowers hung from the ceiling, and prints of ancient Japanese art scrolls covered the walls. The floor, though, was littered with fluff bags instead of furniture, empty food wrappers, dirty clothes, and a teacup set that stank of alcohol.

Geisha graffiti decorated the wall above the rumpled bed. Large characters written in red paint, which Roxie had been told spelled out 'Amai Shi'. It meant 'sweet death' in Japanese, a pre-Telluric language only found on the Caravans now.

"Sit anywhere you want." Amai Shi flopped onto a fluff bag and unbuttoned her tunic. "I was about to have a smoke."

"Thanks." Roxie removed her duster and lay it atop her bag in a corner.

A vidscreen played one of those Mannequin comedies that Amai Shi liked, while an old melody bot played the koto music. Hanging in an open closet were Amai Shi's weapons and gear, all polished and pressed.

"So what brings you up here?" Amai Shi lit a bong in the shape of a handgun and sucked from its pipe. The scent of hemp stung Roxie's nostrils.

"I need a place to crash, love." Roxie sat on a fluff bag.

"You're broke already? Fuck, you got that bonus and everything—"

"*La Rèsistance* tried to kill me earlier," Roxie said. "Before we met at the *Salon*."

Amai Shi blew smoke at Roxie. "Well, you are number one. Who cares, you killed their assassin, right?"

"I'm bloody serious." Roxie stood and paced around. "The assassin said I'd betrayed 'her', the one to deliver them all, or some shite. You think they mean Daedala?"

Smoke wafted from Amai Shi's painted lips. "Who knows what those assholes mean. You're all fucked up over her these days, though."

Roxie frowned, then sat beside her "What are you on about? You're smoking and watching naughty vids all by yourself, you don't clean this place—"

"I haven't been getting as many kills lately," Amai Shi said. "I barely made enough at Syrtis to keep my ass in this *apāto*."

"Doggie Boy says the flats are cheaper down on Level 9," Roxie said.

"I'm not living down there." Amai Shi grimaced.

"I could—"

"Stop trying to help me, goddamnit!" Amai Shi cried. "You might be Street Angel to everyone else, but—"

"But right now I'm your friend." Roxie squeezed Amai Shi's hand.

Moments passed as Amai Shi puffed on the bong. Her body tensed against Roxie, and she forced smoke through her nose. Finally, she threw the bong across the apartment.

"Maybe I'm jealous."

Roxie had to quell a laugh. "Of me? What a load of bollocks!"

"I know about your mission tomorrow," Amai Shi said. "Protecting Daedala for the cameras and all that. The whole Solar System will know your pretty face, *tenshi*."

Roxie shrank back. "How the fuck—?"

"Word gets around." Amai Shi faced her. "You're already super famous, and after this, well, who the hell knows? Dirty Cool and Styra watch you all the time, and now you're number fucking one."

"And I still live on Level 7." Roxie's brows lowered. "I've got nothing!"

"It's all about you these days," Amai Shi said. "That's every fucking thing."

"Sod this crap." Roxie stood and reached for her things.

"Don't walk away from me!" Amai Shi leapt up and blocked the door. "Everyone's got eyes for you. And if *La Rèsistance* tried to kill you—it's got something to do with all the fucking *tawagoto* you've stirred up. That makes you somebody in this goddamn system. But you don't want to be anybody."

They stared at each other, lips tight, eyes wide with rage. The words cut into Roxie's heart because they were true.

"You don't know shite," Roxie muttered.

"What will you do if you leave Mars?" Amai Shi asked. "You haven't a clue. They give you this opportunity and you don't even know what to fucking do with it!"

Roxie shoved her against the wall. "You think you deserve this instead?"

"You're not the only one who's lost and suffered." Ami Shi held up her arm where Roxie had pushed her. A small bruise had formed, which the Ronin tattoos snaked over. Within seconds, the bruise was gone, replaced with a small tattoo of a star.

Roxie hung her head back and closed her eyes. "I know that."

"You're not the one who will be left behind." Amai Shi slumped to the floor, her eyes sparkling with tears. "If you leave Mars, who will I turn to? Doggie Boy likes to party too much, I can't count on him…"

Arms limp at her sides, Roxie gaped at her. No one had needed her in a long time.

"Fuck your pity," Amai Shi whispered.

Sitting beside her, Roxie tossed aside an empty amphetaline bag. "Shi…?"

"I take that shit so I can make it out there." Amai Shi wiped her eyes. "The Cinn isn't enough. Fuck, I wish it were… but I'm so afraid of who I'll see out there, Roxie. Afraid of what they'll see in me."

"Even Dirty Cool and Styra have their tricks." Roxie leaned closer to her. "They claim to hunt without Cinn, but I bet they bloody well use it."

"When I got the Ronin *irezumi*… motherfucker, these nanobots hurt going in, no matter what they say." Amai Shi touched the glittering dragon tattoo snaking across her torso. "I did it to protect my family, I swore my life to the Geishas. Here on Mars, not even the *yūrei* we hunt can deactivate this thing. It'll last forever."

"I hope it does." Roxie smiled.

She placed Roxie's hand on the dragons head, right above her heart. "I'm sorry."

Roxie had to swallow before she could answer. "It's nothing, love."

They watched the Mannequin comedy, laughing and sharing their own shag stories. Both took turns smoking from the bong, making jokes about Doggie Boy's manhood all the while. Amai Shi ordered up thick and greasy cheese beefers, along with chocolate fondue pastries. Roxie paid the delivery bot, and when they ate the food afterward, they laughed about how it would ruin their figures.

While Roxie tossed the food wrappers into the trash can, she glimpsed Amai Shi from the corner of her eye, sniffing an opium popper. They were costly little trips to chemical paradise, and almost as addictive as Cinn.

It would be hypocritical for Roxie to chide her friend on the drug use, or for her jealousy. They both did whatever it took to survive Mars. Beyond the dope, booze, and cheap thrills, they needed each other to make it.

"Come back, *tenshi*, there's another vid coming," Amai Shi called.

An hour later, Amai Shi fell asleep, leaning on Roxie's shoulder. Soon, Roxie closed her own eyes. Colors flickered behind her eyelids, and more than once, she opened them to see humanoid outlines walking in the corridor outside. Other people going to their flats, or policemen walking a beat.

Whatever was in that bong was some good stuff.

CHAPTER 7

Level 24 gleamed with such a high-grade polish, Roxie was glad she'd left her shades on. Tiled walls, floors scrubbed to a mirror sheen by sanitation bots, flowers encircling water fountains—it reminded her of those romance vids her Mum loved.

Citizens in diaphanous clothes stared at Roxie in her new black duster, synthskin jumpsuit, and gelled-up hair. On Harmon's insistence she'd applied lipstick, mascara, and a little rouge—with Amai Shi's help. Just enough so she wasn't as pale, the shadows under her eyes less pronounced. With the Draco revolver slung in her belt, an unlit cig in her mouth, and a swagger an Astro Bunny would kill for, she strolled through the crowd.

She passed cafes where people dined on gourmet steaks, fruit salads, Earth wines, and desserts chilled in Europan ice. The scents of baked bread, broiled meat, sensuous perfumes, and fresh air ducts reminded her of how paltry Level 7 was. A reminder that Mars was just one big interruption in her life.

Once she did this mission for Harmon, she could leave.

Two squads of soldiers appeared on either side of her. None spoke as she arrived at Daedala's private suite. This made more people stare. Roxie sighed.

The suite's door swooshed open. Roxie entered while the soldiers remained outside. The interior made her pause. White walls, chimes blowing above a vent, spacious windows granting glorious views of distant Valles Marineris. The plush furniture was arranged to maximum space, giving the illusion of a larger room.

Roxie's jaw squared as she took it all in.

While the poor wallowed in cramped quarters, the rich dwelled in high rise mini-palaces. Defying the masses, gravity, even the idea of a shared community with other human beings. It was like the state she tried to reach with Cinn.

Higher and higher, leaving everything else far below.

"Roxie Trent." Daedala exited an observatory filled with plants and telescopes. "It is good to see that you have healed since our daring escapades on Syrtis Plain."

Daedala's strapless dress hugged her like a second skin. Silver bracelets and rings accentuated her mahogany skin.

"Looks like you've mended too, love."

Daedala grinned. "That is the gift of the cosmos. The Covenant forbids all artificial alterations to the body. When we are our natural selves, we are all beautiful. You are quite stunning yourself."

Roxie tensed as Daedala touched her cheek.

"Even more than your body, though, I sense an inner beauty in you." Daedala looked her up and down. "One I hope to show our war-torn system in this debate."

"I'm just a bloody escort, not a politician."

"You are many things," Daedala said. "Like Street Angel."

Roxie stared out the window.

"I heard you earned it after risking yourself for others." Daedala circled Roxie, studying her. "Rebels, other hunters. Even the mentally challenged Babblers."

"Wasn't always a hunter," Roxie muttered.

"The security officer on *Jubilee*, the largest pleasure cruiser in the Solar System?"

Roxie stiffened. "What of it?"

Reclining on a couch, Daedala motioned for Roxie to join her. "I accepted Harmon's idea of a hired escort only after I read your full profile. Though you proved courageous at Syrtis, I wished to consider my options."

Roxie sat on a couch opposite Daedala. "You already know, then."

"You don't like to talk about it." Daedala smiled. "That makes it all the better."

"Better that I fucked up?" Roxie started to rise, but Daedala raised a hand.

"No. Better that you still know what shame is. Responsibility. No other hunter in the UGPD shows these traits."

Roxie glared at the floor. "I'm still just a bloody criminal."

"Why did you do it?" Daedala asked. "Why did you kill those children?"

"You've read the report."

"I want your version." Daedala sat beside her.

Despite all the Cinn she'd taken, all the years she'd been on Mars, the memories clawed back into Roxie's mind with ease. Screaming passengers, gunfire in *Jubilee*'s shiny corridors, bloodied cots used to barricade her from terrorist bullets...

"There were sixteen of them," Roxie said. "Part of the Titan Liberation Front. They took over the bridge after diverting me with a fire on the lower decks."

One of the chimes tinkled with banal metallic notes. Daedala rested her chin on her hand, focused on Roxie's every word.

"They wanted every bloke in Colonized Space to know what the UG was doing to Titan's population," Roxie said. "They started by...started..."

The recollections sliced through Roxie's thoughts. The TLF butchering the crew and taking over the bridge. Raping the show-girls. Burning people alive in their cabins. And all of it broadcast on *Jubilee*'s vid feeds, displayed in every part of the ship.

"But I gunned down five of the fuckers," Roxie said in a vengeful rasp. "In the hallways. Two tried to drown me in the sewage duct."

Memories of liquefied sewage made Roxie nauseous. Ever since then she'd hated deep water, darkened pools. "I slashed two more up in the ballroom. Those twats thought they knew how to fight."

"Yet they still held the bridge," Daedala said.

"I shot one's head off outside the bridge, wounded two others," Roxie dug her fingers into the couch. "The rest holed up inside … using children."

"Wired with explosives," Daedala said.

"They let the frightened little buggers loose, knowing they'd run straight at me." Roxie was surprised at how hollow her voice sounded. "I had to shoot them before they were … detonated. The terrorists weren't about to detonate them that close to themselves."

"But you avenged them?" Daedala whispered.

As Roxie glared out the window again, the red landscape mirrored the red images in her mind. "When I entered *Jubilee*'s bridge … oh, how the TLF screamed. How I made them scream."

"You still saved hundreds of passengers." Daedala touched Roxie's shoulder.

Shrugging her off, Roxie stood. "Cut the shite."

"I only want to—"

"I'm not here to confess my sins." Roxie scowled. "I don't need a savior."

"Mars does."

"And it's you?"

"No." Daedala gestured at a set of stairs. "Please, after you."

The stairs led to a gravjet dock where a silver-hulled Jovian yacht waited. Two guards waited at the open entrance ramp. Roxie entered the vehicle.

The interior was decorated in typical Jovian fashion, with furnishings crafted in the style of classical Greece. Images of Caryatid columns holding up the planets adorned the walls, and a brazier of Helios contained a humanoid-shaped flame.

There was no other hunters or mercenaries aboard. Just the attendant and pilot.

"Fortunately, the Jovian embassy loaned us this yacht, *Icarus*. Those gravjets stink like sweaty soldiers." Daedala sat in a plush seat. The ramp slid shut and *Icarus*'s engine thrummed as it left the dock. Level 24 and New Paris receded in the back window as Roxie turned around.

"You expect me to protect you from all the crazy gits on this marble? Alone?"

"Who else can I trust?" Daedala accepted a glass of white wine from the attendant. "Harmon wouldn't have sent you unless he thought he could gain from it."

Roxie slowly sat on a cushioned divan. "What're you gaining?"

As *Icarus* sped up, Daedala sipped her wine. "Do you have any idea what your so-called 'phantoms' really are?"

Roxie removed her shades and declined a glass of wine. "Aliens? Ghosts?"

"Yet humanity never encounters them until they colonize Mars?" Daedala arched an eyebrow. "That dispels the myth that they are remnants of the dead."

"You call them 'spirits'—you tell me."

"A spirit need not be dead. They are something else. The Covenant has studied them for centuries." Daedala set her wine aside and gauged Roxie with shrewd amber eyes. "How many Cinnamon tabs do you have on you?"

Roxie sat up straight. "Why?"

"I don't want them, though they are illegal. How many?"

"Half a packet, maybe."

"Do you know where they come from? Who makes them?"

Roxie shrugged. "Little Cinn fairies that live on Deimos?"

"The New Jovian Covenant researched chemical compounds that alter human perception," Daedala said. "Outside of UG constraints, we were able to experiment with many compounds. Our test subjects were always volunteers from among the faithful."

"Bollocks," Roxie muttered.

"It is true," Daedala said. "None were forced. It was regarded as a religious duty. In time, we uncovered a way to see into other light wavelengths. By extending the reach of our senses, we could finally experience the universe in all its glory. Cinnamoxidil 9 became the most successful of these chemical mixtures. It granted us sight into the electromagnetic spectrum."

Roxie's mouth fell open. "It's a bloody religious tool?"

Daedala offered a thin smile. "It is used in Jovian rituals, yes. The holy sacrament. Like the Tellurics who used to eat a wafer of—"

"Shite, why didn't your crew use it to see the phantoms and fight back at Syrtis?"

"We will not harm the spirits," Daedala said. "We came here to understand them."

"Those things kill people!" Roxie cried. "I've seen entire villages laid to ash, I've found people scorched to pink fucking blobs, I've—"

"They are violent to those who have wronged them. To them, all humans are enemies. Think back to the early days, when the Tellurics tried to force the Martian colonists to serve them."

"You're not going to quote Fleurant, are you?" Roxie asked.

"He defeated the Tellurics for a time," Daedala said. "The Neo-French freedom fighter was quite an idealist. Now his language and culture are sacred to the *Glorieuse Révolution*. Even he sought the spirits' help. That's when the kill bots targeted people as well as the spirits."

Roxie started to speak, then considered the kill bots on Mars. Necrostructs, Burners—all were deposited on Mars by Telluric starships centuries ago. Equipped to seek and destroy phantoms, built to last lifetimes. Implying that the phantoms would not go away. That something would always need to be there to fight them.

"Is that why some of them ask for conversion, like the Burners?" Roxie asked.

"It wasn't only spirits that the Tellurics were exterminating," Daedala said.

"Just because Fleurant wanted to use phantoms?" Roxie shook her head. "The kill bots target every sodding thing that moves, even UG troops."

"Mars was a miserable place," Daedala said. "Those who prepared it for others didn't want to give up the fruit of their labors. This world was never intended for them."

"Genocide?" Roxie grabbed the wine glass and took a gulp. The sweet, burning tang gushed down her throat.

"The Tellurics wanted it all for themselves and the UG are following that policy." Daedala sighed. "That is why the UG excavates all the old sites. Cydonia, Hellas Plain, ruins built into the Valles Marineris. They want what the ancients knew. Before there was a need for the Caravans. Before Earth was permanently ruined."

"Are they aliens?" Roxie asked in a low voice.

"Who knows?"

"What are you looking for, then? Why pick me?"

"You hesitated on Syrtis Plain," Daedala said. "You did not destroy that last spirit. It did not harm you, or me. That means something."

"Well, what?" Roxie asked.

"I intend to find out. First, we must calm the situation here on Mars. If the natives see a UGPD hunter, someone they hate, supporting me in this debate, they might reconsider a few things." Daedala drew her legs up into her chair and leaned back. "Now rest. You have many things to reconsider yourself."

So many thoughts raced through Roxie's mind that she fidgeted for several minutes before sitting still. More than once she glanced at the drink cabinet, but she needed a level head. She was being used for something … but she had no idea what.

After exiting *Icarus* at the small dock in Chasma City, Roxie gazed around. Valles Marineris stretched from horizon to horizon. The largest canyon in the Solar System, it was several kilometers deep, scarring the surface of Mars as if some primeval god had gouged it with a cosmic sword.

Daedala walked down *Icarus*'s ramp, robe tossing in the wind, long hair fixed into a thick braid. "Look. Now you see why I selected this for the debate's location."

Roxie scanned the stratified walls of Tithonium Chasma nearby. Billions of years lay bare, shown in layer upon layer of rock. Epochs exposed to a sun of a different shade than when the lower layers had formed, and revealed to eyes that would could only view them in quaint human light. Roxie wanted to eat a Cinn tab right then, since the electromagnetic spectrum revealed certain ancient features built by the original colonists. They must have been a strange lot, with all those hieroglyphics and lion-headed statues.

"Do you admire the ancient's work?" Daedala gestured at conical structures within the canyons. "The Covenant is studying how they built such places, even how they stored information in streams of light. There is much to learn."

Constructed right into the layers were several vertical cities. Nothing but ruins now, they still jutted from the canyon sides in megalithic glory. Broken bridge spans protruded into the canyon air. Causeways bypassed crevices in the canyon walls. How the early colonists achieved it all, when Mars had yet to be fully terraformed, awed Roxie.

"See how the UG portrays this?" Daedala asked. "This will insult the natives."

Roxie tore her eyes from the canyon and stared over Chasma City. Built atop the northern lip of Tithonium Chasma, it consisted of low-level buildings spread out over a wide area, then walled in by a series of wind barriers. Huge sand dunes had built up outside the barriers. On the side facing the canyon, brutal winds could sweep a person right into the abyss. A sprawling windfarm spread out for half a kilometer from the city.

UG gravjets flew in tandem overhead while armored convoys drove along the roads. Gunbots wheeled alongside them, gleaming in the sun like chrome ants at this distance. Roxie guessed there was at least two thousand troops, maybe more.

Harmon's military carrier, *Crimson Aegis*, hovered above them. Over four hundred meters long, its trapezoid shape cast a distorted shadow on the canyon walls. Huge gravthrusters kept it aloft, generating a constant, titanic hum.

"Sykes Corp just requested UG military aid in containing a miner revolt here before I left Io's orbit," Daedala said. "This much force adds insult to injury."

"The UG does what it's best at."

"Did you ever think this is what you would be best at?" Daedala asked.

"Someone has to bloody well do it."

"For now." Daedala walked down a steep staircase carved right into the canyon's side. Roxie followed. The staircase led to a wide causeway connecting Chasma City with mining settlements on either side of it.

"So how is a piece of crumpet like you going to convince a cunt like Lorne Harmon to be all peachy?" Roxie lit a cig and puffed.

"The same way a skilled hunter like yourself succeeds: perseverance." Daedala strutted along the causeway as crowds waited ahead. She certainly knew how to draw attention. Doggie Boy would cream his pants if he could see her in that tight dress.

Thinking of him made Roxie wonder about the other hunters. Jealousy and competition would be even greater now. Ranked number one meant an obligation to show others why she was that good. Amai Shi was right: all eyes were on Roxie now.

There could be no mistakes.

Throngs of native Martians watched them from behind guarded barriers. Tension weighed the air as nothing but frowns greeted them. The glares Roxie got made her blood chill. Sure, she'd dealt with natives from Amazonis Basin to Cassini Valley, but these people wanted her blood. What had the UG been doing out here?

"Tough crowd." Roxie kept her hands at her sides, ready to draw at any moment.

"These people wish to hear what will be said. If they wanted to harm us, we would both be dead." Daedala smiled and waved at the crowds.

One Martian held up a sign that read '*Nous Sauver Rue Ange*': Save Us Street Angel. Roxie turned away and found Daedala grinning at her.

"You have religion and your do-gooder bollocks," Roxie said. "I'll trust my gun."

"After today, you may trust other things." Daedala kept waving.

CHAPTER 8

Roxie wanted another cig bad, but the wind wouldn't allow her to light one. Gusts barreling down Tithonium Chasma physically moved her a few millimeters as she waited on the platform beside Daedala. The sun forced her to squint despite her shades, making her a useless bodyguard if someone really wanted to murder the Jovian beauty.

The causeway below was packed with Martians and several UG platoons. Roxie caught snippets of Simp Speak as the soldiers ordered the crowd to remain calm. No wonder they hated the UG: Simp Speak was a simple dialect an infant could understand. Using it always pissed people off. Maybe the UG wanted to anger the natives and give those jarheads an excuse to open fire. She'd seen it before.

A floating camera bot whizzed by. Roxie wondered how many people across the Solar System waited by their vidscreen as minutes passed before the signal reached them.

"There they are," Daedala said.

A blue-uniformed entourage walked up the platform stairs. Militaristic to the tee, the United Government representatives all wore full insignia, headgear, and armored vests. Even Lorne Harmon sported the martial look, though his uniform was a lighter blue. A giant vidscreen shimmered behind them as he joined Daedala beside a holographic lectern.

Right beside Harmon was Styra. She ignored Roxie, focusing on the crowd.

The UG fanfare played, an overbearing march with imperious drum rolls, merciless cymbal crashes, and staccato strings.

Roxie recalled hearing it every morning at the academy. She still hated it.

Roxie glanced at the lectern. Harmon's speech was prepared, but on Daedala's side, there was only a hologram of an ever-burning flame.

Harmon swiped the lectern's microphone icon. "People of Mars, we have come together this day to discuss our differences in order to discover a solution to the phantom problem. As you all know, order has been kept by the United Government Paranormal Division for the past two decades regarding the phantom issue, and…"

Ignoring Harmon's hot air, Roxie watched on the crowd. The Martians' slight physiques, born in lower gravity, made them look starved. Butternut complexions, dark hair, and darker eyes were leftovers of the genetic work done on early colonists.

The crowd watched with tense expressions. Most of them were dressed in the traditional Martian hues of brown, red, and orange; blue was despised because of the color's association with the UG. Wearing black and gray, Roxie avoided showing any allegiance. At least that's what she kept telling herself as hundreds stared at her.

"That is why we must educate the population about the spirits' wishes." Daedala's voice brought Roxie's attention back to the debate. "The 'phantoms', as you call them, do not desire land, wealth, or even the lives of your children. They desire justice."

Thousands of Martians shouted in approval. The sound traveled down into the canyon, reverberating back in an amplified wave of anger and frustration. The soldiers stirred on the causeway. Two gravjets flew over Chasma City, no doubt carrying a deathly payload in case the natives became too enthusiastic.

Harmon tried to reply but the crowds chanted in Neo-French. It echoed over the canyon and Chasma City, vibrating the stone platform under Roxie's feet.

"*Souvenir de la Bastille!*" The cry referenced the legendary prison of ancient Earth, where a small band of courageous men and women freed starving people from malicious rulers.

Roxie wasn't sure how much of that fairytale was true, but there was no denying the mob's power. She glanced at Daedala, who offered a slight smile. Harmon rubbed his jaw, swiped a few controls on the lectern, and waited for the crowd to calm down.

"Justice must be decided by the courts," Harmon said, which garnered him ten thousand boos from the riled audience. He again waited for them to relent. "The phantoms are a threat we can defeat together. First, the UG must have full control of Martian facilities to—"

The crowd yelled in disapproval. On the causeway below, a few troops drew their batons. The gravjets flew lower. Every instinct urged Roxie to draw her revolver but she resisted. The tension was smothering her.

Daedala swiped the lectern and held up her hand. The massive vidscreen made her a gargantuan holographic statue standing on the side on the canyon. Every bit the evangelist goddess.

The mob calmed enough for Daedala's voice to be heard over the megaspeakers. "The phantoms can help reshape Mars, Governor Harmon. They possess a great amount of energy—natural energy. This is the path the New Jovian Covenant suggests that all human beings take. A synergy with the universe, acting in concert with it, not against—"

"This is not a sermon." Harmon swiped the lectern. The vidscreen displayed the Caravans in orbit around Luna, Mars, and the asteroid belt. "Our fellow humans need respite, the one Mars can provide with the correct administration."

Roxie stepped closer to Daedala as the crowd fumed.

Batons rose and fell, smacking Martian faces. A nullifier shot immobilized a man and sent him into violent spasms. Styra shot Roxie a glare.

Daedala opened her mouth to speak when a figure below the platform caught Roxie's attention: a person dressed in a brown farmer's smock, wearing a full-face breath mask—just out of the camera bots' view.

The figure aimed a crossbow up at them.

"Down!" Roxie shoved Daedala under the lectern, drew her gun, and fired.

The figure recoiled and limped to the causeway's railing.

"What the fuck are you doing?" Styra aimed her own gun at Roxie. UG troopers stormed the platform and surrounded Harmon.

"There's an assassin—"

"Put it the fuck down!" Styra shouted.

"He's beneath us, you twat!" Roxie cried.

Below, the would-be assassin leapt from the railing to the hovertram that glided along the canyon walls.

"Drop your weapon and lay your ass down!" a trooper yelled.

In Roxie's peripheral vision, the assassin scrambled over the tram cars. No way would she let him escape. If she caught him, they'd believe her.

Roxie jumped onto a tarpaulin shade extending from the platform. She slid down it to the hovertram. Shouts echoed from above. Harmon's voice blared through the megaspeakers. The Martian crowd broke through the UG barriers.

A shot zipped past Roxie's right arm, ripping the tarpaulin. She rolled left and dropped several meters until she slammed atop a hovercar. Gritting her teeth against the pain in her knees, she rolled again into a vent declivity. The hovertram glided from the causeway toward the mines east of Chasma City.

Roxie risked a glance back at the platform. Blue uniforms were everywhere. Martians and soldiers fought on the causeway. People plummeted over the railing into the reddish-brown chasm. Gravjets buzzed the mob, blaring sonic weapons. *Crimson Aegis* hovered into position above the city. All because she was trying to do her job.

The hovertram ran past a loading depot as Roxie slid down the declivity onto the other side of the car. She grappled with a railing as a black object pinged off it.

She faced forward and spotted the same figure reloading the crossbow. Gripping the railing, Roxie aimed.

The tram whisked into a tunnel.

Momentary darkness gave way to harsh yellow lights along the tunnel's sides. Roxie couldn't make out the figure anymore, but kept the gun aimed forward. Soon as she got a shot, she was taking it. Why the UG tried to shoot her, though, she had no idea.

Well, she had fired from the platform. They probably thought she'd tried to kill Daedala. If she'd wanted a death wish, she'd have shot Styra first.

But with all those camera bots, how could they think she was responsible?

The hovertram jolted to a stop. With only one hand on the safety rail, the momentum jerked Roxie off. She hit the track's edges two meters below.

She wanted to curse but the assassin was still out there. After getting to her feet, Roxie stumbled along the rail's edge. Her back throbbed. She righted herself and took a deep breath. Aimed the gun forward. Scanned every shadow.

The only way to absolve herself was to find her target.

Boots skidded off metal, then thumped into dirt up ahead. Something clicked and hummed. Roxie rounded the hovercar corner as a shape ran along the train far ahead.

Roxie jumped from the rail onto the dirt lip along the tunnel's side, then broke into a run. Her knees ached in protest.

The figure looked around and ran faster.

Roxie picked up her speed and fired. The shot echoed in the tunnel and ricocheted off the far wall. The figure ducked and kept running.

The tram hummed and started moving slowly. Hot exhaust blew from vents parallel to Roxie; she had to duck under each one. The figure leapt up and grabbed a railing. Roxie fired again. A yelp reached her ears. Smirking, she kept running.

The tram sped up and she latched onto a railing. Voices echoed back to her. The tunnel lights grew brighter. The scent of iron dust and chalk stung her nose.

When the hovertram stopped again, Roxie landed on her feet and broke into a run. The figure staggered and collapsed against the tram. The voices grew louder.

"Stay there or I'll splatter your brains!" Roxie cried.

The figure looked up. A man, with the mask halfway off his face.

"Please don't shoot! She was supposed to—"

A gun fired. The man's crown exploded into red mist.

Roxie wheeled around as two figures raced toward her. A bullet slammed into her armored vest but the material absorbed the shock. She popped one person in the neck before the other managed to fire. The round grazed her right thigh as she dodged. Another bullet ripped through her duster. Hitting the dirt, Roxie fired twice. The man crumpled against the rail.

Covering the area with her gun, Roxie got back up. Her right thigh burned, and the skin under her left breast stung from the first round's impact. Her bruises from Syrtis were still tender, adding to her aches. But any second now the UG would arrive.

She had three bodies to prove her innocence.

The graze burned, her knees throbbed…with Cinn everything would feel so much better. But she couldn't. She had to remain presentable for when the UG picked her up.

Moving ahead, she came across the two corpses. One woman, one man. Both wearing tram worker jumpers. Each had carried cheap pistols.

"Put the gun down," a male voice said.

Roxie dropped the revolver.

A man in olive fatigues stood on the tram railing. Aiming an SMG at her.

"Walk," he said.

"Where to, love?" Might as well stall since he wanted her alive. For now.

"Forward."

She trudged over the dirt, heart beating faster, the graze burning hotter. The tram started up and inched forward.

"Faster."

"I took a shot in the leg, right?" Roxie limped for emphasis. A gun barrel appeared on her right as the moving tram brought her captor parallel with her.

"Move!" he shouted.

Hovertram exhaust whistled in super-heated geysers. Roxie pretended to stumble as the man leaned down over her.

"I said to fucking—!"

She clasped his neck and yanked him off the rail. He fired, the muzzle flash lighting up the tunnel. An exhaust jet scalded the man's arm. Screaming, his skin bubbling, he tried to bring the gun around. Roxie wrenched his head and snapped his neck. As he slid off her into the dirt, she snatched the SMG.

A thin cable snagged her boot.

Roxie toppled face first into the dirt. Hands tore away the SMG then whacked her face. Another person rolled her in her own duster, zipped a rope around her, and toted her into a service passage branching off from the main tunnel.

"What the bloody hell?"

Someone shoved a rag into her mouth. It tasted like motor oil.

Her captors carried her down another passage lit by red warning lights. The stink of chalk dust overpowered her nose and she couldn't breathe. Grunting, she squirmed until someone slapped her.

As they entered a cooler passage lit with bright overhead fixtures, Roxie realized that two people carried her, with two following. Olive drab fatigues, worn boots. Gunbelts crammed with pistols, knives, bullets.

La Rèsistance.

After passing carts filled with raw iron, her captors dumped Roxie onto the ground. Someone yanked the rope off and her duster fell open. Feet pushed her onto her back. A shotgun barrel pressed into her right temple. The rag was jerked from her mouth.

"Sorry I'm late." She coughed. "I'll take a round of Lunar whiskey."

"On the rocks, Street Angel?"

The familiar voice made her look around but the overhead lights were too bright.

"Sure, love. Let's drink to your four dead friends out there."

"They are not our friends. Neither are you."

A boot nudged her onto her side and she looked up. A man two meters tall, with wavy black hair and a stubbled jaw, peered down at her.

"Locust?" She gave him a mocking grin. "Still trying to save Mars, then? Right-o. Not going to stop you. Now let me shove off and—"

Locust yanked her up to face him at eye level. "You killed all the assassins. Now no one can tell us who they work for. Why they wanted that Covenant priestess dead."

"They killed the assassin themselves! The rest, I had no bloody choice." Roxie tried to think, desperate for a plan. "C'mon, love. You know me. Remember Amazonis Town? Remember Mount Arsia? We had a jolly good time then, right?"

A thorn in the UG's ass for the past fifteen years, Locust was a key *La Rèsistance* leader. She'd aided him a few times when the UG harmed innocent settlers.

"I still recall how you gunned Salvaire down. How you left me at Cydonia when you had a change of heart outside Pyramid Eight." Locust shook her like a doll in his grasp. "How you're still a UG bitch getting wealthy from stealing my people's heritage."

"So you didn't try to off Daedala? She's all about your crazy heritage."

Locust frowned. "You are the hunter that escorted her?"

"We flew. On a great big bird with pink wings."

"Goddamnit." Locust glanced at his followers, two men and a woman. "Pierro, get the scrambler. Chev, keep a look out. Etienna, turn on that wash cart from the cleansing station over there."

Roxie stiffened. Filled with water, the cart had to be at least three meters deep.

"What else do you want to know? Just ask me, love."

Locust released her and she collapsed onto the floor.

"We will ... love."

Chapter 9

An older, husky rebel held the shotgun against Roxie's head as Pierro ran the scrambler over her ConRec tattoo. The hand-held device beeped five times. The skin around the tattoo numbed with piercing tingles.

"Thanks," she said.

"Now that your masters can't track you, we can discuss things," Locust said. "Take off her boots and that silly duster."

She locked eyes with Locust as Pierro and the woman obeyed. Next they removed her armored vest, G-ballasts, and gunbelt.

"What's on your mind?" Roxie tried to be nonchalant, but her heart beat so hard it hurt. The other times Locust had caught her, he'd never ordered her to be undressed. Especially with water nearby. She remembered the isolation tank during her academy training. Preparing for zero-G, she had barely withstood submersion. The sewer fight on *Jubilee* had unhinged that fear.

So how did Locust know about it?

"That scrambler won't work for long," Roxie said. "The UGPD will track my last known location. They'll find me."

Locust shackled her wrists to a small crane hook. It stood beside the conveyor belt filled with carts. Without the ballasts, the lower gravity already churned her stomach.

"Your masters have their hands full with a riot in Chasma City. Some news feeds are already blaming *La Rèsistance*. We are everyone's favorite scapegoat."

He nodded to the others, who formed a circle around her and watched. Roxie's equipment lay piled on another chair. She glowered at them.

"What are you going to do?"

Locust slid a magknife from his gunbelt. "We're going to cleanse you."

Her chest pumped up and down with painful breaths. "You won't enjoy it."

"Won't I?" Locust tugged her synthskin and slit it down the middle. He yanked it off her, exposing her halter top and bottoms. Her bruises only embarrassed her further.

"Are you sure this will work?" Pierro asked.

"The only certainty on Mars is death," Locust said.

"Your friends don't have the mickey to torture me?" She tried to sound tough.

Locust sighed. "This isn't about gaining information from you."

"Then let me go."

"The drugs, the drinking, the killing … it's eating you, Street Angel."

"Don't fucking call me that."

He gripped her chin. "Why? Because you don't deserve it? Because those you try to save, you sentence to death anyway? You are a goddamn hypocrite."

She spat in his face.

After wiping his cheek, Locust tapped the crane controls. Roxie gasped as the device jerked her over the water-filled cart. It was only three meters deep, she could see the bottom, Locust wouldn't drown her …

"This isn't necessary," she said in a shaking voice. "Torture isn't your style."

"Torture? For such a clever woman, you can be so fucking stupid."

"Don't," she whispered. "I mean it. Please."

The crane released. The chains rattled.

She plunged into the cart.

Cold liquid surrounded Roxie. Weighed down by the chains, her feet touched bottom. She clawed at the surface over a meter above her. Memories of the isolation tank, of drowning in *Jubilee*'s shit, squeezed her heart. Roxie flailed.

A fat bubble exited her mouth. Then another.

No. She would not give up that easily. Let Locust wait for it, let him have a corpse instead. He'd not beat her, he'd not batter her down. She would rise above it.

Another bubble escaped her lips.

Roxie flailed about, started to rise. Her skin prickled all over. The chain banged against the side of the car, the vibrations rammed into her ears…

Spurting more bubbles, she drifted to the bottom.

She imagined herself on Cinn. Hitting that high, climbing above reality. Colors flickered in her vision. For a moment she saw Locust's outline, standing near the cart.

More bubbles trickled up from her lips. She sank all the way down.

The shackles jerked and the chains lifted her from the water.

Shaking, water coursing down her body, Roxie coughed and sputtered.

Pierro manipulated the crane controls until Roxie was lifted from the cart and deposited onto a pile of towels. They weren't there before.

Roxie sucked in air. "Fuck you."

The husky man grunted and spat. The woman glared at Roxie.

Locust paced around her while studying a small device.

"You're cleansed." He put the device away and undid the shackles. As soon as her hands were free, she reached for his neck. He grabbed her wrists.

"Easy. You had-"

Roxie head-butted him.

"What the hell are you doing?" Locust wrenched back, his nose bleeding.

The others aimed weapons at her, but Locust raised a hand.

"That's the Roxie Trent I want. Not sniveling and begging. So stop this bullshit. I doused you with Daedala's nanites."

"What? Why?"

"So you can help us." Pierro unbuckled the shackles on her ankles.

"With the phantoms?" Roxie asked. "But the nanites will be bloody inactive—"

"Jovian nanites are like the old Telluric ones," Locust said. "They feed off of your natural electricity and react when placed near certain types of radiation. The phantoms can't affect them."

Roxie lowered her foot from the shackle. "But Daedala?"

"She's aiding *La Rèsistance*. The nanites are from her. She told us about—"

She pounced on him. "You cunt! Why didn't you tell me that was the reason?"

"Would you have believed me?" Locust flung her back onto the towel pile.

"Of course not." She rubbed her stomach as the rest of her wounds flared up.

"Here. Shut up and dry off." Locust dumped a towel over her head, then dug through a satchel on his chair. "Take this med kit, fix that graze on your thigh. Then get dressed in those new clothes over there."

She gave him the finger.

"Maybe someday, *Ange de la Mort*." He left with the others.

After drying off, she walked back to the cart and gazed down into the water. Though her throat constricted, she swished the water around. Liquid immersion was a quick way to get nanites into the body, short of an injection. But they were so tiny, she shouldn't have felt anything in the water. If they reacted to radiation—well, maybe her irradiation shots had expired, but…

Roxie backed from the cart as her hand prickled. She studied her fingers.

Millions of nanites were crawling through her body now.

Daedala had a lot to answer for.

❦ ❦ ❦

Roxie tucked the evergreen shirt into the gray field trousers the rebels gave her. The boots squeezed her toes but at least the new gunbelt hugged her hips the right way. The only thing she'd been able to keep was her Draco; everything else might contain tracking devices.

That and the Cinn packet, which she'd hidden in her bra.

Pierro incinerated her old clothes with a gas torch.

"Need a light? Too bad your cigs went in there. They're my favorite brand."

Roxie nudged Locust. "So talk. Who sent those assassins?"

"We aren't sure," Locust said.

"Maybe it was Harmon? Then he could blame it on you sods." Roxie plopped onto the chair. "Or me. Looks like I was the fall girl. Literally."

Pierro snorted. "Don't ever become a vid comedian."

"The joke's on me," she said. "First you berks try to kill me on Level 7, and now you try to—"

"That is untrue." Locust leaned toward her. "*La Rèsistance* has bigger issues than you. What happened?"

After Roxie explained the attempt on her life in the latrine, Locust and his followers shared uncertain glances.

"What do you *Bastille* blokes want? I told you once, revolutions only pay in wounds and dead friends."

"There is something afoot here in the canyons," Locust said. "Phantoms have started appearing, but doing no property damage. UG patrols have increased but there hasn't been as much unrest in the mines as the news feeds claim."

"And Daedala wanted a debate in Chasma City," Roxie said. "Convenient."

"She was supposed to bring you here after the debate was over, to show you herself." Locust shrugged. "You are fortunate we were waiting nearby."

"So she's all that?" Roxie rolled her eyes.

Locust bristled. "We know the Covenant is not all it seems. They are interested in Mars because of what the ancients left here."

Daedala's words came back to Roxie.

"All those old sites…"

"The fossil prospectors dig up everything." Locust stood and kicked his chair over. "For the UG, for private contractors offworld. The Covenant has its own excavators, though you'd never tell them apart from the rest. They all want it."

"What?" Roxie asked.

"That which can earn Mars its freedom." Locust buckled on his gunbelt. "We need your help."

Roxie paced the chamber. "Everybody wants me these days. Nobody wants to let me in on the bloody secret, though."

"The secret of the phantoms is found in the old temples and pyramids," Locust said. "Have you ever noticed how phantoms haunt those areas, yet the kill bots never come near them?"

Roxie snorted. "They come pretty damn close—"

"But they never enter."

"Again, why?" Roxie asked.

"We want you to help us get these answers." Locust nodded to Pierro, who dug out a paper map from his pocket.

"Paper? What museum did you get that from?" Roxie smirked.

"The same one you got your fashion sense." Pierro smiled. "Holo equipment leaves a traceable signature, so this will have to do. Look. There have been new installations built along the canyon walls here around Valles. No local employees were hired. Not even the large corporations had a hand in this."

"Installations?" Roxie browsed over the map.

Pierro had circled in red a section east of Chasma City.

"Subterranean installations," Locust said. "Protected by phantoms."

She blinked. "The fuck? Protected? You make it sound like they are controlled."

"Maybe they are." Locust met her eyes.

"You once said, with one of those discs from Pyramid Eight, that you would summon phantoms to attack the UG. What makes you any better?"

"The phantoms direct their aggression at offworlders," Locust said. "The only local places they attack are ones the UG have meddled in. Increasing security, building more cyclers, reshaping the land and claiming that they are terraforming—it's all a lie."

"For what purpose?" Roxie asked. "Why implant me with Daedala's nanites?"

Locust said nothing for a long moment.

"There will be chaos in this region for a time. Whoever sent those assassins will wonder what happened to them. To you. If you use the scrambler every three hours, your little UG badge won't show up on their satellite scanners. You have a window of opportunity here. Help us."

"The installation isn't far from here," Pierro said.

"Then what? I'm taking a whopping risk if I do this." She raised her brows.

"My people have already moved the dead assassins to that location," Locust said. "You can say you chased them there, killed them, and then awaited pickup."

"And this is why Daedala brought me here?"

"If you find nothing, you're not out of anything. If you discover something, though … *La Rèsistance* will be in your debt."

"Your account's overdrawn," she said.

"The Salvaire issue will be settled." Locust's jaw tightened.

The woman glared at Roxie. "She isn't worth such forgiveness."

"Etienna … it has been discussed," Locust said.

Salvaire had been a close friend of Locust's. Years ago, both men had been among the best gunfighters on Mars. For him to forgive—or at least gloss over—her successful duel with Salvaire, meant Locust really cared about this.

"I'll give it a go," Roxie said.

They exited the conveyor room, leaving the water-filled cart and another smoldering with the ashes of her clothes. Like she'd been reborn, her past burned away.

As they wended through the tunnels, Roxie walked alongside Locust.

"Why do you care?" she finally asked.

"About?"

"My fear. Daedala had no business telling you."

"For what you are about to undertake, there can be no fear."

Locust led them from the maintenance tunnels to an elevator. The ascent lasted a minute. Etienna shot Roxie a cool stare every so often, while the husky rebel always looked like he wanted to piss down her throat. At least Pierro offered her a cig.

The elevator led to a wide platform atop the canyon. Eight more rebels waited, with hoverbikes for everyone. Four riders each had a corpse wrapped in black plasti laid across their vehicle. Wearing masks and goggles, they'd been waiting.

Roxie wondered how long Daedala had planned all this.

"What would you have done if I hadn't chased that sod on the tram?"

Locust strapped onto a hoverbike. "I would have found you. Your face has been broadcast all over the Solar System now: 'the hunter who refused to shoot a phantom'. I bet the UGPD wants to fuck you without heat jelly."

"Get in line," she muttered.

"Keep up. Or have you forgotten how to patrol the sands, stuck in New Paris?" Locust hit the accelerator. His hoverbike darted away in a cloud of dust. The other riders followed suit, and soon only her and Pierro were left.

"You want me to start it for you?" Pierro asked.

"I know how to drive these damn things." She sat down and buckled on the harness. The narrow seat agitated her cramps.

"Offworld women." Pierro rolled his eyes and jetted away after the others.

Roxie gripped the handle and thumbed the accelerator. The hoverbike skimmed over the sands beside the lip of Tithonium Chasma. Wearing a filter mask, goggles, and jacket, Roxie ignored sand and pebbles that struck her as she reached 300 kilometers an hour. She hoped the installation was close, because SATSCAN would pick them up soon.

The landscape blurred past on her left. A few dingoes tried to follow her, but she blew them a kiss and continued. On her right, Valles Marineris was so immense it seemed to remain still. Like a destination she could never quite reach.

Maybe that's what Cinn had done to her these past few years. Making her think she was speeding along, leaving all her pain and guilt behind, while going nowhere.

Now, though, she had to follow this through, in hopes of restoring her reputation. She'd left Daedala, inadvertently started a riot, and killed people. There'd better be something huge after this ride, because she wanted Harmon to keep his word.

Finish this mission, and she could leave Mars.

But Amai Shi and Doggie Boy…well, she could sent funds to Shi in private, so she could buy out her sentence. Doggie Boy, though, would want to stay.

She wished they were here now.

A gust blew up from the canyon, sounding like the screams of children.

Gritting her teeth, Roxie mashed the accelerator again. 350 kilometers an hour.

She blasted past the other riders and rode parallel with Locust. The hoverbike shuddered, a big rocket she was riding into darkness. Not knowing what she'd find.

But she knew what she wanted to leave behind.

CHAPTER 10

Roxie decelerated at a hand signal from Locust. They coasted down an incline along the canyon's lip, her boot millimeters from nothingness. The wind made her vehicle wobble but she thrilled at her proximity to death. It was like flying that gravjet, or facing her water phobia.

It was like taking Cinn.

Cold sweat dampened Roxie's shirt. She banked away from the chasm.

Locust veered into a small basin. Sand gusted over into the canyon from his engine's blowback. Roxie skirted past the gritty cloud and stopped beside him.

As the others drove up and shut off their engines, Roxie shook dust off her body.

"I don't see anything special."

"You rarely do." Locust got off his bike and loosened the pistol in his holster. "Keep taking Cinn, though, and you'll see nothing but flames like the Jovians."

"For someone expecting my help, you're a sodding asshole."

"That's the only company you ever keep." Locust smirked and walked to the other side of the basin.

Roxie followed, the breeze flapping her jacket. A metallic taste hung in the air. Two cyclers towered in the distance along the canyon edge—normally they kept the air cleaner than this. She examined the sands around her.

A proliferation of dark flecks stained it.

"Rust wind deposits?" She nudged her boot through it.

Locust motioned Pierro over, who connected a small datapad to the scrambler. He pointed it at the ground. The others waited.

"So you've done this before," Roxie said. "What do you need me for?"

"That was one of my friends." Etienna pointed at the flecks and gave her a scornful glare. "Disintegrated by the energy field under us."

Roxie jumped back. "Fuck. I thought you were on Daedala's side?"

"We always like to make sure," Pierro said.

"I hope you're powering it down?" Roxie pushed her goggles up and squinted. Colorful splotches passed in her vision for a split second, then vanished.

"Are you okay?" Locust asked.

"Considering I was shot at and drowned? I'm bloody fine, love."

"You will have just a few seconds to slip through once we open the hatch." Pierro gave the scrambler one final tap and helped Locust pull a ring inset into the basin's side. It had looked like a piece of stone until it rose in a circular shape.

"Aren't any of you blokes coming?"

Locust gave her an exasperated look. "If we could do this, do you think Daedala would have chosen you?"

"So the nanites alone won't let me into this place. What's this really about?"

"You are wasting time," Locust said.

Roxie drew her revolver and aimed it at her hoverbike.

The rebels drew guns on Roxie, but Locust shook his head at them.

"Let's not create a small fireworks show for SATSCAN."

"What bloody game are you at? This isn't for Mars or all those poor blokes who write your silly slogans on loo walls. It isn't just for Daedala. What is it?"

Wind stung Roxie's uncovered face with sand particles. She didn't blink.

"If you really don't care why you have spilled so much blood on this planet, for all these years, then pull the trigger and alert your masters. Or you can enter."

Moments passed as they stared at each other.

"Fine." Roxie holstered the revolver and walked through the hatch.

An immediate shock traveled through her body, as if she'd touched an electric fence. Her flesh tingled with the sensation of something digging into her pores—but not like the nanites. A different energy slid between her skin cells.

Answering the shock with one of its own.

The hatch led into a narrow tunnel constructed of sturdy masonry. It turned a corner a few meters ahead where a faint bluish light shone.

"Hey, I—"

The hatch slammed shut behind her. Martian daylight vanished, leaving her in azure-tinted gloom.

Roxie drew her revolver and crept forward. A slight humming resounded through the masonry blocks. The air's ozone-like taste clung to her mouth. Her boots crunched over sand blown in from the hatch, but otherwise everything was clean.

Nearing the corner, she hesitated.

What did Locust expect of her? He had an ulterior motive for taking a piss, let alone helping Daedala. There must be something here he wanted.

Roxie snuck around the corner.

Yellow-green dots blinked in her vision.

She flinched. The dots faded.

Cinn couldn't have damaged her eyes already. If nothing else, she could see quite well despite the slight blue luminance. Around the corner she encountered a holo panel on her left. On her right, a box generator hummed, its counter stating a power output in mega joules. The holo panel displayed a large On/Off button, plus diagnostics regarding energy consumption and signal disruption. The latest was thirty seconds ago.

Roughly the time she'd entered the hatch.

She studied the graph until she found a disruption before that. A day ago. Maybe that had been Locust's comrade, blasted to ash giblets for trying to get in.

She considered swiping the Off button, but no. She'd not deactivate the field until she discovered what was down here.

The next room was filled with rows of alcoves. Each was enclosed with a transparent shell. The blue light came from shimmering forms inside them.

"Holy fucking…" Roxie dug a Cinn tab from her bra.

Every alcove housed a phantom.

Though amorphous in shape, their cerulean glow was unmistakable. She studied the clear shell and recalled the panel's data. The shells must be wired with an electromagnetic reflector field, making the phantoms visible.

There were dozens of alcoves, stretching on in a subterranean mausoleum.

Though she spotted no evidence of Covenant activity, it had to be them. Daedala had ordered Locust to dust her with nanites, after all.

Roxie cocked her revolver and held a Cinn tab ready. She'd seen phantoms destroy solar relay stations outside New Paris and wreck cyclers in the Amazonis region.

Whoever had the power to contain them had the power to rule Mars.

Roxie slowed her breathing and popped her neck. So she'd gotten in. What did Locust or Daedala expect her to do next? If only she could report this to the UGPD, then take out each one. The creds she'd get. The reputation.

She blinked and edged back from the nearest alcove. If the phantoms could be corralled, there was no reason to keep it a secret. Not a good reason.

Maybe this was what Harmon wanted her to discover.

Roxie mopped sweat from her forehead. She was in the middle of the biggest thing to happen to Mars since the Tellurics seeded kill bots all over the place. It was too much. Too insane. Roxie backed up, thinking up a lie to tell Locust.

One of the shapes in a nearby alcove shifted violently, then coalesced into a humanoid shape.

Roxie froze, finger on the trigger.

The phantom felt around with feline paws, its face a mixture of human and leonine features. Furry skin, hair like an auburn mane, cat-like snout. Its eyes blazed bright blue. A display at the base of the alcove read: Cultist 18 A, Modified Genome.

She walked down the aisle, reading the names on every alcove. Each one she passed, the phantom morphed into a human figure. Colonists in old jumpsuits regarded her with stern stares while a few more leonine forms appeared. None tried to break the transparent shells or made any obvious attempts at communication.

They had to be weak Class Cs, or even Class Ds, something she'd rarely encountered. She wondered if that had anything to do with their imprisonment.

A familiar whirring noise drew her attention to a corridor leading from the aisle. Roxie walked down it and stopped on a platform overlooking an open chamber. It was filled with electromagnetic emitters, which could attract a phantom within a kilometer. This many in one location could attract them from dozens of kilometers around.

Maybe hundreds of kilometers.

"What the fuck?" she whispered.

Not only did someone have captive phantoms, they used emitters to draw more.

Something heavy clacked in the aisle.

Roxie remained still. A suctioning, hissing noise. Another. Then another.

The alcoves were opening.

Azure forms stepped out. The air crackled with energy. Spots filled Roxie's vision. The prickling sensation became a burning one.

As soon as the phantoms left the translucent shells, they vanished from sight. Invisible to her eyes.

Without thinking, Roxie popped the Cinn tab into her mouth.

She scooted back onto the platform above the emitters, swishing the tab inside her mouth. The tangy, spicy taste tingled her gums and slid down her throat. Her breathing quickened and she licked her lips.

But she had to resist the coming euphoric rush. It was the only way she could find out what was going on down here. She wasn't a slave to it anymore. It was just a chemical compound the Jovians had created. Nothing more.

The masonry blocks along the walls came alive with ancient hieroglyphics. She swept her gaze over the platform and the lower chamber. Though she'd witnessed the electromagnetic light pulsing off an emitter while on Cinn, seeing so many at once, their EM light saturating everything, numbed her senses. Was this what the phantoms saw?

She wrenched her gaze from the spectacle and face the aisle. As she neared the corner again, her vision exploded with a million shades her natural eyes would never see.

Dozens of phantoms stared at her, their glowing bodies giving off such collective radiation, she'd probably get cancer within a day. Even with irradiation shots, her skin warmed to the point of making her breathing labored. Her eyes, unused to so much electromagnetic light, hurt from the strain.

Cinn made these sensations feel good, but Roxie knew she had to get out.

One phantom, a woman in old-fashioned cotton clothes, neared Roxie.

"Back, love. Just let me out."

The phantom came closer.

"I'm not one of you. I'm not supposed to see you. Oh fuck, what have I done?"

Other phantoms drew near. Roxie giggled even as her heart wrenched with terror. There was no escape. As soon as she shot one, four would scorch her to ashes.

One of the phantoms neared the holo panel.

"Don't you bloody try it."

The phantom leaned over the panel. It sparked and shorted out, as did the generator box. An alarm sounded, only to be silenced as the phantoms' natural EMP blacked out all 'tronics. The dim lights powered off, leaving only the azure nightmare before her. The phantoms closed in on her. Throbbing in her eyesight.

By now their closeness should be singing her hair, burning her flesh. Blue, transparent fingers came within centimeters of her face, but Roxie ducked and scrabbled away. Reds, blues, purples, and every shade in between fluttered across her vision.

Cinn made her laugh. "Come on, you glowing pricks. I'm not afraid, see?"

Nausea spread through Roxie's gut. Compounded with her cramps, she doubled over while laughing. Anxiety, pain, love, hate—all her emotions, all her nerve endings, were chained to her pleasure centers. This time she burned from within as if each molecule were boiling in lava.

The phantoms came ever closer. A low hum rose in volume until hot liquid ran from her ears and nose.

"Stop!" Roxie stumbled and sobbed. "Just stop, I…"

Her vision leveled off into an even brighter selection of hues.

One phantom, a female with a leonine visage, laid a hand on Roxie's arm.

The jacket sleeve burned away but Roxie's skin was unharmed. Glowing violet smoke wafted off her flesh.

She met the phantom's eyes. The anguished humanity therein wilted Roxie's heart. Cinn transformed the emotion into stupefied rapture.

"I'm not one of you!" Roxie whooped and giggled. If she was going to die, she'd go out with a whopper of an orgasm. As she staggered near the floor, still laughing, she glimpsed waves of electromagnetic power wafting off of the emitters.

A phantom girl stepped out from the rest. Her cerulean form burned so bright, Roxie had to shield her eyes.

"Don't… I had no choice…"

A phantom boy came near her.

"I mean it!" She raised the gun, giggling and sobbing in the same breath. "Don't make me shoot you again …"

Another child stepped close.

Screaming, Roxie fired at the emitters.

The round streamed through the air. Hot, desperate, unstoppable.

Like she saw herself. Like Cinn made her feel.

Blue arms encircled her.

A brilliant purple-red flash blinded her for a moment. She turned aside as the emitters blew. A roaring wall of sound struck her ears and a roiling energy wave flung her into the air. Heat and flames licked at her. The sky collapsed, darkness gave way to harsh, yellow light—then she was free.

Blue arms held Roxie as she sped from the exploding complex.

Floating in the air, she felt as if she were ascending to Heaven. Like Mum had told her in the old Byrgius Cathedral on Luna, around those priests in the nylon robes, doling out the sacrament with a lead-lined glove …

She slammed into the ground. A tall leonine form stood over her, then fled.

The aches in her back made her jerk with orgasm. Roxie guffawed with joy and flapped her arms as blackened smoke rose several meters away.

Through fluttering eyelids she made out clouds, gravjets. Flipping over, she glimpsed a huge canyon on her left, then a burning blast crater in the ground far below. Shapes zipped here and there in her peripherals.

A tall, burning contraption stalked over the red soil nearby.

Her ears popped so hard that Roxie cried out in pain and pleasure. Staggering up, she coughed, then tumbled down. End over end she rolled until she collided with a stream of sand, rushing back toward the crater.

The loose sand deadened her fall but filled her eyes, nose, ears, and mouth. Roxie laughed anyway, Cinn making it all feel fantastic, until she rolled to a stop against something hard. Feeling about, she realized she'd rolled against a burning hoverbike.

The pain in her body became electrifying pleasure, allowing her to stand up and laugh while hoverbikes raced from the rising smoke. Other bikes smoldered in crumpled piles. Four bodies in brown clothing lay scattered over the sand.

Roxie laughed even as a distant part of her brain realized the man at her feet was the assassin. A quick glance revealed the other three bodies were those she'd killed in the hovertram tunnel.

Cinn forced her to laugh again, but it hurt this time.

Blue forms slid through the crater, the sand smoking from contact with their heated bodies. One flung aside a hoverbike, and the craft sailed through the air until it clipped a gravjet's wing. The aircraft spun out of control into the lip of the canyon. A fireball belched into the sky. Burning metal flew in all directions.

Roxie shot one of the phantoms, dissipating it in a puff of blue dust. As the dust fell to the ground, though, she could barely see it. Glancing around for other phantoms, she made out a few faded blue wisps—then nothing.

"No…no!" Roxie dug into her bra for a Cinn tab, but her clothing hung in tatters.

Smoke rose from the barrel as she aimed at nothing.

Roxie gasped and fell to her knees as the Cinn wore off with searing abruptness. Pain crawled along her body from new bruises, raw sores, oozing scrapes. Licking her lips, she tasted sand mixed with blood. She doubled over and vomited more of the same.

Shaking so much her teeth chattered, Roxie managed to look up as a four-meter tall monstrosity stomped through the sand toward the crater.

Its skeletal frame was charred, with plasti flesh hanging off it in melted clumps. Fire guttered from both its hands. A spout of flame continuously burned atop its head.

A Burner. The kill bot was no doubt attracted to the phantoms.

"The Flame is your salvation," the thing uttered in a grating, mechanical voice. "The Flame ignores poverty, wealth, stagnation. Obey the Flame!"

Jets of merciless fire shot from its hands and whooshed over the crater. Humanoid forms, wisps of fire popping off them, scattered from the crater. An invisible force slammed into the Burner, knocking it onto its back. Sand and fire spurted into the air as the Burner continued its ancient declarations.

Roxie tried to move but slumped onto her side. Heat from the Burner's flame jets warmed up her skin. The edge of her right boot caught fire, which she managed to stomp out as she winced in agony. Moving felt like death, and even breathing brought scratching aches inside her throat.

Tasting more sand and blood, she cocked her revolver anyway.

She fired at the Burner. The EM round blasted both phantom and kill bot in a blue-orange explosion. The Burner's limbs lay at odd angles, but its internal power source still fed its arm jets. Pointing up, they gushed angry flaming tongues at the sky.

Roxie dragged herself a few meters from the crater as two more Burners appeared on the other side. They clanked through the sand, the wind making their burning craniums flicker with deathly light. Another gravjet blew past, disturbing sand, sending it into Roxie's face. It circled around the crater and slowed. She cocked the revolver again, trying to keep it up as the Burners came closer.

"Rox!"

The voice reached her ears like a whisper from a dream. She laughed until she coughed again.

The gravjet drew near, the ramp extending while hovering in midair. Two figures jumped from it and landed near Roxie.

"Nice party, Rox. Why no invitations?" Chewing a Cinn tab, Doggie Boy raised a Draco pistol in each hand.

"Get on up, honey." Legs knelt beside her, wearing a layered mesh suit and knee-high boots. "You ain't fucked up that bad. There, now. Open your mouth."

He held a small orange capsule centimeters from her lips. His silver nail polish reflected the flames around them, the pinkish Martian sky. The inferno inside her.

If she didn't take it she might die right here.

Roxie lapped the Cinn tab from Legs's palm. He beamed, the darkness in his gray eyes devouring her. She chewed, swallowed. Laughed as he helped her up. Her fingers gave off a violet glow.

Standing on her own, Roxie aimed at a phantom appearing in her vision.

It had her face.

"The fuck?"

She stumbled, but Legs elbowed past her and fired. The phantom blew apart in cerulean fragments, vanishing before they hit the ground.

"Get your shit together, Street Angel." Legs fired his other Draco barrel. "That one wasn't on the house."

Roxie saw her face in all the phantoms' visages. Screaming, she blasted away until the revolver clicked empty, then she grabbed one of Doggie Boy's. Ignoring his protests, she squeezed the trigger again and again. Trying to prove that she was better, that she could survive without them. That she wasn't one of them.

Cinn didn't make it feel good anymore.

Chapter 11

"Eat this!" Doggie Boy shot a phantom. It disintegrated like snow over a heater.

"Watch this shite." Roxie fired twice, blasting a Burner's hand off and destroying the phantom it'd been fighting. "Now that's the dog's bollocks."

"Woo-hoo!" Doggie Boy groped his crotch and laughed.

On a dune across from them, Legs reloaded his double-barreled piece. He smiled at her, but her knees wobbled and she flopped onto her rump.

"Smoke break?" Doggie Boy plopped down beside her and laughed.

Two gravjets flew over. Shots echoed down into the canyon like thunder, but the storm was the one she'd unleashed from the bowels of this little hell she'd uncovered.

A Burner crept toward them from the crater. It blasted everything before it with duel flaming hands. All around it, sand shriveled and popped into glass shards, then melted again into disfigured heaps. Doggie Boy popped off two shots into it, but the Burner's armor merely smoked as the kill bot came closer.

"Let me try." Roxie aimed as Doggie Boy tossed aside his empty gun and stuck his tongue in her ear.

Squirming, she still managed to knock the side of the Burner's head off.

"Here, this might help."

Doggie Boy stuck his finger into her mouth, but Roxie shoved him off. Her next shot went wild, puffing up the sand in a dust cloud.

Why wasn't the Cinn making all this awesome? How many times had they done this, every second singing with ecstasy?

"Wait, this will do the trick!" Doggie Boy got and unzipped his pants.

Roxie shivered, flame and phantoms scintillating in her Cinn-drenched vision.

"Doggie Boy? Just…just stop."

The Burner trod up the incline, its empty mechanical eyes fixed on them.

It fired.

While Doggie Boy whooped, Roxie ducked, the flames going right over her head. Some of the hairs on Doggie Boy's arms curled over and smoked. The tip of his ponytail was now ashes. He looked at her with awed eyes, then burst into laughter.

"Run, goddammit!" Roxie aimed lazily at the Burner right atop them.

She knew she should move, at least shoot, but she waited for Cinn to make all her wounds a miniature bite of chocolate, a lick on her clit, a sup of good whiskey. Enraptured in so much pleasure she wouldn't want to move, fearing it would end.

Agony ripped through her body instead, heightened by her expanded senses.

Snickering, Doggie Boy pissed in the Burner's direction just as something blew it apart in a cloud of black shrapnel. The explosion knocked Doggie Boy back two meters, while Roxie rolled away until her left arm and leg scraped over the canyon's edge.

Flames ran up her right pants leg.

She patted it out and wrenched away the burning fabric. Her hands glowed again.

Little of her clothing remained. Already she had a slight skin burn from so much flame exposure, and the cool Martian air cracked it. Cinn should have transformed every bit of that into another orgasm. She groaned on the canyon's lip and wished the drug would make everything alright.

"Get up, you dumbasses. You want to die, do it on your own time."

The gruff voice made Roxie roll from the edge and look up the incline.

Dirty Cool stood there, shotgun smoking as he nudged Doggie Boy with his boot.

"I almost had it," Doggie Boy breathed.

"Get the fuck up." Dirty Cool nudged him again, then walked down and yanked Roxie to her feet. "That thing was right on top of you both."

"I had it under control," Roxie muttered as her limbs ached.

Two hundred meters distant, she spotted a phantom slowly vanishing while making for a gravjet. Cinn was leaving her again. Abandoning her when she needed it most so she would come back begging for it.

"That fucking wanker." Roxie leaned on Dirty Cool. "He brought me here."

"Who?" Doggie Boy chuckled.

Dirty Cool's expression was covered by his synthskin mask, but his eyes stabbed into her. "You can give a deposition when we get out of this little fuck hole."

"Good. Then I can get paid." She wiped soot and sweat off her face. "How did you get here so fast?"

"Necrostructs and Burners been all over this backwater." Dirty Cool loaded another concussive into his shotgun. "Right after you botched a simple little job for Daedala. You know how fucked up this planet is right now?"

"Not as fucked up as my head." Roxie groaned and stumbled.

Dirty Cool grabbed her arm and held her steady.

"Get it together. If HQ didn't want your ass so bad, I'd leave you out here. Fuck, Roxie! You will never get it. Never fucking get it."

He stomped off, aimed at three necrostructs, and fired. The concussive shredded the skeletal trio into junk. Other coilguns fired nearby.

The rolling dunes north of Tithonium Chasma was dotted with necrostructs. She turned all way round, spotting a group of Burners clanking in from the west. Near the crater where she'd discovered the secret chamber, a gravjet had landed. UG soldiers gathered up the four bodies Locust and his rebels had left. To the south, *Crimson Aegis* floated above Valles Marineris, gravjets and drones exiting its docks. The carrier's huge shadow still looked tiny in the bottom of the cyclopean canyon.

Eastward, several hunters battled phantoms, among them Amai Shi. Mingled in with them, though, were a few armored UGPD officers, something she hadn't seen in the field for years. They acted more as support, carting two dead hunters back to a gravjet. Fifty meters away two gravjets lay crashed into the sand, burning.

Bodies hung from one of the cockpits.

Roxie sank to her knees. She had unleashed war on Mars.

What did the UGPD think she had done? She'd saved Daedala's life, and those soldiers had…no, there wasn't time for that now. Dirty Cool was right. She needed to prepare for what was coming. Either she'd be a heroine, or a pariah. A scapegoat for every little mishap that had taken place over the last few hours.

She still didn't know why.

Grunting, Roxie kicked aside a necrostruct's charred head. She needed Cinn so it would all make sense.

She reached into her bra, but found only ashes in the cleft of her breasts.

Dirty Cool shot another phantom. Roxie shook her head.

"How can you even see these buggers?"

He didn't look at her. "Because I've been here longer than you. Now move."

While Dirty Cool covered them with his shotgun, Roxie caught up to Doggie Boy, who zipped his pants and groaned. His Cinn had worn off too, but he'd recovered both of his revolvers. Roxie blinked. She'd lost her own gun.

"Give me one of those, love." Roxie reached for Doggie Boy's holsters, but Dirty Cool blocked her.

"Hey, stop fannying about, I need—"

"To shut up and keep walking," Dirty Cool said. "You've stirred the shitstorm enough today."

Before Roxie could argue, Amai Shi approached, eyes glazed over with Cinn. Magblade in one hand, SMG in the other, she barred their path to the nearest gravjet.

"*Nantekotta i?*" Amai Shi gestured at Roxie. "You really don't think you can just shoot a few kill bots and take her out of here?"

"I do what the fuck I please." Dirty Cool fired at something Roxie couldn't see.

"So you can collect?" Amai Shi asked.

Roxie whipped her head around. "What?"

Doggie Boy snorted. "Don't worry, Rox. You're a person of interest, not a damned criminal."

"Better if one of us brings her in," Amai Shi said. "Not an old UGPD fart."

"Shut the fuck up. I mean it." Dirty Cool raised the shotgun.

"Tell me what the bloody hell is going on." Despite all her aches, Roxie brimmed with alertness. She reached for one of Doggie Boy's pistols again.

Dirty Cool and Amai Shi casually leveled their guns at Roxie.

Explosions and gunfire boomed around them, but no one flinched. Roxie glowered back at their emotionless stares.

Shrugging, Doggie Boy tried to take her arm. "Listen, Harmon just wants—"

"What the fuck does he want?" Roxie shouted.

"Come with me, *tenshi*," Amai Shi said. "We'll split your bounty and laugh about all this later, when your name's cleared."

"Bounty? I'm a bloody hunter like you. I'm ranked number one!"

Their silence only made her angrier.

"You Geisha bitch," Roxie said. "Is this how you'll get off this sodding planet?"

"Shut the hell up and we can all come out of this with plenty of creds," Amai Shi said. "Now put your hands—"

Roxie leapt at Amai Shi, but she rammed the handle of her magblade into Roxie's stomach. Roxie crumbled into the red soil.

"You can barely walk, I'm trying to make this easier on you, and you want to *tatakai*?" Cinn lit Amai Shi's eyes with eagerness. "You stupid bitch."

"I could fight you with my fucking eyes closed." Roxie clutched her stomach.

Amai Shi's laugh was strained. "You have no clue what they're doing to us—"

Dirty Cool crunched the butt of his shotgun into Amai Shi's face. She collapsed into the sand and dropped her weapons.

"I'll eat your fucking eyes if you say anything else, you painted cum nugget." Dirty Cool loomed over Amai Shi. "HQ wants Street Angel. So they get her."

Amai Shi scrambled up. Her bruised cheek and crushed lip darkened and then reformed, whole. A new dragon tattoo appeared on the healed cheek.

"You've got her—for now." Amai Shi took her weapons and walked away.

In all her years on Mars, Roxie had never seen hunters fight each other with so much danger around them. There must be a huge price on her head. And no amount of Cinn would have made Amai Shi say that without a reason.

"I've never seen anybody attack a Burner with piss before," Roxie said, trying to take her mind off her pain and trepidation.

"Told you I had a big—"

A screech drowned out Doggie Boy's words as something flung a Burner at a passing gravjet. The kill bot exploded, sending the craft careening into a nearby hillside. It blew apart in a yellow-orange mushroom.

A shockwave of heat blew over the dune and knocked them all down.

A flaming wing swiped past Roxie's head. Fiery slag pelted the sand with bone-crunching thuds. A scorched helmet with hair still attached rolled past her leg. Dirty Cool lay still, bleeding through his mask. Doggie Boy sat up, then lay back down, yelling in pain. Roxie gave herself a quick scan. No new wounds she could see.

"Motherfucker!" Doggic Boy cried. "I'm not in the mood to die today!"

"Makes two of us." Roxie felt Dirty Cool's neck. Still had a pulse. "It'd take a meteor to kill you."

"I swear you were about to suck me off back there." Doggie Boy laughed. "Not about to die yet, and—motherfucking son of a bitch, ouch!"

Roxie yanked a burning piece of shrapnel from his right thigh.

"Hey, now you got one to match mine." She shook her heated hand.

"That mean we can screw … oh goddamn, I need a smoke!"

"Sure, love. Once the sand fairies give you a blowjob, eat my vag, and rescue us."

Roxie coughed and studied their surroundings. A giant flame blocked their path. Nothing but two dead hunters, one decapitated UGPD officer, and a pile of smoking necrostructs all around.

She dug out Doggie Boy's earbud and shoved it into her own ear. "Bugger it all, you ever eject the earwax?"

"That's what … oh fuck … that's what I got your tongue for."

Doggie Boy tried to smile but winced. Blood leaked down his right side where another shard of metal had pierced the skin. Real pain shone in his eyes. Real fear.

"We gonna make it, Rox?"

"You bet."

She clasped his hand and smiled, though her heart ached seeing him wounded.

Ever since he'd come to Mars, it had been all partying, shagging, and Cinn-laced firefights. The same as her. She could never imagine him growing old. Or herself.

"Well … what happens now?" He reached for one of his pistols, but the barrel had been bent in the blast. "Damn it. That was my favorite one."

"Got any Cinn left?"

"You think if I did, I wouldn't have…fuck!…I wouldn't have eaten it?" He grasped his thigh and writhed in the sand.

Roxie crawled over to one of the dead hunters, a man in a purple tunic with a shaved head. Half of his face was burned off and a hole still smoldered all the way through his chest. The tunic and shaved head gave him away as Shaolin. He'd been on Mars less than six months. The UGPD was getting pretty thick-headed, sending out rookies like this. Or desperate.

Not as desperate as she was. She dug into Shaolin's pockets, under his armpits, even into his waistband, until she finally grabbed a plasti wallet tied around his leg. It contained two orange tabs. Two more one-way rides to paradise.

Roxie gulped one down and slid the other into her bra.

"Don't be a stranger." She patted Shaolin's stiff shoulder and crawled back to where her friends lay.

A clanking noise reached her ears.

"Did you just…ha ha. You checked under his junk?" Doggie Boy's face was pale.

"Shh."

Roxie kept crawling, eyes searching everywhere as the sweet taste rose in her mouth. She willed it to act faster, flood her system so she could get her friends to safety.

Wherever that was.

A necrostruct lacking its coilgun came over the opposite dune. It saw her and walked in her direction. It would pass Doggie Boy first.

Though the drug still provided no pleasure, the Cinn energized Roxie. She ran on all fours to Dirty Cool's shotgun. The necrostruct maintained the same patient pace.

Her fingers closed around the shotgun handle. The necrostruct was a meter away from Doggie Boy. She grabbed the weapon and aimed.

The necrostruct's blade came down.

"Nope." Roxie pulled the trigger.

The heavy-duty round knocked the skeletal bot all the way back down the dune without its head and shoulders. Its blade arm stabbed at the air twice, then went still.

"Nice," Doggie Boy said. "But Dirty Cool will fuck you up for touching—"

He gasped and coughed. More blood seeped into the sand.

"Shut it." Roxie walked a perimeter around the dune. One hand holding the shotgun at hip level, the other pressing the earbud.

"Spotter Control?" Her voice cracked, raw with dust and pain.

A necrostruct clawed up the dune, its legs blown away.

She blasted it to bits and tapped again. "Hey, nanny wagon, you copy me?"

A blue form slithered over the canyon lip on her left. Roxie whipped the shotgun around, then remembered she hadn't reloaded it.

"Come on anyway, love." Roxie's heart swelled with confidence. "I'll rip you apart before you take them."

The phantom took on the form of a leonine-faced woman. With feline grace it padded over the sand, leaving no footprints. All the while it maintained eye contact.

A body-wracking shiver came over Roxie. "What do you buggers really want? You want me off Mars? I'd be glad to oblige."

The phantom cocked it head and studied Roxie.

Roxie kept the shotgun aimed. Sweat streaked down her face and stung her bloodied lips. Cinn kept her standing, but a thousand hungry agonies chewed at her body.

With a bare foot the phantom traced something in the sand.

Heart slamming against her ribs, Roxie waited. All her training and experience urged her to shoot. Judging from its size, the phantom had to be a Class B.

The phantom stopped tracing. It had drawn a hieroglyphic similar to those she'd seen in Cydonian pyramids and temples. They stared at one another for several long moments, the hairs on the back of Roxie's neck on end.

Rippling like azure water, the phantom skimmed over the plain until it disappeared into Tithonium Chasma.

Roxie stared at the hieroglyphic. It was rounded, with a cross on one end and a spiral at the other.

"Trent? This is Spotter Control. Evac is ETA three minutes on your position. Copy that?"

She tapped the earbud. "Copy. Trent out."

"Who were you … talking to?" Doggie Boy's lips were blue.

"Angels, love." She felt Dirty Cool's pulse. It remained strong.

"Only angel on this red marble is you." Doggie Boy coughed and moaned. "Now fly away … before they take you to Hell."

"Been there. Their drinks suck." Roxie forced a grin as she gripped his hand. "Why don't you fly instead?"

She placed the extra Cinn tab into his mouth.

"Don't leave," he said. "Even when they get here … don't leave."

"I'm right here, love." Roxie looked away as he closed his eyes.

CHAPTER 12

As Roxie exited the gravjet, she squinted at the bright lights shining from UGPD's dock. More aircraft than usual filled the skies above New Paris. Far below, klaxon curfew alarms rang out. Even the hovertrams were shut down.

Two squads of soldiers waited past the dock doors. Glaring at her.

Maybe this was worse than she thought.

Stumbling down the ramp, Roxie sealed the jacket given her by the attendant. Each step felt lighter since two of her g-ballasts had been destroyed in the battle. After coming down off Cinn, the attendant had administered nano gauze to seal her cuts and deaden her bruises. It was expensive, like nothing they'd ever given her before.

Doggie Boy had paid the highest price of all, though.

During the flight from Valles Marineris, Dirty Cool had remained unconscious. The gravjet's crew had ignored her questions about the fiasco in Chasma City, saying she'd be briefed at HQ.

The silent treatment. That's all she'd gotten since leaving Tithonium Chasma. She didn't even know if Legs or Amai Shi had survived. Judging from what she'd seen as the gravjet carried her away, casualties were high.

She forced herself not to look at Doggie Boy's body bag again.

Once inside HQ, Roxie passed a line of hovering camera bots. She unsealed her jacket and tossed it over her shoulder, revealing her tattered shirt and bruised flesh. One pant leg had been ripped off at the hip, and one of her boots was melted through.

The cameras followed and shot her at every angle.

"This is what Mars does to you," she said.

Four soldiers flanked her. The camera bots took a few more shots and left.

As she passed the *Fantôme Salon*, other hunters rose from their tables and stared. Some nodded in respect, while others shook their heads or made anxious murmurs.

Around the corner, Amai Shi was turning in her kill tally at the contract booth. She gave Roxie a neutral glance, though her painted lips were tight.

"Sugar, you've sure assed it up this time," Legs said as Roxie turned the next corner. "Fellas, wait a minute."

She eyed how close his hand was to his gunbelt.

"Guess you're not selling little bits of orange forgiveness this time."

"They still need you," Legs said. "So play nice. Don't be stupid like him."

Two attendants wheeled Doggie Boy's body bag past.

"He's not even fucking cold yet." Her voice cracked on the last word.

"But you gotta be cold now." Legs gave her a forlorn nod. "You gotta be."

She glimpsed Amai Shi leaving the booth. She needed to talk to her. Dirty Cool had prevented her from saying something…

Legs lit a cig and blew smoke in Roxie's face. "Ain't gonna be the same again, you understand?"

"What the bloody hell are you—?"

"Roxie Trent, report to Conference Room A, South Wing," a voice said over the intercom. The soldiers nudged her on.

"Give 'em what they want, honey," Legs called after her. "It'll go easier for you."

Her blue-clad escort led her down another hallway and through a security detection terminal. She'd already been cleared once en route to New Paris.

This time the terminal emitted a long beep. The soldiers looked at each other. The terminal operator cleared his throat and hurried with the next scan. Her ConRec tattoo stung for a few seconds while she blinked away more colored dots. Finally, they continued to a set of double doors. One soldier motioned for her to enter.

Roxie pushed open both doors. Conference Room A was small with no windows. Vidscreens along the walls showed current footage from Chasma City.

Only two figures waited within: Lorne Harmon seated behind a desk—and Styra.

Harmon looked her over.

"Too bad you don't look worse. I might be willing to hear your case, were you crippled and dying."

A vidscreen displaying her profile went dark before Roxie could read the new additions in red letters. She loosed a slow, deep breath.

The vidscreens reflected off Styra's half chrome-skull in a whorl of televised destruction. She wore more armor than usual, with magdarts strapped along her forearms.

"What am I accused of? Think I tried to off Daedala?"

"Would that you had. It would make this process much easier." Harmon kept glancing from the vidscreen on his desk back to Roxie's face.

"You drew a weapon and fired," Styra said. "At what, who the fuck knows. The camera bots recorded nothing unusual."

"I saved her life." Roxie crossed her arms.

"Then left her open to further attack by jumping onto a hovertram," Styra said. "Very professional. Very predictable of you."

"I was chasing the assassin—"

"I was there and saw nothing!" Styra shouted.

Harmon raised a hand. "We have footage of what happened afterward. Over two hundred dead and three thousand wounded in that fucking riot you caused. And that's just in Chasma City."

Roxie shook her head. "Your goddamn jarheads need to—"

"We also have four bodies, all of them natives. Then we have an explosion followed by the appearance of eighty-six detected phantoms east of Chasma City, right beside the canyon."

"How many did I—?"

"According to STASCAN, you shot seven," Harmon said. "Impressive, unless one considers how much the UGPD lost in responding to such a huge threat. All of those phantoms attracted twelve Burners and sixty-three necrostructs."

"How many did we lose?" She recalled the final smile on Doggie Boy's face.

"Eight hunters. Nineteen UGPD officers. Four gravjets and their crews." His stare was ice. "The UGPD was already short-handed. Now it is almost inoperable."

"If a phantom herd of any size attacks a UG facility," Styra said, "we will not be able to counter it."

Roxie leaned on the desk. "You blokes ready for the best part? Those phantoms weren't there for some big smash, hoping someone would come along. They were contained within that crater, in a bloody lab or something. Someone linked a bunch of emitters together to attract them."

"No evidence was discovered of such a thing," Styra said. "You are making up bullshit to save your ass."

"The bullshit is that you're in this room talking to me," Roxie said.

In a split-second Styra aimed her pistol at Roxie's head.

Roxie didn't flinch.

"Put it away." Harmon's calm voice chilled her far more than Styra's iron-melting glare. Styra holstered the weapon, never breaking eye contact.

"Styra is here because she was charged with overseeing riot control in Chasma City. The entire city is on lockdown. There have been similar instances of civil unrest in Ilios on the Icaria Plain, as well as a starport at Tharsis Mounts."

"Daedala?" She continued staring at Styra.

"She is safe in the Jovian compound atop Tharsis Tholus," Harmon said. "A group of Covenant members arrived and are seeing to her. We have two platoons in place there, as well as other security measures."

"So what's my story going to be?" Roxie finally looked away from Styra and focused on Harmon. Her stomach started to growl, but she shifted weight from one foot to the other and tensed her abdominals.

Never let them see you starve, a Martian proverb went.

"The Covenant has come to the conclusion that you abandoned their priestess, thus endangering the pact the UG has signed with them regarding ambassadors. The UG has decided that you incited the riot at Chasma City, and afterward, tried to use your newfound popularity to sensationalize a hunting trip gone wrong."

"The fuck—?"

"On said hunting trip, you used emitters to summon phantoms outside of UGPD contract. Thus, not only will you not be compensated for your kills, but you are held liable for all damages, deaths, and destruction of property suffered by the UGPD—"

"Got to hell."

Styra's steel-like fingers encircled Roxie's neck and lifted her off the floor.

"You first."

This time, Harmon did not reprimand her rival.

"I saved hunters out there," Roxie managed, her windpipe closing together. "Someone planted that lab there…"

Styra smiled as she mashed Roxie's larynx, bruising her throat.

Harmon stood and adjusted his tunic. "Indeed they did. Had you not been so reckless and leveled the place, we might have found out who. Had you shown some mercy, we might have been able to question one of those 'assassins'. Put her down."

Styra let Roxie drop to the floor.

Blood popped from Roxie's nose and lip and she gasped for air. Her throat wouldn't cooperate, as if the flesh and esophagus had melded together.

"If she's damaged, I'll sell your ass for scrap." Harmon jabbed a finger into Styra's chest. "Don't forget how you fucked up, too."

Rubbing her throat, Roxie gave Harmon a confused look.

"You are correct." Harmon knelt beside Roxie. "You did save fellow hunters. You did discover a troubling secret beneath those sands."

Roxie coughed, bloody droplets spattering the floor. Her guts curled up into a tight ball but she forced the vomit back down and glowered up at Styra.

"And?" she rasped through an aching throat.

Harmon stood. "For the public's sake, and to assuage our slighted Jovian guests, you will be held here in New Paris. In our detainment facilities on Level 5."

"How … long?"

"Until we can work out what to do with you." Harmon nodded to Styra, who yanked Roxie to her feet. "You cannot be in the public eye right now."

"Why?"

"My scientists wish to run some tests on you first," Harmon said.

Roxie's eyes widened.

Styra's scowl deepened.

"Think of this short vacation as a benefit for your own safety. Afterward, based on those tests—I will reevaluate your situation." Harmon sat back down.

Styra shoved Roxie to an elevator as two squads of soldiers flanked them. Roxie tried to remain calm but one of the soldiers carried a yellow jumpsuit and handcuffs. As the elevator descended into the depths of New Paris, she trembled. She'd heard the rumors, saw the bodies carted down to Necro Row.

"You won't break me."

"You have already broken yourself. Look at you. You can barely stand, Street Angel. Who started that shit? Legs? Bastard wishes he had a cunt as wide as yours."

"I bet your cock is bigger than his."

"You're going to learn all about big cocks where you're going." Styra grinned. "You'll be popular. Real fucking popular."

"Then I'll still number one in two things you suck at: hunts and shagging."

Styra snatched the handcuffs and clamped them onto Roxie's wrists.

"We'll see."

The cuffs, though not connected, kept Roxie's wrists held together via internal magnets. The painful, awkward position made her arms pinch into her chest. Her hands numbed from the tight magnetic force.

The elevator stopped.

A soldier shoved Roxie into a narrow hallway. Cameras, gun turrets, and a nanite displacement terminal waited at the end of it.

The overhead sign read Prison Block 8, Level 4.

"This isn't where I'm supposed to bloody go. Harmon said Level 5."

Styra grasped the back of Roxie's neck and walked her forward.

They paused at the terminal, which ran a lighted ray over the length of Roxie's body. She stiffened, waiting for the Jovian nanites to be found.

The terminal beeped a negative and Styra pushed Roxie through the door.

The device didn't detect them. Was Locust lying?

The door led into a larger room with cubicles, vidscreens displaying camera feeds in prisoner cells, and several detainment personnel that all regarded Roxie as a smelly turd. One approached with a nullifier, but Styra waved him off and led Roxie into a cell block. Each cell was nothing but a small dark space with a camera in the ceiling.

She wondered how many *La Rèsistance* members had been brought here.

Never to return.

Would she return? Roxie never gave dying much thought. Like not thinking about next month's rent, or running out of food.

The prospect of dying just made her want a hit of Cinn.

Styra paused before a cell door and shoved her inside.

No cot, window, or chair. Just a drain in the middle of the floor, catching whatever would leak from her body in this little death hole. A thick bleach stench stung her nose. Harsh light shone from above.

Six troopers entered behind Styra and the door slid shut.

Roxie breathed so hard that her lungs hurt.

"You must change into this jumpsuit," Styra said. "It will protect you."

"From what?"

Styra lifted Roxie up and ripped her pants and boots off.

"Now we'll see what you're really good for." Styra yanked off Roxie's shirt. "A slut who bents over for a hit of Cinn."

Now she stood in her halter top and underwear.

"Fuck you," Roxie breathed.

Styra beckoned for the soldiers.

One held each of her bound hands while another slapped Roxie's rump.

She swallowed as her sweat splashed onto the floor.

First payment to that drain.

Styra moved to the doorway—out of the cameras' view.

"Fuck all of you!" Roxie shouted.

Styra smiled. "They can hammer your vag all day, but it won't matter. You're neutered. Like a bitch dog in one of those rich people's houses above us. Neutered and kept like a slave."

"At least I'm still human. You're just a collection of fuck-knock off the UG dug up in a junkyard."

Styra nodded to the soldiers.

One of them unzipped his fly.

Fear stabbed through Roxie's heart.

"You fucking coward! This is the only way you can take me!"

"You think this is about ego? I'm not so petty as that, you little cunt. I tried to have you killed by those fake rebels in that latrine. Then those assassins at Chasma City. But you're not going to replace me."

"Then why?" Roxie squirmed in their grasp.

A soldier slapped her face.

"You see how much I've lost?" Styra tapped her half-skull. "So they could have what they wanted? You dumb bitch, you don't even know what Harmon's got planned for you. But I can still be what he wants—with you out of the way."

"You recording this for him to jack off to later?" Her voice became a whine.

The soldier punched her in the stomach. Another one unbuckled his pants.

"I'm recording it so when they find your body, Harmon will think you were fucked over. Like everyone else on this goddamn planet."

Roxie tensed, trying to keep her legs clamped together.

"No matter what you do to me, you'll never—"

Styra shoved something into Roxie's mouth, then forced her lips shut.

She tried to spit it out, but Styra rammed a knee into her stomach. After the third strike, Roxie sucked down the object, her guts quivering with agony.

"I want to watch you fuck every one of these soldiers while on Cinn. Each thrust into you, every time you gag on their cocks. You'll even thank me while they do it."

The sweetness saturating her mouth made her sick. Bile crawled up her throat.

"I gave you a quadruple dose because I know you're past Phase Two. The chemicals have already saturated your cells, but you still might feel that high. Now, guys—show her how we treat angels."

The Cinn made Roxie laugh even as a tear slid down her cheek.

Second payment to the floor drain.

Steaming hot water blasted over them, followed by billowing steam clouds. It shot from the walls while lime-green powder fell from the ceiling. Roxie giggled as the water scorched dirt off her flesh. The cell's yellow light made everything waver with orange-yellow shadows.

"What the hell?" Styra jerked back.

The door opened and the detainment warden walked in.

"Hey, she has to be deloused first! Put those dicks away or they'll fall off, you dumb bastards. She's still radioactive!"

The Cinn erased Roxie's hurts, fears. Everything glowed with ultraviolet majesty.

The soldiers shoved Roxie away and tried to zip their pants while heated water continued to spray them. Their bodies pulsed in her vision, in a variety of hues.

Red most of all.

Roxie rammed her knee into a soldier's groin. His genitals cracked under the impact. Yelping, he crashed back into Styra, who stumbled into the warden.

Though the Cinn drowned her with its typical elation, Roxie had full control of herself. Her skin crackled with energy. Water hissed into steam upon contacting her.

The other soldier fought with his zipper, but Roxie brought the edge of the cuffs down and jerked to one side.

The soldier screamed as blood and urine gushed from his ruptured penis.

"You dumb sons of bitches, put her down!" the warden cried.

"I'll have your guts for this!" Styra yelled into his face.

"Fuck off, you Psycoid bitch. Leave now and nothing gets reported!"

Roxie laughed, her body afire with Cinn. It lent her inhuman strength.

She stared down at the drain as red and yellow liquid swirled into it.

Third payment.

"This isn't over!" Styra shoved past the warden and out the door.

Two prison guards ran in, batons raised.

Roxie covered her face as a baton slapped against her stomach. She elbowed the guard's neck, snapping his head around. The warden screamed for more help.

By the time she finished crushing the other guard's skull into bone splinters and pulp, nine more ran in with batons and brass knuckles.

Three more guards fell before they put her down.

Chapter 13

Roxie forced the rest of the nutrient gruel down her bruised throat. Its clobbered chunks tasted like rotten cabbage that had been shit in by someone with milk diarrhea.

After emptying the cup, she tossed it away. She had to piss again but the cell's cleansing system wouldn't activate for another three hours—if she recalled the passage of time—and she didn't want to smell the urine for that long.

This was her ninth day in the cell … maybe the tenth.

She hated math.

At least she was off the jam rag. They probably got tired of her squatting over the drain ten times a day. They gave her plenty of tampons now.

Styra had visited the day after her attempt at staged rape, but the warden had accompanied her. They'd watched Roxie got deloused, but that was all he would allow.

Styra was waiting. So was Roxie.

Maintaining energy to fight back was the only reason she ate the horrible meals.

Roxie leaned her head against the wall and recalled her arrest after *Jubilee* returned from that hellish cruise. The relatives of the wealthy victims had spat on her as soon as she was escorted through the starport. The UG blamed her for all the deaths, claiming she could have sealed the terrorists in the aft section to safeguard the passengers. They sent her to Mars, plying the only trade they thought she knew.

Killing.

During her first month with the UGPD, Roxie had tried to save a Martian family from a necrostruct, but its coilgun struck a power grid, killing them. The blast had thrown her twenty meters, leaving her in the infirmary for two weeks.

Dirty Cool named her Street Angel afterward.

Most hunters went by an alias, though when a more experienced hunter doled one out, it always stuck. Ever since, her fellow hunters had called her that.

She smiled sadly. Even as a little girl, Roxie had never believed in angels like Mum. But she did like the flying bit. Her gaze rose from the floor, climbing along the walls until it reached the ceiling. Her smile faded. There was no escape for this angel.

As she counted the steam sprinklers inset into the walls, she blinked.

Purple and red spots passed through her vision.

The cell door slid open.

Roxie inched forward. It was now or never.

"Now step inside. Slowly."

The voice made her heart leap into her throat.

A prison guard stepped in, hands at his sides. Behind him came a UG soldier.

Just as she was about to say his name, Legs held a finger to his lips. His other hand pressed a pistol into the guard's back.

"Now … tell her she's beautiful."

"Uh … you're beautiful?" The guard gaped at Roxie, sweat dotting his brow.

Legs shut the door and shoved the guard to the floor. "It's not a question, cumstain. Say it and mean it."

"You're very beautiful," the guard said.

"You added a word. Dumbass."

Legs shoved a detoxer needle into the guard's neck. The guard spasmed and collapsed onto the floor.

"So I'm just beautiful then?" Roxie asked in a rough voice, her throat still healing.

Legs smiled. "Here sugar, get into this choad nugget's uniform. The cameras will come back on in two minutes."

Energized with hope and purpose, Roxie peeled off the yellow jumpsuit and undressed the guard.

Legs winced at her bruised nudity.

"Not how I wanted to be seen, right?" She pulled a shirt over her head, grimacing at its cheap cologne and body stink.

"Not how I wanted to see you, honey. I would've been here two days ago, but security is tight as fuck right now. Not just here, but everywhere."

"Anyway…thanks."

"Ain't outta this yet. Now c'mon."

They walked past the other cells. Legs crammed a UG cap over her head and handed her the dead guard's baton. Neither spoke as they entered the room with cubicles, vidscreens, and the main elevator.

Two clerks and a guard conversed in a cubicle, but everyone else was gone.

"Night shift," Legs mouthed to her.

A trundling noise made them flatten against the wall.

A gunbot rolled past. Its minigun swerved back and forth.

Legs pointed at a different corridor where another elevator waited. They hurried to it, just out of sight of the gunbot. Two cameras watched them go but nothing happened. No alarms, no shouts.

She spotted the other cell doors. A fury rose deep inside of her.

"We should break them all out," she whispered in his ear.

Gripping her shoulder, Legs shook his head. Roxie finally nodded.

He punched a code into the pad and the elevator opened. After they got in, the weightless feeling of descent sloshed the gruel in her stomach.

"We should have released all the blokes up there," Roxie said.

"No time. I had to go through a lotta shit just to get you out."

"How did you manage all this?" she asked.

"I was a hacker for a Caravan gang."

"That's why you're on Mars? You said it was so bad you couldn't talk about it."

"Sugar, you ever try busting through UG military codes? Shit like that made me wanna take a hot shower afterward."

"You lying bugger." Roxie squeezed his arm. "But if we make it, we'll never work for the UGPD again."

Legs checked his pistol. "Nothing lasts forever, Street Angel."

"Don't call me that."

"After this you'll have to pick some other name. Roxie Trent and Legs ain't gonna be seen again after today."

The elevator stopped and the door slid open.

They entered a maintenance area crammed with generators, ductwork, pipes, and tool cabinets. The hum of machinery barely muted the sound of their footsteps.

"If that database was right, this leads to Necro Row where they deposit dead inmates." Legs tiptoed as they passed a row of empty gurneys.

One bore bloodstains. Gnats buzzed around another, stinking of sex.

Coming around a corner, they spotted a guard.

He was watching a porn vid, pumping his fist into his crotch.

Roxie raised the baton.

"At least let him finish," Legs whispered into her ear.

"Oh, for fuck's sake."

Roxie whacked the guard's temple just before he climaxed. He toppled to the floor and groaned. She bludgeoned him again, making him go limp.

"Poor bastard." Legs sighed.

"You sick fuck. Where'd that database say the exit was?"

"Exit? It's a disposal chute, honey. No more doors where we're going."

She gaped at him.

"Trust me."

If only he knew what he was asking for. She still felt dirty, could still see Styra watching. Still feel the soldiers' hands on her. Cinn could have taken her above it. Taken her so high, so far that she would have forgotten all of this.

Things were different now.

"One at a time. I'll go first." Legs pushed a lever.

A small hatch opened before a conveyor belt.

"Just lay flat and don't freak out. The chute dumps into a collection basket on the level below. It might contain dead bodies."

"You believe a sodding database?" Roxie frowned at the conveyor.

"It's been right about everything so far." Legs lay on the conveyor. In seconds he was gone, passing through the hatch into darkness.

She wanted to escape, make Harmon and Styra pay, find out Daedala's game—but this was beyond desperate. Even on her darkest days she'd still had a contract, a gun, some creds to buy a bag of amp powder.

Back then, she hadn't cared about the future. Now she wanted to discover what was happening on this planet. Why she was caught in the middle of it.

Roxie got onto the conveyor, but it moved so quick, and she was still weak, it shoved her through the hatch before she could lie on her back. At the last second she rolled onto her stomach, heading face-first into the blackness.

The chute's dimensions just cleared her shoulders; Legs must have hunched up to make it. The rattling conveyor rolled her along for a few meters, then zipped down at a sharp angle. In complete darkness, unable to move, Roxie zoomed down into an abyss reeking of rot and grease. She gritted her teeth as her hair brushed the chute wall.

Her eyes burned.

She rubbed her eyes, then opened them. The burning continued. Closed them again, then opened them to see a few bright orange specks.

For a brief second Roxie glimpsed the conveyor belt's outlines, the rivets in the chute wall. Everything had a slight blue glow.

She shot through rubber flaps and plummeted into a metal basket.

It was filled with plasti-wrapped corpses.

Roxie jerked back and flung imagined germs off her body. She rolled to the basket's side and jumped. Four meters down, her feet thudded onto a concrete floor.

Legs steadied her. "I didn't like the welcoming party, either. This way. There's supposed to be a morgue. C'mon, stop making that face."

"I've been beaten, choked, almost raped, and rolled over a pile of dead berks. How the fuck's a girl supposed to feel?"

"Alive, beautiful. Alive."

They crept through a large room containing collection baskets. Disposal chutes led to other parts of New Paris, up to Level 8. Further up in the city, the dead were collected by mortuary services for proper cremation. Some of the wealthy were buried in the ground, complete with a marker and coffin like the ancients.

The room was lit by long cylindrical bulbs. Every few meters a UV light shone, revealing details on the corpses as they were carted away by large lifters. Driven by poor natives, the lifters were the size of a small tank. Many were painted with iconography of the Flame, one of the successors to the old Telluric religions, and the progenitor of the New Jovian Covenant.

Roxie shivered, wondering if any mourners might have Cinn on them. Daedala claimed it was a religious tool. A few tabs could energize her.

Each lifter clamped onto a basket and drove to a large incinerator two hundred meters away. A red glow emitted from the ovens like an atonement pit from the Telluric Bible. Though most lifters dumped their loads into an incinerator, a few carried baskets through an opposite door. Municipal guards in red uniforms manned a booth there.

"These prison outfits will draw attention," Roxie said as they ducked into an aisle filled with the latest baskets.

"Don't worry, the fashion boutique is open."

Legs nodded at a basket filled with recently deceased people. They still wore their clothing and hadn't even been wrapped in cheap plasti. Gnats buzzed over them, glittering crimson under the incinerators' ambiance.

"Bollocks to that!"

"Either we take their clothes, or we lie down with them."

He climbed up a basket and tugged a stiff leg.

"That database tell you about this? Bloody fucking hell, Legs." She clambered up after him and covered her nose. "Pry the boots off that one. No, the one on your left."

In a few minutes Roxie wore knee high black boots, a leather skirt, a strapless top with the midriff cut off—she'd not wanted to wear the poor woman's blood—and a dark red jacket. All of it smelled of death.

If she had her way, she'd be smelling quite a bit of it soon.

"This is the best you could find? This isn't a sodding date!"

"You look nice, sweetie." He shrugged on a brown duster. Wearing a woven red and orange shirt with rancher chaps, he looked like a steer herder.

"This better work." She eyed the lifters as they cleared out the nearby aisle. They'd be gathering baskets from hers next. "Now what?"

"We could walk out that door." He pointed at the one with the municipal guards. "Or, we look for a crewman exit. Even though this area is darker than Fleurant's poetry."

"Both of those are shite plans, love."

"I'm listening." He felt around in the duster, smirked, and drew out a crumpled cig pack. "Sweet Mother Mary of Sol's dildo."

While he lit up with a lighter from the same duster, Roxie tried to formulate a plan. If the lifter drivers spotted them, they'd be reported. Dealing with the municipal guys was out, too. They needed to hurry. Her next prison meal was due in an hour, and someone may have already discovered the guard in her cell.

Spotting the graffiti on another lifter reminded her of the Necro Rites.

"Follow me and go along with what I do."

Roxie walked with an agitated gait toward the end of the aisle. Keeping the prison guard's baton under her jacket, she lowered her brows and tried to look as arrogant as possible. She stopped short as a lifter chugged her way.

Its brakes screeched. The operator stared out his window three meters above her.

"Ain't nobody supposed to have their asses down here." He pushed back his helmet and ogled her. "Not even your cute little ass, lovesie."

As he reached for his mic, Roxie rapped the lifter with the baton.

"I want to speak to your supervisor."

"The hell?"

"Somebody told us the Rites were through that door," she said.

The driver squinted as if he had to fart. "Rites? The Flame stuff? Lovesie, you in the wrong place. This look like a Rites chapel? Goddamn."

Roxie grabbed the handrail and pulled herself up until she faced the man. He pushed a pair of panties under the driving console, his face red.

"We paid good creds to come down here and pray. Either you show us where it is, or it's your creds that'll be gone, berk."

He wiped his face with the panties, balked, then tossed them out the window.

"Uh. Yeah, yeah. Get yourselves up here. And keep your fingers outta my stash."

Roxie motioned at Legs, and together they climbed up and sat behind the driver's cage. As the lifter thrummed back to life, Roxie frowned at the boxful of panties nearby.

"So what? Their original owners won't be needing 'em anymore."

"You fucking kidding me?"

"Everybody needs a hobby, sugar."

The lifter entered a cul-de-sac, turned around, and drove across the incinerator chamber. Roxie tried to relax but her stomach knotted up. They needed to get as far from New Paris as possible. Heal up, resupply. She recalled one of Aparajita's caches hidden at the northern edge of Lunae Plain. It was filled with a few Dracos, EM rounds, and enough amphetaline to choke a basin boar. They'd been friends then, partners in hunting phantoms. Rivalry had torn them apart.

Phantoms had torn Aparajita apart.

"Does Amai Shi know you did this?" Roxie asked.

"I didn't tell her. She's all about her ranking now. I saw her at the *Salon*, after you got back, but goddamn, she was like a Psycoid. Just staring at nothing."

"She knows something," Roxie said. "Dirty Cool knows it too."

"I know we'll be joining 'em if this driver doesn't hurry the hell up." He pointed at a lifter dumping corpses into an incinerator.

She stared at the bodies falling into the flames. She didn't believe in Heaven or Hell, not since the phantoms filled her reality. She was already in Hell, trying to get out.

Get out so she could send Harmon and Styra back down here.

CHAPTER 14

The driver stopped the lifter inside a concave opening on the far wall. He turned and glared at Roxie through the window cage.

"Alright, lovesie. Get your ass on through that there door."

Blushing, he grabbed a pair of purple panties.

"You keep quiet, I know where you can get a whole goddamn pile of these. Look really good on you."

"No thanks. We're late for the Rites." Roxie climbed off and hurried to the door.

"Those would look good on you," Legs said. "Should've taken him up on it."

"Just come on and hope you remember those Flame prayers taught in school."

Legs lit another cig. "Fuck that. I went to a Second Earth school."

"No wonder you're such a twat." She smiled, thankful to joke about something.

Tension still smothered her as the lifter drove away. The only routes she knew from Necro Row were the elevators: either leading to the upper levels where she'd get caught, or to the lower ones, where she risked rape, murder, and robbery. She couldn't flash her ConRec tattoo to drive off people now.

The door flipped open as Roxie stepped through. Though the air was cleaner, a bleach and lime stench tainted it. The lower ceiling was covered in Telluric illustrations of the burning Earth and winged individuals escaping from it to Mars. A nano fresco dominated one wall, though most of it had ceased morphing and now resembled a clogged morass where a woman in a spacesuit held a blood-filled chalice.

"Mother Mary of Sol, after her third transfiguration," Roxie said.

Legs scratched his stubble. "She's got nice tits."

"Is there anyone you wouldn't shag?"

"That guy in the lifter."

Candles fashioned into *Roux Nouveau* nudes flickered in small alcoves. Most had melted into deformed figures resembling Babblers or Psycoids strewn across Mars, forgotten by society. Roxie poked a finger into a half-molten figure.

She'd once sold Mum's Telluric crucifix to buy Cinn. The orange tablets had brought her closer to enlightenment than any silly prayer.

"You're gonna hex yourself," Legs said.

"Only if we don't hurry."

Roxie entered the Rites Chapel. Its higher ceiling was festooned with hanging incense bowels. Pulse cloths flapped like a curtain over a window. Roxie avoided walking under them. The nano objects writhed like red and white tentacles.

Less than a dozen people waited beside counters where loved ones lay dead. Unlike the bodies in the chute baskets, these were brought here by their families.

A lump rose in Roxie's throat. She'd never considered who had watched over Mum back on Luna during the Flame ceremony. And now she'd lost Doggie Boy...

She needed to get out of there.

Roxie fixed her stare on a wrinkled old man lying on a slab nearby. A UV fixture bathed the corpse in violet hues, highlighting lint, hair, and a scar above the left temple.

For a moment Roxie viewed everything in the Chapel with the same light. She blinked. The effect faded.

"You okay?" Legs asked.

"Sure, I'm ... just not the religious type. Come over here."

Two young women frowned over the old man. Both wore synthskin corsets with plasti cheekies, revealing their bottoms. Their hair was spiked into three shafts with bangs combed over their eyes. Two strumpets burying their granddad.

It would have to do.

"Sorry I'm late." Roxie stood beside the dead man and bowed her head. "The Flame purifies, glorifies, and burns forever."

Legs murmured the same, trying to keep a straight face.

The women looked at them with bewilderment.

"You knew him?" one asked.

"I did, love." Roxie smoothed the dead man's hair, then pretended to look away in grief. In truth, she was seeking the priest who scanned every visitor. And…there he was, a skinny man in gray robes waiting beside the exit. He glanced at her, frowned, and checked his holoboard.

Time for a spiritual awakening.

"He taught me so much…bloke helped me out whenever he could." Roxie wiped her nose and made herself shiver.

Legs coughed and glanced at the priest.

"Are you…related?" the other woman asked.

"Only in our humanity." Roxie needed a distraction. Something to make the priest move away from the exit.

"We should go," one of the women whispered, but her companion waited.

"You owe us a hundred creds."

Roxie's head shot up. "What?"

The woman's face reddened despite her thick makeup. "Your kin here, whoever he is…he owes us that much, but died before he paid up."

"For what?"

"Both of us," the woman said. "At the same time."

"That horny bastard!" Realizing she'd yelled, Roxie glanced at the priest, who was heading their way. The other mourners gave her sharp looks.

"We have the bill here." The other woman showed a thin screen to Roxie. It displayed the old man's picture, thumbprint, and the price: 100 creds for sex.

"He's deceased. That nulls the contract."

Roxie nudged Legs. He walked slowly toward the exit.

"No, his thumbprint is here. As next of kin, you have to pay us!" The woman shoved the screen at Roxie's face.

The priest came over. "Please, ladies, this is not the place. I have a small vestibule where this matter may be discussed. Be respectful of these others who—"

"Did you hear me?" The woman waved the screen.

"Let's see what old wrinkly flapper cock says."

Roxie pushed the dead man onto the woman.

She shrieked as the priest tried to keep the body from hitting the floor. It dragged him down while knocking the prostitute into her friend. Legs yanked a pulse cloth down, its fabric enveloping them like plasti around fresh beef.

Roxie and Legs fled through the door.

Outside the Rites Chapel, other mourners waited in line to watch their loved ones get burned to ashes. They gaped at her, so she wept the best fake tears she could manage.

"I can't…I can't believe he's gone!"

Legs ushered her past the line. "There now dear, everything will be okay."

Once they passed the Chapel entrance and traversed a catwalk over the incinerators, Roxie pushed him off.

"Bugger me, that was weird. Any more ideas?"

"Let's get the hell outta here first. Past this catwalk, we should find an elevator to take us down a level."

After stepping off the catwalk they passed a cadaver mart. Corpses, most of them young and attractive, lined the street in upright boxes. Hawkers yelled out prices. A few well-dressed buyers eyed the rigid merchandise.

"Look here, a fresh cadaver free of radiation, no Telluric nanites, with all the organs intact!" a saleswoman cried. "His musculature can accommodate any modification, and we have a dissection special if you act now!"

A woman accompanied by four armed guards pointed at several bodies. "I'll take those. My family's due to arrive from the Caravans next month, and we need more to work the land."

One man cursed as his purchase, a cute young woman, puked during reanimation.

"You told me she was dead!"

"It's just a reflex," the saleswoman said. "With the newer vascular pumps and serums, this Psycoid will sync with the software after a few hours."

A husky man bumped into Roxie. "Move ya ass, I got two Psycoids reserved."

"Surprised the UGPD doesn't buy new recruits down here," Legs muttered.

"Yeah…"

Every corpse glowed purple in Roxie's sight for a second. For a tiny eternity they all lived again, staring at her, latent energy simmering through their cold flesh. She gagged and bumped into Legs.

"Get me out of here."

"Sure thing, sweetie." He helped her stand straight.

They trudged through the mart. She tried not to look at all of the bodies.

The UG burned all lower-class corpses. Most were either poisoned by radiation in the city's lower levels, or drank water from old aquifers tainted with Telluric nanites. Some people still carried the microscopic bots, passed from generation to generation, ensuring they would attract the occasional kill bot. Other nanites activated a purge virus, killing the host at a certain age. All were atrocities meant to dispose of those who'd made Mars habitable. All of it put in place to prepare Mars for those on the Caravans.

And she'd contributed to it.

"I have to find Daedala. She might help us."

Legs eyed the passersby as they entered the district outside Necro Row. Filled with dilapidated apartments, trash-filled streets, and fewer patrols, it was a hotbed for gangs and rebels.

"She's a politician, honey, not a savior. She'd turn our asses in to make herself look good with the UG."

"She's on Mars for something more than shite speeches about friendly ghosts."

Several teenagers trailed them in an adjacent alley.

"There, on your right."

"I see 'em." Legs kept a hand near the gun hidden in his duster. "Babblers, from the look of 'em."

They walked faster to the nearest elevator. Graffiti covered everything in slogans, vulgarities, and murals. No beggars lay on the curbs. Down here, the invalid, weak, or unarmed ended up in the Row with the rest of the dead.

As they neared a corner of abandoned sex boutiques, seven teenagers popped from behind a barricade. They wore oversized garments and had tattooed foreheads.

A teenage boy splayed his fingers at Roxie as if they were knives.

"Wrong turn, wrong turn, you money termites, wrong!"

The other teenagers tried to outflank her and Legs.

"Where's the right one?" Roxie smacked her palm with the baton.

"Barr … barri …" a teenage girl said, her gangly legs covered in ripped fishnet. "Barri-cade! B-barricade!"

As they tried to get past Legs, he stomped a foot.

"Nope, I don't think so."

Roxie's heart sank. They weren't a gang. They were survivors.

The kids she'd shot on *Jubilee* would be this age had they lived. Babblers never had a chance anywhere, and were used for cheap labor—or worse. Their brains had been tainted with water toxins near the old farms and ranches. Since most natives couldn't afford to move, each generation bore the mutation.

"Kill, kill you, you, and both of you!" the male leader shouted.

Legs reached into his duster, but Roxie touched his arm.

"How about a trade? This jacket for information."

"Kill? K-k … kill kill?" The boy rubbed his hands.

Though the faces of *Jubilee*'s young victims floated through her mind, Roxie stepped forward. She was tired of seeing frightened children.

"Barri … cade?" the girl asked.

"No. This for a way out." Roxie removed the jacket and tossed it to them.

"Stinky stinky, cow feed, stink stinky," the girl said.

Voices rang out over the cadaver mart.

"Let's go," Legs murmured.

She turned and glimpsed a skinny form in gray robes and two females asking people questions. A municipal guard accompanied them.

"Kill?" the boy said, but the girl shook her head.

Roxie's eyes widened in realization.

"Cow feed? Stinky cow feed? You mean a silage lift?"

The girl nodded with enthusiasm.

"Take us there and you can have the baton and jacket. His duster too."

"Bullshit," Legs said.

"It might be our funeral next time if we don't."

Roxie nodded back to the cadaver mart. He grunted and gave them the duster. One Babbler drew out the cig pack and lighter, and all of them yelped with joy.

"Little fuckstains," he said. "Those were good cigs."

"I'll buy you a crate load later," Roxie said.

After the Babblers gathered the items, the girl led them down an alley piled with junk generators. Roxie and the rest had to climb over them. Some contained skeletons; others were filled with sand rats squirming in traps. The lanky girl hopped down into one and disappeared from sight. Roxie tensed, then followed.

The generators dropped off into a busted grill—leading down into darkness.

She stepped off the edge. Air rushed past her before she landed atop a pile of stale, rotting grain. It dusted the air around her, which she fanned away as she rolled off the pile. Legs came next, followed by the other Babblers.

They stood in a square shaft littered with grain in various states of decay. Spare clothes, tools, a broken frack rifle, and other belongings lay here and there. There was a small firepit with a blackened ceramic bowl hanging over it.

Her gut churned upon realizing the children had been eating fortified cattle feed.

The boy leader snatched the jacket, but the lanky girl grabbed it and put it on.

"Stinky stinky? See? No barricade, barricade. Stinky."

"They make Simp Speak sound like pillow talk," Legs said

Roxie knelt and pulled the collar up on the girl's new crimson jacket.

"You look gorgeous, love."

"Gor … gor …"

It was the first time she'd interacted with a child since the incident on *Jubilee*. Her hands lingered on the girl's shoulders. There was so much she wanted to say, even if the girl didn't understand.

Gor … gor-gee-us?" The girl stood straighter and smiled.

Roxie swallowed and grinned back.

"Right-o."

The girl beckoned for them to follow while the other Babblers argued over the baton and duster, smoking the cigs. Roxie hurried the girl along as Legs drew his pistol, face drawn into a frown. If they couldn't get out this way, it'd be a short trip to Necro Row. Without a gun and Cinn, she was powerless.

Roxie rubbed her forehead, then studied the unarmed, unwashed, uneducated Babbler girl. The child lacked weapons, a home, even parents, but wasn't powerless.

Neither was she.

The grain shaft terminated into the wall of a massive silo built onto the side of New Paris. Roxie gazed at it, towering ever upward. Holding thousands of kilograms of silage, the lower level gangs had likely tapped into it, selling it to poorer citizens. All that Martian beef cooked for offworlders and the rich, while these people ate cattle feed.

Legs opened a metal flap cut into the silo.

"How far down does this go?"

The girl shrugged. "Down, down, down …"

He smirked at Roxie. "You first, Street Angel. You got the wings."

"Told you not to call me—"

Something whizzed past her ear and burst into Leg's back.

Hot blood struck her face. He grunted, tried to turn and aim, but a second shot knocked him into the silo's waiting chasm.

Back in the chute, muzzle flashes lit up the dimness with terrifying brilliance. They glowed red, blue, and orange in Roxie's sight while shrieks and stuttering pleas ended with curt abruptness.

The girl passed the baton back to Roxie and smiled.

"Come on, love, you can't stay—"

A round burst through the girl's arm. Another exited her throat.

"Come on goddamnit!" Roxie tried to grab the girl.

A third shot tore off the girl's face.

White hot flashes crossed Roxie's vision as she screamed. For a brief hellish instant, she sensed UG soldiers aiming in the darkened chute.

Glowing like specters of death.

A bullet nipped Roxie's leg. Another scraped past her right shoulder. She fell into a ball and rolled backward into the abyss that had claimed her friend.

Claimed her heart and all hope she had for Mars.

Chapter 15

Silage-tainted air rushed past Roxie, stinking of vinegar and alcohol. The darkness was pierced far below by a circle of yellow light.

She sucked in a deep breath and kept herself in a ball.

In a shower of corn grains, Roxie plowed through the silage. Mouth closed, she refused to exhale. Silage slid past her limbs, rolled into her ears, up her nostrils, and invaded her clothes. After plunging a meter into it she struck hard-packed silage. Pushing herself up, she slid right back down into a loose deathtrap of corn husk and cow feed.

She couldn't breathe, she wanted to blow silage from her nose so bad her lungs were burning, the stuff was tickling her throat…

Wait. It was like water. She had to calm down or she would die. Remain calm, find a way out. Remain calm, find a way…

Bracing her legs on the hard silage, she dug back up.

Her fingers met resistance, then grasped an arm. Legs.

Heart burning with desperation, Roxie tugged him through the silage. Fiery agony built in her lungs. Her grip slid off him, but with maddened wrangling, she found it again.

She latched the crook of her arm around his wrist and tugged.

Sloughing through the reeking mess, her boot struck the silo wall. Light peeked down. Risking such a glance filled her eyes with grains. She squeezed them shut. The silage's chemicals made them burn. As she struggled, the colors teased her vison again.

Blues, reds, oranges. The outline of a body—it had to be Legs. The shape of a brighter square section glowed just above her head.

Following it, she dragged him and pushed her head up through the silage.

As she sucked in a breath, a light shone down from above.

A SMG burst rattled in the silo with metallic reverb. Rounds popped into the silage. The light wavered as Roxie shoved Legs through the glowing section she'd just visualized—the silo's maintenance hatch.

The hatch slid open. Silage spilled Roxie out in a cornmeal waterfall as bullets zipped past her arm. Coughing up silage, she slid from the silo and crashed onto a chute feed. It led to a canal outside New Paris where excess silage entered a vat. She tumbled into it, slammed into Legs, and skidded to a halt in the vat's drier contents.

Roxie pushed air out her nostrils, ejecting silage. Then she hacked up a gob of it. Wheezing, she crawled over to Legs and felt his neck. He still had a pulse.

"Get up."

Roxie crammed her shoulder under his left armpit and brought him up. He groaned. His pistol was gone, lost in the fall.

As she staggered with him to the vat's side, Roxie took in her surroundings.

Spotlights roved over the grounds while hundreds of meters above, the metropolis's lighted terraces, platforms, docks, and windows gave a semblance of normality. Night covered the land with Earth, Deimos, and a smattering of stars greeting her. Her old navigational training came in handy as she studied them.

They'd exited one of the silos on New Paris's eastern side.

Some stars twinkled in different hues than normal. Maybe Cinn had finally screwed up her eyesight like Dirty Cool always said.

Thinking of him reminded Roxie of who'd be hunting her now.

"Come on, you silly bugger." She urged Legs to a safety ladder on the vat's side.

New searchlights blinked from the silo above.

"Now, asshole." She slapped his face.

The hum of gravjets weighed down the air. Alarms screamed.

"Either that or bleed to death here, so come one!"

Leg's eyes fluttered open. "Fucking stop already, I heard. Bastards got mc twice." His voice was lighter due to the thinner atmosphere.

"Let's not wait for a third." Roxie eased him over the side. "Slide down like we used to at Cydonia. You remember—"

"The excavation pit ladders. I remember, sugar."

He grunted, grabbed a ladder rail in each hand, and slid down. Every few meters he caught his feet on the rungs. Despite his wounds, he made rapid progress.

Roxie followed in a similar fashion. Without gloves the cool metal burned her palms. Several times she mashed her fingers on the rungs or clomped her boot onto a rung too soon. Finally she glided the rest of the way down. The metal blistered her palms until she leapt off. After hacking up more silage, she made herself stand.

"Where to now? I forgot my ticket." Legs kept his right arm close to his body.

Under New Paris's lights, she saw a second bloody hole in his back.

"They winged me. Lucky fuckers." His cough had a wet sound.

"Yeah. Lucky." Roxie's skin rose in goose bumps as gravjet engines hummed louder. "We can't take a tram or any of the outlying spaceports. Fuck."

"Go to ground." Legs nudged her toward a ranch a kilometer away. Their feet scrubbed over crusty grass, the only kind that grew after generations of experimentation.

"Go native? Bollocks to that. You know how the locals hate us."

Gravjets darted over Lunae Plain.

Roxie and Legs ran.

"At least they might not shoot first."

He stopped when they reached a long silage carryall fitted with twelve meter-high wheels. Ares's logo, a winking bull, shone on its side in biolume paint.

Roxie gaped as he climbed up the ramp to the carryall's driver cage.

"The fuck? Get back down here!"

Legs turned as the searchlights scanned the vat behind them.

"Head to that ranch, honey. Grab a horse, ride it so they can't trace you. Find a scrambler and get that fucking tattoo off."

She rushed up to the ramp. "You're not doing this."

"If we stay together we'll both get caught." He dug a Cinn tab from his pocket and ate it. "Heh. Little fuckers didn't get everything."

Her heart squeezed into a frigid ball.

"Damn it, I said—"

"I'll find you, okay, sweetie?" Legs ran a small device over the cage's lock and the door slid open. "Get outta here. Prove 'em wrong."

Roxie started to charge up the ramp but searchlights fanned over the end of the carryall. She shrank back in time as bright, lifeless luminance reached the driver's cage. Legs flipped the light a bird and shut the door.

The carryall started and the gargantuan wheels turned over the ground.

She fled over the plain and ducked into rain collection sluices as gravjets followed the carryall. Legs drove it away from the vat, which was yanked loose from the silo's dispersal chute. Chute and vat both flipped over and spilled thousands of kilos of feed onto the ground. Even from that distance, the impact vibrated the ground under Roxie's feet. A yellow-brown haze filled the air.

The carryall ripped along the road, bashing aside hovercars, guard stations, and even a steer corral as the unstoppable vehicle drew the UG's full attention.

"Fuck." She stumbled behind a kilometer-long aisle of solar panels. "Fuck you, you should have come with me!"

A low howl carried over the plain.

She raced from the panels to a service ramp connecting the fields to another road.

A second howl sounded.

Jovian wolves. Raised in Jupiter's orbit in high-G stations, the canines were the UG's hound of choice. On a world where a stray phantom could disrupt sensors or obfuscate SATSCAN data, they always found their target. They could bite her in half.

She ran faster.

By the time Roxie exited the ramp, she was close to the ranch. Her lungs hurt with each breath. Exhaustion made her nauseous. Without the g-ballasts, her equilibrium was off in the lower gravity.

Across the plain, the carryall shuddered as gravjets strafed it. Tracers lit up the night, followed by low thuds of impact. Rockets darted from the sky and blew craters into the road. Still the carryall surged on, crashing through a tram station. Geysers of flame devoured the darkness for a second.

"Please let him make it," she breathed.

The gravjets loosed another salvo. The carryall exploded in a grandiose fireball worthy of a Jovian psalm. The rest of the tram station blew apart.

"Doggie Boy… Legs… I wish I could have …" Her sobs hurt her chest.

More alarms resounded over the plain.

Her run became a jog, and finally the jog slowed to a meandering gait. She covered her mouth, fearing her sobs would carry to the ears of her pursuers. Sure enough, not two hundred meters behind, handheld lights darted over the field.

Wolves yelped and howled. A gravjet sped by, then another.

The glow of the burning carryall made shadows flicker over Lunae Plain as she stumbled past a cornfield near the ranch's fence. Too tall to scale, electrified, and monitored by cameras, it was hopeless to even try it.

Roxie doubled over and pounded her knees.

"You stupid berk. Should have just let me die."

Standing straight, she gritted her teeth. Stuck her hands out and approached the electric fence. It would be quick. She wouldn't let go.

The fence glowed yellow in her sight.

As the current hummed up and down, so too did the yellow glow flare and fade. She waved a hand before her face, stepped back. Ignored the howl a hundred meters behind her. As she gazed around, everything glowed with shimmering, pearlescent life. New Paris was brighter, bluer. She could pick out even more colors among the stars. The carryall's fire, the funeral pyre of her friend, roared with red-orange vibrance.

It was as if she viewed the world with Cinn in her system.

She ran along the fence, its glow guiding her to a section that emitted no light: an unmarked security entrance through the barrier. She yanked it open and ran through.

The corrals were watched by cameras, but the devices' laser guide now became visible: a single red beam slicing over the area. Showing her where it could see.

Waiting until it swiped in the other direction, Roxie slipped into the corral. After slogging through mud and cowshit, she reached the stables.

Horses of the Ares pedigree waited inside, bred for centuries to survive Mars's gravity and terraformed atmosphere. UGPD hunters studied them since *La Rèsistance* rode the animals into off-road areas. The same places Roxie would have to go.

The howls came closer. Roxie held her breath, then grabbed a handful of fat, round turds from a stall. Legs had died so she could survive.

And so she would—whatever it took.

Roxie smeared herself with equine feces. Rubbing it on her cheeks, into her hair, even lathering her boots. The stink made her gag but she remained still.

Outside the electric fence she spied lights. A huge furred form, tall as a man's shoulder. Soldiers in full kit, frack rifles ready.

Taking shallow breaths, Roxie waited until the wolves lost her scent. The gravjets finally searched another section of the plain. By now, the carryall fire had been extinguished. Rescue personnel mobbed the scene, but there was no one to save. The UG had to make it look good, probably blame it on *La Rèsistance.*

Roxie remembered Amai Shi's comments back at Tithonium Chasma: a bounty remained on her head. Styra and all the rest would be searching. The highest-ranked hunter on Mars was now the most infamous escapee.

After saddling an Ares, Roxie rode from the stable and out the dead place in the fence. Once she got her bearings, she urged the horse into a canter until she reached grazing land outside New Paris. She might pass as a ranch hand on SATSCAN.

"Get me clear of this place and I'll set you free," she whispered into the horse's ear. "We have a deal?"

It blew through its lips and she rolled her eyes.

"Berk."

She nudged the beast's flanks and galloped over the landscape. Wind dried the feces into her hair, skin, and clothes. Bumping in the saddle, her rump and thighs ached after a few minutes. She'd not ridden a horse since coming to Mars, and even then she'd not cared for the beasts.

Using the stars as a guide, Roxie found Aparajita's old cache on Lunae Plain. Distant ranch lights offered enough illumination for her to see it. It took two minutes to get her leg over and slide down from the saddle, her thighs hurt so much.

She dug with one hand while holding the horse's bridle in the other. The hard-packed soil resisted her cracked fingers until she lifted out a military supply capsule.

The ground gave it up too easily. She flinched upon seeing the overturned loam.

Someone had already dug it up.

She kicked the capsule open.

Instead of spare guns, ammo, and Cinn, a sheaf of paper blew out of it.

Roxie tossed the bridle aside and scrambled after the paper. Once she finally snatched it, the words on it froze her heart.

It read 'Fly Away Street Angel.'

"Fuck, fuck, fuck!"

She shoved the message back into the capsule, reburied it, and saddled up.

For over an hour she slapped the horse's flanks, galloping away. Looking over her shoulder often. Finally her neck cramped and she stopped abusing the poor animal. As the beast carried her further into the night, her eyelids drooped a few times.

Two gravjets blasted by, making the animal buck.

She hung on until she slumped over its neck. The reins dangled from her limp fingers. Her mouth was so dry, the name came out as a rasp.

"Doggie Boy … don't go …"

She managed to open her eyelids, crusted over with dried sweat, shit, and silage.

The landscape was awash in cool shades. Blue shrubs, purple horizon, navy blue sky punctuated with distant azure twinkles. It hurt her eyes, jolted her brain. Hugging the horse's neck, she closed her eyes again.

"Legs? Please …"

A crash made her sit up in the saddle.

Pink grayness appeared just above the horizon. It was already morning already.

Roxie rubbed her eyes, then gasped as they watered up with dried nastiness from her hands. Using the inside of her shirt, she cleaned her eyes and retched at the stink.

A second crash.

The horse neighed and cantered. Roxie fought with its bridle as she gazed ahead.

Two necrostructs lay smoking in the sand.

A figure in white face paint, holding a magblade, sat atop a hoverbike.

Roxie blinked more choad from her sight.

"Amai Shi?"

The figure now wore a blonde wig and lifted a wine glass in toast.

"Legs? Sod this shite, what's going on?"

The horse neighed again.

Wind blew red dust over the necrostructs like a sacrament in Necro Row. Her vision warbled and swam. Dizziness made her sway in the saddle.

"I..."

Roxie slid off the horse and thudded to the ground. The pain didn't register, just summoned more spots in her vison. Purple, pink, green.

A figure stirred on the hoverbike, holding a shotgun.

As she rolled onto her side, the horse whinnied and galloped off. She coughed, tried to stand, then slid back to the ground. Dust floated around her like crimson snow.

"Go ahead, turn into Doggie Boy." Roxie's laughter hurt her parched throat. "I know he's dead. We're all dead."

"Who are ya?" a rough voice asked.

Roxie shielded her face from the rising sun. It stained the sands a deeper crimson as if she lay on a plain of blood. Licking her cracked lips, she fought another dizzy spell.

She couldn't give her name. That person was dead. Mars, the UGPD, and the whole Solar System needed to believe that.

She needed to believe that.

Something metallic clicked.

"Answer or I'll blast ya."

"Call me *Ange de la Mort*, love."

Chapter 16

"She's drawing them like pecker gnats to a dingo dick."

The male voice resounded in Roxie's ears as she stirred.

Her back ached, her ass hurt, her stomach growled. A terminal lethargy tugged her limbs down to the ground. Her left hand brushed over coarse soil while something heavy hummed around her right wrist.

"So we should dump her into a sand sink and continue like we always have?"

Locust's voice.

Roxie tried to sit up but she plopped back down.

"I already told ya what we should do with her."

Her eyes opened. Yellow and blue swaths passed in her vision.

"With her, we can win," Locust said.

"Win what?" she asked in a croaky voice. "Asshole of the Decade?"

"Great, it talks."

"Can you move?" Locust asked.

Roxie blinked. Her vision normalized.

She lay on the bed of a hovertruck, staring up at the blue-yellow Martian sky. Locust stood on a sprayer platform welded to the bed's left side, while a husky man with a shotgun sat on the other side, glaring at her. His lanky gray hair and blue eyes marked him as an offworlder. The hovertruck slowly floated over a wide field, not kicking up dust. Armed figures walked behind the vehicle.

"Finally, you came to back us. Covered in shit, no less." Locust smirked, now dressed in dun camo fatigues with a pistol strapped to each hip.

Roxie grimaced as she tried rolling onto her left side.

"No amount of boost work will fix her." The husky man snorted. "I think I see a sand sink over there."

Locust frowned at him. "Roxie, meet your rescuer. He's—"

"Use my new name," the man said.

"Chev," Locust said.

"Obliged … Chev." Roxie sat up and coughed.

A scrambler was strapped to her right wrist. The clothes she'd stolen from Necro Row stuck to her in a reeking medley of dried mud, sweat, and horseshit.

She craned her head around at the others following the hovertruck: native Martians, their butternut complexion matching their camo fatigues. None looked happy to see her. Etienna gave her the finger.

"I see you brought my fan club along." Roxie scratched at her hair, a stiff spiked morass. She narrowed her eyes at Chev.

"I've seen you before. In that tram tunnel … you bumped into me in Necro Row."

"So ya did." Chev aimed his shotgun at her face. "Want to explain why the UG wants ya so bad?"

"Maybe I won the Lucky Stars Lottery." Roxie stared back him.

So *La Rèsistance* had been following her since her escape.

"Then I'm here to pay up." Chev cocked the shotgun.

Locust laughed. "Never put two hunters together. They will never get along."

"This bloke's a hunter? Of what, sand rats?"

"This morning, I downed two necrostructs to save ya." Chev took an inhaler from his coat and sprayed its contents into his mouth. "And now, I have the most wanted piece of ass this side of Saturn."

"Jolly good, then. So what am I supposed to help you win?"

Locust studied the sky, then consulted a datapad.

"We'll talk as soon as you're secured."

"Fucking look at me. I'm covered in shite and can't stand. How am I a threat?"

"It is not you. Is it what they put inside of you." He tapped his right wrist and pointed at hers.

"Oh, right." Roxie rolled her eyes. "You can at least tell me where we are."

"Mars," Chev said.

She glared at him. He chuckled.

The hovertruck traveled for another hour. Few in the group talked and Roxie didn't ask questions. Sweat rolled off her as the day's heat rose. Though still a chilly planet compared to Earth, Mars's thinner atmosphere filtered less UV light, making concentrated sunlight more dangerous—at least for an offworlder.

None of the native rebels seemed affected. To her surprise, Chev extended a canvas flap over the bed as the sun rose higher.

"And here I thought you blokes were going to let me cook," Roxie said.

"Oh no," Chev said. "I'd eat ya pretty ass raw."

As the other rebels laughed, Roxie grinned.

"Would you, now? Bet you're used to swallowing turd-covered tarts."

Chev drew a blade.

Roxie tensed her leg muscles, ready to kick until Locust stood between them.

"Both of you shut up."

Turning away from them, she focused on the landscape. Judging from the rocky, barren soil, it hadn't been terraformed, which made her wonder where she was. That horse couldn't have traveled more than seventy kilometers from New Paris, plus her heavier offworld body had slowed its progress. With craters and ancient riverbeds appearing on the eastern horizon, she ventured a guess: Xanthe Terra.

The hovertruck bumped from the flat plain onto a region bisected by gullies, ravines, and long crevasses. A few craters here and there added to the area's epochal damage. Jackals trailed the hovertruck for a time, no doubt starving since the old colonial buffalo were nearly extinct. Mum used to tell Roxie that herds still roamed the red planet.

She'd been such a romantic, unlike Dad, who'd been stern. He left when Roxie was four. Why, Mum never said. He was more of a ghost to her than any she'd met here.

Irrigation channels dug by the original colonists, then re-excavated by the UG, crisscrossed the area. Stagnant water pools filled some craters, while rusted pump stations and kilometers of busted pipeline gave Xanthe Terra an unwelcoming aspect. Tufts of grass and a few wildflowers sprang up near the channels. At least something had grown.

A deep alluvial flat, swampy with exposed pipelines, blocked the hovertruck's path. Locust jumped down from the sprayer platform and nodded.

"This is the place."

"They'll track us here by nightfall," Chev said.

"Pierro will get here in time. Then we can start." Locust smiled at Roxie. "Your bath awaits, madame."

Roxie slid until she sat on the edge of the truck bed. "You first."

Locust nodded to Etienna, who fired an empty magdart into a pipe lock release nearby. The lock popped and one of the large pipes opened.

Two rebels peeked from it, pistols raised.

"Clever. No wonder SATSCAN can't find you."

Roxie stood, wobbled for a moment, then recovered her equilibrium.

"You berks have a Drown machine in there too?"

No one answered as Chev pushed her into the pipe. It measured three meters in diameter, caked with age-old mud, dried sodium, and potassium flakes. Inside there was no decoration, trash, or even a spent cig butt. It was a staging area, not a home.

"Nice place," Roxie said. "Is the rent expensive?"

"Staying here will not be your problem," Locust said.

"Leaving might be." Chev nudged her on.

She scowled at him, then smiled.

"A hunter? No one retires from the UGPD."

"You did," Etienna said.

Continuing through the pipe, their footfalls echoed in the dimness. Several rebels used flashlights to pinpoint an intersection with a hatch. Past the hatch, Locust led her into a circular room containing bilge controls and crank wheels. He sat on one of the wheels as Etienna pasted a Martian map to the wall.

"Going on vacation?" Roxie asked.

Locust indicated the map.

"These are the places *La Rèsistance* has spotted Jovian ships landing in secret. All within the last thirty-six hours—while the vids show Daedala making statements about equality, freedom, and transparency."

"Guess you need me and my Jovian nanites to investigate?" Roxie asked.

"We didn't help you escape for nothing."

"Help?"

"Your friend sent us a message. That he was breaking you out of that prison."

Roxie sat back, mouth open. "Then why the fuck did you let Legs die? Why didn't you help us?"

"He was supposed to meet us at Hebes Chasma—not this far east."

She glowered at Chev.

"Then what the bloody hell were you doing in Nero Row?"

"If I hadn't distracted those other two UG squads down there, ya girlfriend wouldn't have gotten ya to the silo at all." Chev smirked as if he'd saved her.

"Will you help us?" Locust asked.

"What, these sods not capable of doing the job, like this bag of shite here?" She jerked a thumb at Chev.

Chev leveled the shotgun at Roxie's head.

"You enjoy waving that thing in a girl's face, don't you?"

"When it's not in my pants." Chev caressed the barrel.

"Your mum was mean to you as a child, wasn't she?"

"I spanked her every day."

"Sick fuck," Roxie muttered.

"If you're through swapping hunter stories?" Locust asked. "It's time to remove you little love stamp from the UGPD."

"How long before they find us here?" Roxie asked. "Only a looney would stay in one place for long, with my record."

"She learns quick." Etienna rolled her eyes.

"An hour, maybe less," Locust said.

"You wanker. It takes 24 hours to break down the ConRec link to my system—"

"We don't have that long," Locust said.

"Fuck that, then." Roxie plopped onto a wheel and winced, the hard metal denting her tired rump. "It could kill me, you know."

"I told ya we should have left her," Chev said.

"Cut off her hand, then," Etienna said. "The hand that killed Salvaire."

"Quiet," Locust said.

Roxie glared at them all. "Bollocks to that. I'll take my chances with the UG."

"Suits me," Chev said.

"Not before we test her." Etienna tapped her pistol.

"Anytime," Roxie said.

Locust sighed.

"What will it be, *Ange de la Mort*? Risk a quick procedure, stay here until a UG gravjet finds you, or we simply cut your hand off?"

"Cutting it off could still kill me, you stupid git. Besides, you just want me for your rebellion. You always have."

Locust smiled.

"I am hurt, Roxie. You know I would never shoot you unless I had just cause."

"What's in it—?"

"For you?" Locust sniffed. "You never do anything for anyone but yourself."

Ignoring Chev's or Etienna's aimed weapons, she grabbed Locust by the collar.

"You goddamned insect. I watched two of my friends die, I saved hunters from that cluster fuck you led me into at Valles, and then threw away what little career I had on this asswart of a planet!"

Locust waved the others off. "Then you have nothing to lose."

She yanked her hands away as if touching him soiled her body. Anger fueled her limbs, making her pace in a circle. There was no reason not to help them. She had no other allies on Mars now. And Legs had trusted them.

"Right-o, then. Let's do it. Before I change my mind."

"It never was really up to you," Chev said.

Roxie whirled and stuck her finger in his face.

"One more word, berk, and I'll make you eat that bloody piece. Got it?"

Locust stood. "That's the Roxie Trent we need. Now please sit while we remove your pledge of love to the UGPD."

Breathing hard, she sat back down.

Chev slung the shotgun over a shoulder and smiled.

One rebel stood by with a clamp-like device while Etienna removed the scrambler from Roxie's wrist. She sneered as Roxie gasped, the skin around her wrist raw.

"Oops. Wouldn't want to ruin those pretty looks of yours."

Etienna yanked the scrambler away from Roxie. Tethered electronically, its removal made Roxie cry out and clasp her wrist to her chest.

Etienna laughed until Roxie's foot collided with her jaw.

Chev's shotgun barrel touched Roxie's cheek.

"That will heal, dipshit. This won't."

Wiping her bloody lip, Etienna reached for her gun. Locust pushed her back.

"Enough! Save it for our real enemies."

Locust grabbed the other device and knelt before Roxie. "And you, stop your bullshit. I said an hour, maybe less. The UG might be outside this complex right now."

Etienna stomped off.

"Why does everyone hate me so—"

Roxie jerked as the device clamped over her wrist. A scorching sensation burrowed through her skin. In seconds, the flesh of her forearm turned light gray. A swelling ache filled her arm as if every blood vessel were clogged. She sucked in through clenched teeth and pushed Chev's shotgun away.

"Told you, berk…"

"If you're this tough, maybe ya really can help us," Chev said. "When I left the UGPD it was filled with a bunch of pussies and addicts. Everybody taking four times as much Cinn as was needed to see those ghosts."

"Bet your ranking…sucked," Roxie breathed as her right arm shivered.

A dull numbness spread from the tattoo.

Locust studied his datapad, then looked at her face.

"It wasn't as good as yours." Chev scratched his balls. "But I never brought the whole damn place down with me when I hunted. You newer hunters, ya just don't give a fuck. The UG rebuilds its stuff, but the homes you destroy? Nobody rebuilds them."

"Phantoms destroy most of that." Roxie's lungs fought to provide more air.

"Always the same excuse," Chev said.

"Fifteen percent," Locust said. "Chev, you know what the UGPD's doing."

Chev shook his head. "Doesn't fucking matter. Any way you can speed that up?"

"Any more and she'll enter cardiac arrest."

"It's okay," Chev said. "She doesn't have a heart."

"So why did you give the UGPD the boot? Lose your nerve?"

Chev scowled.

"I fucking knew it. You might gun down a necrostruct, but phantoms…that takes something you don't have."

Chev cocked the shotgun. "And that is?"

"You never gave in to it. You have to let everything go and shoot. Sod the consequences, the cost—your life. Because most of us convicts have no life outside this. But you did, love. Had a family, then lose them after you left the PD?"

"This is my family." Chev raised the shotgun.

"Forty-two percent." Locust blocked Chev.

Roxie's throat hurt from talking but she continued.

"What, then?"

Chev lowered the shotgun.

"Those fuckers gave me Cinnamoxidil 8. It irradiated my lungs. I couldn't hunt phantoms anymore after that."

"Seventy percent," Locust said.

Roxie tasted a spicy metallic flavor. She felt so swollen, she wondered if her cycle had kicked in already.

"So you were a Grade 1? No wonder you went bloody AWOL. You were barely good enough to hunt rogue Psycoids."

"They experimented on me, ya stupid bitch!" Chev yanked out the inhaler, face turning red. "Because of me, ya stupid drugs finally worked!"

"A Grade 1 twat. Moloch used to get you sods to polish his guns. You enjoy cleaning the loo after Dirty Cool dropped a deuce?"

Chev stalked from the chamber.

Locust arched an eyebrow at her.

"For a person with no friends, you seem uninterested in changing that. Eighty-nine percent."

"With friends like that, who needs—oh shite!"

Limbs quivering, Roxie slid off the wheel and struck the floor. Saliva dripped from her mouth and her lungs compressed.

Her heartbeat reached a crescendo, then stopped.

Her eyesight transformed everything into blue, violet, and red shades. Locust glowed maroon, much like the planet he'd sworn to liberate. This time, though, Roxie traced visible lines in her arm, connected to the ConRec tattoo. They snaked through her blood cells, her receptors. She waved her right arm. They arced from her skin.

The scrambler blew in a shower of sparks.

"Holy shit!" Locust yelled.

The scrambler slid off her wrist. Gazing around, she spotted the heat signatures of Chev, Etienna, the other rebels—through the pipe walls. Waves of heat radiated from Locust. Through his flesh, a heart pumped in swelling red hues.

Roxie scrabbled back against the wall. "What the fuck did you do to me?"

Genuine concern showed on Locust's face. "What?"

"I see those buggers out there! I see your heart pumping, I feel the heat coming off all your sodding bodies—"

"Then Daedala was right. You're well into Phase Two." He tapped his datapad.

"And you are free."

She raised her arm. The ConRec tattoo had faded. Nothing more than a dark skull and pistols just beneath her skin.

"Phase Two? What did they do to me?"

Locust helped her up.

"No time now. The UGPD can't pinpoint you, but SATSCAN will detect you even without that tattoo. Let's get going."

"Tell me."

Leading her back through the pipes, Locust kept an arm around her waist.

"A Phase Two radiates the same electromagnetic signature as a phantom. SATSCAN will think you're one of them."

"What a bloody crock!"

"Why else would they want you?" Locust forced her to walk faster.

Styra's comments flooded Roxie's mind. The way she reacted differently to Cinn now, all the crazy things with her eyesight—and Daedala's nanites.

"That's why the necrostructs followed me," she said.

"That's why we can help each other."

The other rebels waited outside the complex, staring at Roxie as if she were responsible for all the wrongs they'd suffered. All the loved ones they'd lost.

They didn't know what she had lost.

Roxie stumbled from the pipe entrance and Locust had to keep her steady.

Chev smirked. Etienna sneered.

"Give me a sodding moment, will you?"

Locust sniffed.

"You're an outlaw. You don't have moments anymore."

CHAPTER 17

Shalbatana Canal snaked north into Chryse Plain, one of the more successfully terraformed regions above the equator. Fed by the Canal's water, as well as irrigation pipes stretching from the arctic Northern Basin, the Plain possessed a fertile green hue.

Roxie pushed up her shades and studied the fenced-in ranchland, agriculture fields, and towering windmills. Solar panel arrays glittered beneath shiny new atmospheric cyclers. She breathed deep, enjoying the air's taste.

Just a few days ago a hit of Cinn would have elevated it all to paradise.

But not now.

She stubbed a pebble over the Canal's edge. It plummeted twenty meters before splashing into the swift current.

Locust stood beside her.

"You offworlders always have to pollute something."

"Then you whine for us to build more."

After a steaming bath and a meal of military rations, Roxie had been provided with a new synthskin jumpsuit. Knee-high gravboots helped her move in the lower gravity, and a short but layer-armored jacket fit her perfectly. All of it brown.

She'd hated leaving the safe house deep within Xanthe Terra. The rebels had even stopped calling her a UG Bitch after a few hours. Now that was respect.

Her favorite gift form *La Rèsistance*, though, was a new Draco revolver, its barrel sawed down and the EM cylinder extended to twelve rounds. She wore magdarts under her left sleeve with an old-fashioned carbon steel blade belted behind her back.

It was like having new best friends.

Until she thought about Doggie Boy. Or what Legs had done for her.

And Amai Shi … wanting to turn her in for a bounty.

She had to get herself together and be in the moment. Or she'd be dead.

"What's that?" She pointed at a tall structure a kilometer away.

Locust peeked through his binoculars.

"That's an old Telluric cathedral, not far from where the ancient Viking set down. Our contacts spotted a Jovian ship landing over there. They have unloaded many crates."

"You think they're the ones building the phantom bunkers. But you said that Daedala wanted your help in freeing Mars. Wanted my help."

Locust hesitated for a moment, eyes on the plain.

"The Jovians, *La Rèsistance*—we are using each other. I think Daedala wanted our help in activating your …"

"I get it, love. The UGPD is really an experiment. And I'm the best specimen."

She'd not believed him at first. The UGPD, for all its faults, had saved people. She had saved people. But the more she'd thought about it …

"No wonder Dirty Cool and Styra never use Cinn to see those buggers." She flung another pebble into the water. "They can see all that shite."

"And with convicts, there's no oversight, no regulations," he said.

"If we die, overdose, whatever, then so what, no one would care. But what's so special about a Phase Two, whatever?"

"The drug has made your body more sensitive to electromagnetic wavelengths."

"Oh come on—"

"At Phase Two, you are less likely to suffer its euphoric side effects. It switches your receptors to be stimulated more by energy than physical sensations. At least, that is what Daedala told me."

Roxie ground her teeth. "This is my body we're talking about. My life."

"You had your fun, no?" Locust smirked. "Plus you are alive."

"But why? Did Daedala tell you?"

"She said that someone who can see would bring peace."

"Someone who is a Phase Three Cinn addict. What happens then? You wouldn't tell me around the others at the safe house."

"Daedala withheld certain—"

Roxie punched his arm.

"Don't fuck with me. What does *La Rèsistance* expect me to do?"

"Control the phantoms," Locust said.

She snorted. "You're crazy."

He grabbed her right arm and pointed at her inactive ConRec tattoo.

"After the crazy bullshit you have seen and done, you think I'm insane?"

Roxie yanked her arm back.

"So we just stroll into that Jovian party down there and they'll tell us?"

"Imagine how much havoc would be caused if that many phantoms were released here. The Chasma was nothing. This? This is billions of creds worth of food, equipment, stocks. The food waiting for the Caravans while we starve. Now that's crazy."

"There are families on those ships. I don't like what the bloody UG is doing either, but I'm not starving anyone."

Locust regarded her with scorn "They would not do the same for you."

"I'm not them."

"Then what are you fighting for?"

She could say revenge, for what had been done to her and her friends. Or justice, for the people of Mars. Those answers were too easy to live with. Too easy to say.

"Forgiveness."

Locust laughed. "From whom?"

She faced him.

"Myself."

They stared at each other until Locust finally smiled. Roxie smiled back.

"Then let us storm this new *Bastille*," he said.

"Hold the revolution blather until after we're finished here, right?" She glanced at the evening sun. "You sure you want to bust their knackers in full daylight?"

"We need information before that ship departs."

Below the Canal wall, Chev waited with Etienna. They wore similar brown clothing to blend in. The rest of Locust's unit had ridden hoverbikes to the Canal's other side, to rendezvous with them on the plain. From what Roxie understood, *La Rèsistance* was moving as one unit across the planet, even as the UG cracked down on more riots.

Chev dug dust from his nostrils and looked at it.

"Hungry already?" Roxie asked.

"Sodium builds up in my nose, asshole." Chev flung it away. "These new cyclers should filter that shit from the air better."

"I can't smell you, so they must be working," she said.

Chev grabbed his crotch and spat.

"Not now you two, we've got to reach that old cathedral," Locust said. "The ranch corps own the land, so the building should be abandoned. Once there, we'll keep an eye out while Roxie checks out the Jovian's little project."

Roxie shook her head.

"Like hell I will. If there are phantoms, I need some bloody way of seeing them."

"She is a Phase Two Cinn whore, remember?" Etienna grinned. "She should be able to sense a fart before Chev lets it."

Chev scratched his ass crack. "So, how many fingers do I have up in there?"

Roxie snorted. "You're fucking having me on, right? I can't just…well, I can't turn it on like that."

Locust pulled a black packet from his pocket.

"I have saved these until now. Do not take one unless a phantom is endangering our mission."

Roxie snatched the Cinn tabs and stuffed them into her belt. "Any cigs?"

"How do we know she won't shoot us just to get herself off?" Etienna asked.

"The same way you left me at Valles while I handled those phantoms myself."

Roxie enjoyed Etienna's furious blush and Chev's glower.

"We must be a team here," Locust said.

"You know I can deliver." Roxie looked them each in the eye.

As they all mounted a hoverbike, Etienna scowled.

"I know all too well what you deliver."

Squeezing the bike's handlebars, Roxie stared until Etienna looked at her.

"What the bloody hell is up with you?"

Etienna returned the stare. "You killed Allard Salvaire."

"And?"

"I loved him."

A dozen smartass remarks came to mind but Roxie slowly nodded.

"He was a good bloke. Had me dead to rights at that corporate ranch. The only way I could beat him was to lure him into the dust storm."

"So you cheated?" Etienna reached for her gun, but Roxie shrugged.

"No. I won. Salvaire knew what he was about. But he was a lucky bugger."

Etienna scuffed her hoverbike into Roxie's.

"Why? Because you killed him?"

"No. Because someone loved him."

Etienna spat, then mashed her bike's accelerator.

"Guess she won't be joining the fan club," Roxie said.

The foursome sped up the side of the Canal then dove over its lip. Roxie braced herself as she plummeted down. Right before the hoverbike's sled jets touched the water, she gunned the engine. The vehicle righted itself and skimmed over the liquid surface.

Solidified magnesium, sodium, and potassium floated at the water's edges, yet to be filtered out. Smaller particles stung her nose as she accelerated.

The others followed suit, water spraying in their wake. This way they'd summon no dust clouds while entering the plain. Nearing the Canal's end, they zoomed down a distribution chute and skidded onto grass and soil again.

After passing the irrigation sluices, they powered down the hoverbikes and dismounted. The constant lowing of steers and the hum of automated threshers disguised any sounds the group made. The cathedral was less than three hundred meters distant.

Locust took out his binoculars, scanned the landscape, then nodded.

"The others are in position within a hundred meters of the fence. The starship is hidden in that graveyard behind the cathedral. Keep low."

They crept along the fences, ignoring the cameras. As long as they didn't climb the barricades or steal livestock, the farm corps ignored who got caught on camera. The stench of cowshit, silage, and mud clogged Roxie's nostrils.

The cathedral rested on a stone platform carved with swirling designs meant to imitate planetary orbits and comet trajectories. Now, cowpats and weeds defaced it.

Roxie hurried across, stepping in cowpats rather than the hard stones to further mute her approach. Appearances didn't matter out here. Winning did.

Near the doorway, Locust used a hand signal to indicate they split up. He and Etienna went around the left side, while Roxie and Chev crept right.

Over the centuries, stones had cracked loose and fallen onto the pavement, leaving rubble piles. Graffiti covered many of them. Some tombstones stood at an angle or had fallen over. Roxie wended among them, hand near her revolver.

Chev kept up, though he huffed louder than she liked.

Coming around the cathedral, Roxie crouched behind a weathered tomb edifice. She spied the Jovian starship in the middle of the field. Over eighty meters long, its silver hull gleamed in the sunlight. Heated air shimmered near its engine cones.

It was prepped for take-off—ready to leave quickly.

"Can you cover me with that thing?" She nodded at Chev's shotgun.

"Just get this over with." He wiped his brow with a blue UG bandana.

"Memento from old times?"

"Usually I wipe my ass on it."

"Bet you're a hit with the rebel skanks."

"Hurry the hell up." Chev motioned her on.

Roxie scurried from tombstones to statues, inching closer to the starship. A low thrum came from it, different than an engine sound. As she sped under a landing strut, she glimpsed a long row of upturned earth.

There were no guards.

Her skin chilled as she looked around. If Daedala had been working with Locust, and with the UG combing the planet after her escape … there should be some guards.

She tried to make her eyesight change to see through walls or detect hidden sentries. Concentrated, held her breath, blinked rapidly—anything.

Like she'd told Etienna, it couldn't be turned on and off like that.

Whatever it was.

Crawling on her hands and knees, she passed under the ship. Its latent heat sucked her breath away and she hurried until nearing the edge of an excavated hole.

Inside it were several alcoves like those at Tithonium Chasma.

A line of electromagnetic emitters sat in a row. A floor, walls, and coolant systems had been installed. All it needed was a roof— and some phantoms.

Boots scuffled over stone.

Roxie lay low, hand on her revolver.

UG soldiers walked around the graveyard walls, hauling more emitters into the complex. Two Jovian acolytes dressed in white jumpsuits accompanied them.

She flattened behind a statue. Thoughts of Harmon, Daedala, Locust, the UGPD, all of those with a stake in the phantoms zipped through her mind. Trying to figure out the connection, the logistics. The reason.

Waiting until after the group passed, Roxie crawled near the starship's exit ramp. It led straight down into the newly-constructed complex. She waited as the soldiers set the emitters down and walked no further. The Jovians went in and out of the aisle where the alcoves stood.

Jovian nanites, then. Daedala's game mystified Roxie even more.

After winding around the other side of the complex, Roxie winnowed though a narrow opening where the ceiling hadn't been built yet. She waited as an electrical rush went through her, like the complex at Tithonium Chasma.

So there was an energy field in place.

Again she focused, tried switching her vision to one of glowing outlines.

Still nothing.

Roxie edged along a long corridor containing dozens of alcoves. Many emitters already hummed on a platform below. Within days they'd have all these alcoves filled. Ready to unleash their azure prizes.

Rounding a corner, she spotted the acolytes facing a portable vidscreen.

Lorne Harmon was speaking to them through it.

"Installation is nearly complete, but the timetable you've provided will not match up with the other sites," one acolyte said.

Harmon waved a hand. "Continue with the original plan. I need everything ready in ninety-eight hours."

Roxie frowned. That was four Martian days. She recalled the map Locust had shown her. If all those circled locations were attacked simultaneously, Mars would be crippled. More people would starve. The UG would declare martial law.

But this acted against the Covenant's proclaimed interests. These couldn't be rogues within the organization. Not with that many starships.

This was wide-reaching and expensive. Daedala had to know about it.

They had gotten her involved, asked for her sole protection at Chasma City, doused her with Jovian nanites,…and then had Locust bring her here.

She was still being used. The game wasn't over.

With the conversation ended, the vidscreen turned off.

Roxie popped a tranq magdart into both acolytes. The serum within the missiles put them to sleep before they hit the floor.

She searched them, found nothing, then walked up the next aisle. The place would never become operational. She'd blow it to Ceres first.

As she stepped into the complex's open area, four UG soldiers turned, then reached for their weapons.

Roxie drew, cocked, and fired.

One soldier's head blew apart, gray-red spray blinding the man beside him.

She ducked as a shot zoomed over her shoulder. Cock, aim, fire.

A soldier clutched her chest and collapsed. The blinded soldier fired wild in Roxie's direction, but she focused on the last dangerous one and ripped half his neck away with a shot.

The last one, trying to wipe blood from his eyes, fired another SMG burst.

"Where the fuck are you?"

"Here, love."

Roxie popped a bullet into his eye.

As the dead soldier dropped, another tackled her from behind.

The revolver flew from Roxie's grip. Fists hammered her back. She rolled away before the man wrangled her into a choke hold. Both leapt up. She dodged two punches before drawing her blade and ramming up into the soldier's chin. He still socked her jaw.

She wrenched the blade, sawing through his lower gum, splitting his lips. Shrieking, he flailed until she thrust into his neck.

Though the armored jacket had blunted the man's blows, Roxie still winced as she reclaimed her pistol. She started reloading as a loud clack echoed over the graveyard.

Chev stood in the open. Aiming his shotgun at her.

She didn't move. The revolver's cylinder remained open. One more bullet to load.

Chev smirked.

She kept her fingers loose on the revolver. Gauged the distance to his forehead.

"So you wiped who's ass with that rag? Lorne Harmon's?"

"I'll also wipe my dick on it when I'm through with ya."

Her ears caught the crunch of boot on stone from around the cathedral's corner.

"How much are you getting?"

"Enough. Though the pleasure is half the payment. Seeing the great Street Angel go down. You'll be cleaning my shitter with your tongue."

Her eyes narrowed.

The shotgun moved slightly.

Roxie ducked as Chev glanced at the corner.

Etienna crept around it. He blasted her.

The round struck her and the stone corner, showering stone shrapnel and blood over the graveyard. She crumpled onto her stomach and twitched.

Slapping the cylinder shut, Roxie weaved behind the starship ramp and fired.

The shot blew out Chev's left elbow. He yelled and fired in her direction. The shot scattered over the ramp, activating the starship's security alarm. It blared over the graveyard, reverberating through the cathedral.

The steer herd raised its voice in anxiety-filled lowing.

A UG squad clambered down the ramp, frack rifles aimed. A Jovian priest gazed at them from a viewport, then disappeared back inside.

Roxie ducked under the starship and fired at Chev again, but he dodged behind a tombstone. The shot crushed the stone edifice in a cloud of dust. Before she could shoot again, the soldiers leapt off the ramp and fired.

Frack fire sizzled the air as Roxie dove behind a horizontal tomb. The superheated rounds gouged through the tomb and struck the cathedral, leaving huge smoking holes. The chalky stink of scorched stone made her eyes water but she rolled right and fired.

One UG soldier's helmet flew apart in red and plastic splatter.

More frack shots blew the top off the tomb, raining heated stone wreckage over her. She rolled again until she found cover behind a rubble pile.

An opening in the cathedral wall was a meter away.

"Come out, Street Angel!" Chev called. "Let's see how fast ya fly to paradise!"

A tombstone shuddered.

Roxie shot it. The edifice toppled over and revealed a soldier trying to flank her. As he scooted back, two rounds pounded into his armored vest, stunning him.

She didn't waste time to see who'd helped her. She scurried on all fours through the hole into the cathedral. Chipped tile floor, rotten pews, and a bell fallen from its tower crammed the once-proud structure. She darted behind the bell as a frack round struck it.

The gong inside rang, filling the cathedral with atonal misery. Roxie clenched her teeth and crouched, holding her ears. She should have known better.

More rounds rained through the hole she'd escaped from. Masonry dust fouled the air. She crawled behind a pew, sighted a blue-uniformed leg, and fired.

The soldier wailed as the bullet blew her foot off at the ankle. On her back, the footless soldier fired all over the cathedral interior. Frack rounds zinged through the air like glowbugs from a nightmare. The dust and smoke thickened.

Roxie ran in a crouch to the entrance, then ducked and rolled left at the sound of Chev's shotgun clicking. A blast impacted the wall on her right. She grasped the revolver in both hands and fired twice. The first shot whizzed past Chev's legs. The second winged his left side. He limped behind the graveyard wall as she cocked a third shot.

"I'll still make enough to repair all this shit when I claim the bounty. If ya could shoot better this would be over, ya dumb whore."

Roxie wasn't about to reply and give away her position. At least one more soldier waited out there, with two others wounded but still able to kill. As she hurried from a tombstone to a rubble pile, though, a breeze blew away the smoke haze.

Chev waited two meters away. The shotgun stared her in the face.

He grinned.

Something blew through Chev's neck and he stumbled.

The shotgun fired, some of the pellets striking Roxie's left arm. The layered jacket did its work but it smoked with heated holes.

Chev gurgled and sank to one knee. Roxie met his eyes.

"Looks like one of us still has a heart."

She shot him in the chest.

Loosing a breath, Roxie turned and spotted Etienna. Her pistol still smoked from the shot she'd fired into Chev's neck.

Roxie ditched the jacket and smiled.

"Thanks, love."

Etienna grinned back until holes ripped through her body. She slumped. Blood spread around her.

Roxie ducked around the cathedral.

A figure in white face paint stalked from the entrance.

"I'm claiming the bounty this time," Amai Shi said. "And thanks to you, I won't have to share it with that *gesu yarō*, Chev."

As they stared at each other, guns ready, a low hum caught Roxie's attention.

Someone had set the emitters off.

Chapter 18

"Hear that?" Roxie asked. "Phantoms will be here soon."

Amai Shi's eyes lighted with feral brutality.

"Good."

Roxie's fingers flexed on her revolver's handle. Pointed down, she could fire from the hip in a split second. So could Amai Shi.

"Doggie Boy deserved better," Amai Shi said.

"Yes, he did."

They fixated on each other while the emitters hummed louder.

"You let him die out there."

"You know that's a load of shite—"

"I know what Legs did," Amai Shi said. "I know he died getting you to these rebels. How many friends will you sacrifice to be the best?"

"It's not about that any longer!"

Amai Shi glowered.

"Styra told me all about it. How the UGPD experimented on you so that you'll be the fucking best. The rest of us hunters won't be worth anything to them after that."

"Killing me won't give you what you want," Roxie said.

"It'll get me off Mars. You could've already left, but you still want it all."

Though orange and green spots scattered over her vision, Roxie maintained her focus. It was always the eyes in a gunfight. Look at anything else and she'd be dead.

Though Amai Shi didn't lower her stare, her nostrils flared. She pursed her lips, then closed them. Her left hand hovered near her sheathed magblade.

A second ticked by.

Roxie didn't blink.

Another second.

Amai Shi's left eye ticked.

She yanked her revolver up as Amai Shi raised her SMG.

Squeezing the trigger, Roxie ducked behind a tombstone as bullets dusted it. One round dinged into her right boot heel. The next second, her right leg felt a little lighter.

Her gravboots wouldn't work properly now. Each reaction would be just a split second slower, giving Amai Shi an advantage.

"Nice, *tenshi*. You almost got lucky."

Roxie crawled over rubble to a different tombstone a meter away from Etienna.

Amai Shi crunched over the courtyard somewhere on Roxie's left.

"Like you were lucky escaping New Paris."

Roxie flung a small stone to her left.

It struck a grave marker. An instant later it was wracked by gunfire.

Rolling from around the tombstone, she blew the handle off Amai Shi's magblade. Shrapnel flew everywhere. Amai Shi screamed and collapsed behind a statue.

Roxie scurried behind a ruined wall alongside the cathedral. The emitters hummed so loud, the noise filled her ears.

"Was I lucky again, love?"

"Fuck—"

The screech of metal drowned out the rest of Amai Shi's retort.

The Jovian ship crunched like an empty Drown can.

She scrambled over the wall as a ball of flame gushed over the courtyard.

Smoking bricks toppled over, ripping the synthskin off her right leg. She jerked from the heated wall, her jumpsuit smoking from the contact. Chunks of flaming hull tumbled over the plain. Heated fumes forced her to grab the breath mask from her belt.

A piece of burning debris had already melted it.

Crawling on her elbows, Roxie studied the ship's remains. The engine cones now faced skyward and the fuselage was a jagged ruin. The back of the cathedral had collapsed, birthing a huge dust cloud. Coughing, she crept into a charred, wet morass.

She was face to face with the scorched remnants of Etienna's skull.

"Fuck…"

She knocked it aside and kept crawling.

As the dust and smoke cleared, a large chunk of masonry rose into the air, then flew into the starship's cockpit. It collapsed in a whine of crushed metal.

Phantoms.

Roxie dug into her belt for the Cinn packet. Not taking her eyes off the starship, she fumbled into another belt pouch. Then another.

The gun shook audibly in her grasp. She'd never had such withdrawals before.

Amai Shi's voice carried over the cathedral.

"My *manjuu* tingles. Cinn ever do that to you, Toilet Angel? Who needs a man or woman when you've got this?"

Roxie's fingers finally closed on the packet. She yanked it out, but the plasti ripped and three tabs flew away from her.

The last remaining tab had been seared by the debris.

Blackened orange dust sifted between her fingers. Unable to breathe, she crawled to the three tabs as something tossed the ship's landing pylon. It sailed end over end onto the plain, slicing through an electric fence. Steers clomped away, voicing frantic bellows.

Amai Shi's SMG sputtered bullets at the wall.

"Ha, ha. I see you!"

Grunting, Roxie reached for the tabs, but another explosion rocked the wall.

A large brick crushed the tabs.

A stuttering cry exited her lips and she shoved the brick aside.

A pile of orange dust lay there.

Amai Shi fired again, the sound coming from the other side of the cathedral.

"That's one phantom for me!"

Something large struck the ground, creating a tremor.

Shaking, Roxie scooted over and stuck her face into the orange dust pile.

With hungry inhalations she sniffed the powder. Tingles erupted over her skin. The gash on her right leg hurt less. She snorted the rest in massive breaths, inhaling ash and dirt in the process. Eyes fluttering, she hacked and coughed, then rolled onto her back. A spicy burning filled her nostrils and cleaved through her sinuses.

She quivered as Cinn flooded her system faster than ever.

No euphoria erased her fear. No ecstasy tweaked every ache into bliss. Like before, the drug let her see into the electromagnetic spectrum and energized her body.

But nothing else.

An azure cloud materialized atop the ruined starship. It throbbed in time with the linked emitters' collective hum. Steadying herself against the wall, Roxie aimed. The cloud became a ghostly leonine man, tossing aside busted bulkheads.

Two more phantoms approached the cathedral.

A low buzzing sound caught her attention and Roxie turned.

Two carryalls filled with ranch hands sped toward the broken fence.

The UGPD had sent Amai Shi, but hadn't warned the locals or Spotter Control.

She was the real target.

Her only plan had been to make a break for the hoverbikes, but not now. And where was Locust? He'd probably left when the shooting started.

As Roxie aimed at the phantom on the starship, a low thud resounded from the cathedral's other side. In her enhanced sight, red and purple waves spread through the air. The phantom atop the ship retreated from them—right in her direction.

The other phantoms followed.

Amai Shi had set off a thermo grenade.

Though Roxie managed to shoot one phantom, the other two pounced over the stone wall and flung tombstones at her. She leapt into an open tomb as slabs of ancient stone slammed overtop her. Pebbles slid into her hair, rock dust filled her lungs. Hacking, she squirmed on her back. The tombstones settled over the hole, trapping her.

One tombstone cracked.

A deep chill roiled her stomach. She raised the gun in both hands.

Laughter drifted above the tomb.

"You're right where you belong, my number one *tenshi*."

The SMG rattled off a full clip. Blue light flashed through the cracks above as the bullets destroyed the phantoms.

Dirt and loose stones rolled into the grave. Roxie waited for the right moment. Already she could see through the tombstones.

"I hear you down there," Amai Shi said. "You're going to cum with each bullet I put into you. You'll beg me to keep shooting."

"The drug doesn't work for me anymore. Don't you see? They want us to fight!"

More gunfire, then a thud.

Amai Shi cursed several meters away.

A blue hand lifted the tombstone and threw it into the cathedral as Roxie leapt from the hole. Stone rocketed from the structure at the marker's impact. A brick struck Amai Shi in the back, flinging her to the flagstones.

Roxie somersaulted over another tomb, turned, and fired.

The phantom held up a hand as the EM round tore through its chest.

Another phantom hurried over the plain as one carryall raced away. The other vehicle was a smoldering pile with blackened ranch hands lying around it. Generators blew apart and sparked in the phantom's presence.

Glowing lines radiated from the steers, the phantoms, and Amai Shi. Cyans, vermilions, violets. Now, the rush of alien colors didn't hurt Roxie's brain as much.

The ground rumbled.

Steers charged through the deactivated fence, frightened by the explosions.

Roxie wondered if she should find higher ground or just aim the revolver at her head and end it before they crushed her. All those hooves, grinding her flesh to pulp...Cinn would have made it feel heavenly.

"Hear that, *tenshi?*" Amai Shi called. "Or can you see it with those new eyes? You fucking bitch, why didn't you tell me? It wasn't enough to be Number One, was it?"

Roxie scurried onto an overturned statue.

"Stop being a twat! They're using us!"

A bullet crushed the statue's face. Roxie jumped behind a tombstone.

"If I win here, I'll get a chance in their program. And I will be better than you."

"Whoever wins here will just be their Cinn poppet."

Roxie didn't care about giving away her position. She had to try reasoning with—

A shot ripped across her back. The graze seared through her shirt and flesh.

"Too bad you're going to lose, *tenshi.*"

Yelling, Roxie wheeled around and blasted apart a tombstone. A slight form dodged. Amai Shi, glowing violet through the smoke. She fired again.

Her bullet took off Amai Shi's ear.

Squeals of delight sung above the incoming stampede's furor.

Roxie wanted to puke. That was her friend out there. A few weeks ago, it could have been her. So high on Cinn that even dying felt good.

Trying to keep her voice strong, Roxie reloaded her gun.

"It doesn't have to be—"

A roaring thunder echoed over the plain as the stampede enveloped the cathedral grounds. Steers clambered over rubble, stumbled into tombs, collided with gravestones. Trampling one another, the animals spilled into the open complex. The emitters ceased humming. Due to the phantom's presence, the anti-stampeding chips planted into each beast no longer worked.

The sound and spectacle blinded Roxie with a cavalcade of color and ripples. She leapt atop a sturdy tombstone, her boots barely balanced on it.

Horns clipped the tombstone. She wobbled, heart in her throat. Dozens of maddened bovines sped past. Dust clogged her nose. Hooves kicked up stones at her like shrapnel. One sliced her cheek.

From the corner of her eye, she spotted Amai Shi, running over the backs of steers. She hopped from one moving animal to another, eyes lighted with savage glee. Her ear had grown back, covered in tattoos.

Roxie aimed and fired.

The revolver's empty cylinder clicked.

As she reached for her magknife, Roxie ducked. Amai Shi jumped toward her, swinging. The magblade swept over her head but the movement sent her off the marker and into another open tomb. No sooner had she fallen into it than a steer leapt over it.

Cowshit and dirt spattered Roxie but she scrabbled up.

Amai Shi jumped down beside her.

While steers ran around the open hole, Roxie thrust with the magknife. Amai Shi side-stepped and rammed her broken mag-blade handle into Roxie's left side.

Crying out, Roxie thrust again, but Amai Shi crammed an elbow into her chest and back-handed her. Blood choked Roxie as she slashed Amai Shi's left cheek in half, then crushed her knee into her diaphragm.

Wheezing, Amai Shi whipped the magblade around and slashed through Roxie's right shoulder—but the swing also struck the leg of a passing steer.

The beast squealed and skidded over the hole. One of its hooves scraped Roxie's right arm, but the other pressed on the magblade.

Amai Shi ducked down as her own magblade was pushed through her left bicep.

"Oh fuck…fuck yes…"

Amai Shi leaned over and licked Roxie's cheek as she pushed the magblade out. Blood squirted them both. Screaming in orgasmic agony, she jabbed the magblade at her.

The glowing ripples in Roxie's eyesight showed her how to move, where to strike. She dodged and landed an uppercut, then a hook against Amai Shi's jaw.

Amai Shi staggered back, then lashed out with her magblade. Roxie fired a magdart but it struck the tomb wall. Dirt sprayed their faces. Knuckles rammed into Roxie's wounded shoulder.

"You can't win!" Amai Shi drew back for another strike.

She pushed Amai Shi to the left and thrust. Amai Shi dodged but Roxie kicked her wrist, shattering the bone. The magblade hit the ground.

Laughing as the final steers ran past, Amai Shi crammed the SMG barrel into Roxie's chest and pulled the trigger. The clip was empty.

"You never had a future," Amai Shi said through bloodied lips. The Ronin tattoos wriggled over her wrist and bicep, healing them. "But I do. I was never meant to be here. You were my ticket."

Roxie clasped her right shoulder. "You were my friend."

Their eyes met, then both reached for the magblade.

They wrestled for it, but Cinn powered Roxie's body. With inhuman force she grabbed the weapon and rammed it through Amai Shi's gut.

The tip stuck into the tomb wall.

Roxie went numb and shook her head.

"No…you stupid…look at what you made me—"

Lips shaking, Amai Shi cradled the magblade as blood poured from the wound.

"Stupid 'cause I want to live? What the fuck will you be now? Without Cinn, without the UGPD, without me and Doggie Boy…you're nothing."

Tears leaked down Roxie's face. "I never wanted this."

"I know…"

Amai Shi's eyes lost their Cinn glaze. The Ronin tattoos clogged around the blade in her stomach, unable to repair such damage.

"Tenshi? My tenshi…"

They stared at each other until Amai Shi offered a slight smile.

"Don't," Roxie whispered. "Shi… please…"

Amai Shi struck out with a hidden knife.

Roxie knocked the knife aside and plunged her own blade into Amai Shi's neck.

Hot arterial spray bathed her. Gurgling, Amai Shi thrashed about.

The fear in those dark eyes tore Roxie apart.

"I'm sorry, I'm sorry…"

Over and over into Amai Shi's ear while she held her close.

"*Tenshi?* I can't feel…"

Amai Shi fell still.

The Ronin tattoos on her chest went dark.

Roxie staggered back as the sounds of fleeing steers faded. The magknife weighed her down and she slumped against the tomb wall. Throbs pulsed in her left side, right shoulder, and her rib cage. Her eyesight was normal again.

Her world wasn't.

For several minutes Roxie stared at her friend's corpse. In her weird eyesight, Amai Shi's body gradually went from red to pinkish gray, losing its heat. She touched the star tattoo on Amai Shi's arm, where she'd bruised her several days ago.

A boot crunched over the rubble around the tomb.

Roxie shielded Amai Shi's body and raised the blade.

Locust stood above her, pistol smoking. Dirt and blood caked his jumpsuit.

"I have what we need. Let's go."

"You should have done it." She glanced at Amai Shi's body.

He lit a cig and offered his hand.

"I had her in my sights, but you owed it to her, *Ange de la Mort.*" She closed Amai Shi's eyes.

"I'm no one's angel anymore."

Roxie took his hand and clambered from the tomb. Her right shoulder flared with pain and a wave of dizziness made her stumble.

"Well, you're an angel of death foretold by this asshole. Hear what he has to say."

Locust nodded at a nearby gravestone.

Behind the marker was one of the Jovian neophytes. Blood ran from his forehead.

He gazed at Roxie with awe.

Locust frowned at her wounds. "Let's hurry, before you bleed to death."

"I've got too much to live for now. Whoever made her do this will pay."

Roxie kicked dirt into the tomb containing her friend.

"Ashes to ashes…"

Locust yanked the neophyte to his feet.

"Blood for blood."

CHAPTER 19

Roxie slid off the hoverbike and bumped against the wall of Shalbatana Canal. Her clothes smeared red over the mortared stone. It could be hers, or Amai Shi's.

It didn't matter now. Mars always demanded blood.

Locust shoved the Jovian neophyte behind a rock outcropping and glared at her.

"Don't be so stupid. Take cover."

"Don't you ever lay off?"

She wished Cinn worked like before. She needed to escape the pain in her body.

The pain in her heart.

Locust planted the cig into her lips and helped her sit on the ground.

"Guilt is a fool's extravagance. It won't help you survive."

She puffed the cig but the its metacaffeine just aggravated her wounds, making her heart thump faster.

"Stuff the Fleurant quotes, right?"

He scanned the area with binoculars.

"His prose is sacred to many natives. Since he resisted the Tellurics, I thought you would appreciate the irony."

"That I'm an offworlder fighting my own kind? Shite. I don't have a kind now."

"Daedala may convince you otherwise."

"Then let's shove off, then."

"First, this."

Locust drew a can of flesh putty from his bike's tool box.

"Are you ready?"

"Do it."

She tensed as Locust gingerly cut scraps of her jumpsuit from around the cut on her right shoulder. The cut was clean, but deep. He sprayed putty into the wound. The tan-colored substance stunk like ass as it puffed up and filled the bloody gash. It still hurt more than a toothache. Like the blade was slicing through her shoulder all over again, but in slow motion. She glared at Locust, who smiled.

"You expected the numbing version? *La Rèsistance* is short on funds these days."

"But never short on assholes."

She bit her lip and closed her eyes as the putty sealed the wound. There was nothing on hand to fix her ribs or left side. At least the gash on her leg had coagulated.

She stared over Chryse Plain, at the smoking cathedral, the empty ranch. Attacked by thousands of hooves, it resembled a huge pile of shit now rather than something people had worked centuries to perfect. Let the Caravans have it now.

"That putty will only hold for a few hours. We must move."

"Wait."

Roxie's eyes flicked over the horizon. Colors rippled across the sky in the distance, then grew larger, as if something approached.

A low hum built over the horizon.

She and Locust shared a look.

"You saw it before you heard it?" he asked.

Still staring at the sky, she slowly nodded.

"What is going to happen to me?" the neophyte asked.

Roxie sucked so hard on the cig, its metacaffeine made her legs twitch.

"What's your name, love?"

"Meleager," the neophyte said.

"You Jovians and your Greek names. So, Meleager? Shut the fuck up."

Meleager looked her up and down with recognition. Maybe he'd seen her on a vid back when she had been Daedala's escort at Chasma City.

The hum grew louder.

Locust snapped branches off a nearby bush and camouflaged their hoverbikes. As he took cover beside Roxie under the outcropping, two gravjets flew overhead. He popped a new clip into his pistol while she refilled the Draco's cylinder.

The gravjets landed near the cathedral. Locust pulled out his binoculars again. Meleager turned, opened his mouth, but Roxie snapped the cylinder shut and scowled at him. Meleager hunkered down and looked away.

"Hunters?" Roxie finished the cig.

Locust swept the plain with the binoculars, then focused on the cathedral again. The smoke plume still rose, but was lighter in color now. Small fires guttered in the complex where the emitters blew. She assumed Locust had something to do with that. A dust cloud rose from the west where the cattle had fled. Carryalls rumbled in that direction, trying to gather the herd back together.

She nudged him. "Well?"

Locust handed her the binoculars. "See for yourself."

Placing the lenses to her eyes, Roxie tweaked the magnification. As it adjusted to her eyesight, her lips formed a defiant line.

"Like what you see?"

Through the lenses, a platoon of UG soldiers formed a perimeter around the cathedral. Two handlers led Jovian wolves over the ruins. Several familiar figures stalked the area. Roxie's teeth ground together.

Styra stormed back and forth, beckoning to the soldiers, kicking at shattered tombstones. Dirty Cool watched two soldiers collect Amai Shi's corpse. With his black synthskin mask on, his expression remained unreadable.

"They are not here for the phantoms. Your precious SATSCAN will have told them that someone other than that Geisha killed a few."

"How the fuck did Chev join *La Rèsistance*?" she asked.

"That pile of shit had us convinced. I've seen him gun down so many UG troopers…" Locust shook his head.

She lowered the binoculars, unable to view her friend's corpse anymore.

"Is *La Rèsistance* that desperate?"

"No more desperate than your Geisha comrade was."

Roxie grabbed Locust's sleeve.

"The UG drove her to it. Putting us through a program to see who can absorb the most Cinn. We hunters never had a bloody life."

Locust gently removed her hand.

"You do now. If you want it. That tattoo is deactivated. Disguise yourself, get some facial surgery, change your looks. Find the nearest spaceport and leave."

"What about your rebellion?"

"You have to choose for yourself."

She glared at the burning cathedral, the gravjets, then at Meleager. Locust made it sound so simple. Unlike Amai Shi, though, she had no family or friends offworld. No goals past surviving. But she wasn't going to let Harmon and Daedala get away with what they'd done to her and her friends.

"I still want to know why. So if you want me for your revolution… I need your help to find answers."

Locust pointed to a row of agriculture fields past the cathedral.

"Pierro's group was still in contact with me after you gunned down those UG bastards. Once they create a diversion, we'll leave with our prisoner."

"Diversion?" Roxie frowned.

A few seconds later a fire spread over the fields. The wind fed it, and soon the horizon was seared with a yellow-orange line. Smoke columned into the sky. Even without the binoculars Roxie made out figures rushing to the gravjets.

A few gunshots carried over the plain.

"Sod that. We still can't use the hoverbikes, they'll detect us."

"You offworlders always think Martians are stupid." Locust eyed the Canal. "In a few minutes we can enter the release gates as this thing refills."

Roxie gaped. "Bollocks to that. You want to drown?"

"There is an aquifer tunnel beneath the plain. *La Rèsistance* has used it before. It will take us to our second rendezvous point, two and a half kilometers northwest."

Chewing her lip, Roxie looked away.

"I thought you had mastered that fear."

"Then what? You really expect us to haul him, the state I'm in?"

"There is no choice."

Locust bound Meleager's wrists with cuffs similar to those Styra had put on Roxie. The memory made her anger flare. If only she were healed … she'd go over there and put a bullet into Styra's brain.

"Stop worrying about your former comrades for now. Until we learn something from this man, we cannot do anything. We must find a secret, a weakness."

"I bet this berk's stuffed with them."

Roxie followed Locust, who led Meleager up the Canal's service stairs. Gunfire reverberated over Chryse Plain, another reminder of what she lived for now.

"You call this a fucking tunnel?"

Roxie backed from the edge of an expansive subterranean aquifer. Only Locust's flashlight lit the narrow walkway alongside it, where centuries-old handholds protruded from solid bedrock. Silvery-white magnesium and sodium stains coated everything.

Locust shoved Meleager onto a pier where a motorboat was tied to the quay.

"No. Just a tunnel."

She took a deep breath, smelling dank earth, chlorine, and mildew. Time to be a big girl and make it through this. But she was sick of being a pawn.

Locust shoved Meleager to his knees.

"Before we go on, we must ask you some questions."

Meleager trembled. "I … I am prepared to face the final—"

"End?" Locust smiled. "You are a neophyte. I do not see the dedication in your eyes that will prepare you for death."

"Death? I thought we were going to question this bloke?"

Roxie didn't look down as she walked over to them. Such deep water.

Locust drew his magknife and knelt beside Meleager.

"I know you Covenant believers consider all things as one, contributing to the energy of the universe."

Meleager nodded. "Yes—"

Locust lay the magknife on Meleager's throat.

"Your contribution would be small. Very small. You conspired on something, though, that will be immense. Something larger than you could ever be."

Lips tight, Meleager glanced at Roxie.

"Your contribution will be negligible."

Chuckling, Locust nodded.

"Probably. What of her? This bounty hunter, now a renegade, whom your ambassador chose to be her bodyguard at Chasma City?"

Roxie rubbed her arms in the aquifer's chill air, wanting her jacket back.

"Well?"

Meleager didn't look at Roxie.

"She is a propaganda tool, nothing more. Daedala wanted to show that there is discontent and insecurity among the UGPD's hunters."

"Then why dust me with your nanites? Stupid berk."

Meleager's eyes widened. Roxie frowned.

The shock in the neophyte's gaze was genuine. Always in the eyes…

"Why are you planting emitters and complexes all over Mars?" Locust asked.

Meleager stared ahead.

Roxie sighed. "Say something, you annoying git—"

Locust clipped off one of Meleager's fingers and flung it into the aquifer.

Meleager's scream was cut short by Locusts' fist into his gut.

"What the fuck?" Roxie cried.

Locust flicked blood off the magknife, eyes on Meleager.

"And so I return part of you back to the universe. I will do so, one piece at a time, until you tell us what you know."

"This is insane!" Roxie yelled.

"Define sanity."

Locust grabbed Meleager's next finger.

"Daedala told us nothing about that hunter slut!" Meleager shouted.

Face calm, Locust lowered the magknife. "Tell me what you do know."

She gripped her holstered revolver as she glared at Locust. They needed information, but getting it this way made her nauseous. After seeing what the TLF had done to *Jubilee*'s passengers, she loathed torture.

"We call the ancients to reclaim what is theirs," Meleager said in a rushed voice. "What is still theirs."

Locust scratched his stubbled chin with the magknife's handle.

"Mars? It once belonged to the phantoms? The dead?"

"They are not dead." Meleager's face reddened with fury.

Roxie stomped forward and grabbed Meleager's chin.

"Then what the sodding fuck are they?"

A dreamy look came over Meleager's face.

"You do not see? You, who has destroyed so many, gazed upon their monuments, seen their alphabet—you still do not understand?"

"There have been times … it doesn't matter." Roxie cradled her right arm, the shoulder wound still aching. "If they aren't ghosts, then what? Aliens?"

"Answer her." Locust raised the magknife.

"Don't be stupid, just tell us," she said.

"You will discover soon enough," Meleager said.

Locust slashed. Blood spurted over the pier.

Meleager screamed as both of his thumbs were tossed into the dark waters.

"Goddamn you!" Roxie drew and aimed at Locust. He ignored her.

"They are the true Flame!" Meleager's agonized voice reverberated through the chamber. "They are those who were not afraid! Those who escaped the flesh!"

Roxie's skin chilled. "Escaped?"

"The technology of the Leonid colonists…it allowed them to go beyond mere physical representation. It could transform them into pure energy. Data within pure light. Traveling to the stars. One with the universe."

Roxie wiped her face as the chill seeped into her skin. Into her heart.

"Then…those buggers were humans, once? They did this to themselves?"

Locust raised his blade to Meleager's throat.

"Why?"

"It is what they came to Mars for." Meleager's voice cracked. "To escape what old Earth had become. To become something else."

Her eyes darted here and there as ideas coalesced in her mind.

The ruins, the fossil prospectors. The reason why phantoms never posed a problem until the United Government's preoccupation with those old sites—and the phantom presence guarding every one. Then there was the kill bots, the Telluric hatred for everything native to Mars. Jovian intervention, their devotion to energy.

Their manufacture of Cinn.

She grabbed Meleager's arm.

"You're looking for it. How they did it. You Jovians, the UG, even the Tellurics centuries ago with their bloody kill bots. You all want the secret."

Meleager stared at the water.

Consternation warred with anger on Locust's face. "What?"

"They want to know how to become a phantom. They think the secret—the technology, the bloody instructions, whatever—is hidden in the ruins."

"You should rejoice," Meleager said. "You, our new Angel. You are the first to near Phase Three. Soon you will surpass it."

Shaking, Locust leaned back.

"Daedala claimed they were spirits! My people, reborn to—"

"They evolved past death," Meleager said. "They are beyond eternity now."

Roxie's breath caught and she closed her eyes. All this time the popular belief had been that they were ghosts. Scientists had always described them as waves of energy, or even a different life form, but the UG banned such ideas from mainstream vidfeeds.

She's helped them contain the secret while they worked to find it. All the UGPD missions, the observations by Spotter Control and SATSCAN, using hunters as test subjects—using them to keep natives and kill bots from the secret. Maybe that's what Harmon had wanted her to find out. To see how much Daedala knew.

"Why is Daedala installing these complexes all over Mars? Is she trying to take over the planet? With the UG's help?"

Locust's jaw set in a grim line. "Talk. You only have so many fingers—"

"The Flame take you!"

Thrusting forward with his legs, Meleager pushed himself into the aquifer. A splash, a few bubbles, and he was gone.

"Fuck!" Locust paced the pier. "That fucking sand rat! I'll dance in the Covenant's ashes! This was to be ours. Our ancestors! Our—"

"Way to win? You're like the rest of these buggers. Wanting the phantoms' secret for yourself. You don't give a shite about Mars and you don't care about me. Only what I can do for you."

Locust wiped the magknife off and sheathed it.

"Have you ever given me a reason? You killed Salvaire, my best friend. You have aided my enemies for years. You've even shot me!"

"I've also saved your ass more than once, you ungrateful fuckwad."

"What compelled you?"

Roxie grimaced as her shoulder throbbed.

"I'm Street Angel, remember?"

"Why?"

The anguish in his voice gave her pause.

"Because I wanted to."

They stood on the pier for several minutes, not looking at each other. Roxie would have killed for a decent cig or a shot of whiskey. A hit of Cinn, to transform her anger into happiness. She rubbed her nose and sniffed, wishing some of the orange powder remained there. Lot of good it'd do her now.

"I do not care what these phantoms are," Locust said in a low voice. "I do not care why you do the things you do. Why you refuse me. None of this must stop us from preventing others from uncovering this secret."

"Refuse you? What the bloody hell are you on about?"

Locust met her eyes. "Not all revolutions are built on hate."

Roxie snorted. "That's the lamest pick-up line I've ever heard."

"It should be. You are the only one I have used it on."

Locust checked his pistol and walked to the boat. Roxie laughed without humor.

"What's wrong, *La Rèsistance* run out of cute tarts? The UG steal all your hot crumpets with big totties? Thought you had a lovely one years ago. She back at the flat, keeping the bed warm?"

Locust got into the boat, untethered it from the quay, and started the engine.

"They killed my wife."

Roxie slowly sat in the boat and stared at her boots.

"You've been doing all this for her?"

Locust leveled a dark gaze on her.

"Who else do you think I have been doing it for?"

"That's why Meleager's words got you miffed. That's why you wanted to summon them at Pyramid Eight. You've been looking for her out there."

The veins in Locust's neck stood out as he adjusted the boat's forward light. It illuminated the wide aquifer, disappearing into the darkness, reaching no end.

"You thought hunters like me…you thought we were destroying her ghost."

"Now she is truly gone. There is nothing to discuss."

Locust gripped the boat controls, looking into the darkness. The look of a man who had bottled his hate along with his hope. Now she'd just emptied him of hope.

Leaving the hate.

"The UG…they did it?"

Long moments passed before he spoke.

"She was afraid of water, like you. A great fighter, but she didn't want children until we had won. Strong and stubborn. She fought until the very end."

Roxie swallowed. The hurt in his voice, his stare…

"I'm not her, love."

"I know."

They looked at each other. She smiled gently. He returned it.

"Let's find Pierro."

Locust piloted the motorboat down the aquifer. The vessel's forward light cast glimmering shadows along the walls, reflecting off minerals encased beneath the surface.

"Then what?" she asked.

Locust increased speed, leaving dark ripples in their wake.

"We find Daedala. Then *Ange de la Mort* turns this planet upside down."

Chapter 20

Roxie tore into the megafood carton as soon as Pierro handed it over.

Hands shaking, she stuffed the dark brown cubes into her mouth. Salty, chewy, and sweet, each gulp made her belch as the high calorie foodstuff filled her eager gut.

"Go easy on that."

Pierro helped Locust from the aquifer access hatch onto a cratered mesa. It overlooked Chryse Plain from the west. After speeding kilometers along the subterranean waterway, Roxie and Locust had finally reached the rendezvous point.

An antiquated carryall waited near the hatch, its treads wearing thin. Over two dozen members of *La Rèsistance* waited in it, outfitted in brown camo fatigues.

"Where is the captive?" Pierro looked down the hatch.

Locust accepted a megafood carton from a fellow rebel

"Jumped into the aquifer during questioning. But we have what we need."

Though Pierro simply nodded, Roxie gave Locust a meaningful look.

She would not forget what he was capable of.

"Did you find out where they are meeting?" he asked.

"Tharsis Tholus," Pierro said.

"The main Jovian temple on Mars?" Roxie asked.

Pierro just smiled.

Locust helped her to the carryall.

"Everyone, let's load up. It is a long drive to that old volcano."

As the other rebels piled into the carryall, Roxie frowned at him.

"Who is meeting at Tharsis?"

Locust stared down the aquifer hatch, then slammed it shut.

"We'll talk on the way."

She knew what he'd wanted down there. All the times they'd encountered each other on this bloody planet, they could have killed each other. She'd never seen real profit in Locust's death, especially since she sympathized with the rebels.

He wanted her … but she wanted answers.

And she didn't trust him.

They were in a desolate region, far from any cycler, ranch, or town. The rebels weren't loyal to her. Choices were limited and she needed proper medical attention.

She had to follow him.

The vehicle, once used by one of many mining corporations hoping to plunder Mars, trundled over the pocked landscape. They all sat in the trailer with the top retracted. Though the air quality lessened the further they drove from Chryse Plain, she refused a filter mask and continued eating. She might not get another chance.

Roxie gazed over the red sand, the tumulus and craters. Many areas remained just as lifeless, untouched by soil reclamation and wind erosion prevention. No irrigated canals reached it, thus dooming any modern settlement to failure. Buffalo and horse bones littered the region.

Pierro nodded at the bones.

"My grandfather saw the last great herds. He said there wasn't enough terraformed graze land to support them."

"Why didn't ranchers collect the poor buggers?"

"The Tellurics bred them in vats and released them out here. No forethought or plan. They simply tweaked genes in a lab and hoped for the best. Just like the rest of us."

She glanced at his butternut flesh and had to look away.

Locust procured two canteens from the trailer's cooler and handed Roxie one.

"This is how barren Tharsis Tholus is. To approach it, we cannot use carryalls, hoverbikes, or anything mechanical that SATSCAN might detect."

Water poured down Roxie's dry throat as she pressed the canteen to her lips. Cool and fresh, it made her sigh in deep satisfaction. She'd never been much for plain water before. Locals often poisoned the UG's supply, leaving mercenaries like her to drink Drown and other offworld swill.

But she'd never been much for acting as bait, either.

"SATSCAN will detect me, love."

The rebels looked from Roxie to Locust. Pierro frowned.

After emptying the canteen, Locust smiled.

"Why else do you think I asked you along? Their sensors will think you are a phantom—just like those necrostructs after your escape from New Paris."

"Ha ha! You dumb fuck. You really think I'm going to—"

"While you draw their attention, we will raid the Jovian compound. We will rescue Daedala from the UG. She cannot refuse, since the Covenant has declared political support to *La Rèsistance*."

"What a crock," she said. "We need to target Lorne Harmon."

Pierro lit a cig and blew smoke in her face.

"That is self-serving ... for you."

"Jovians are pacifists. Harmon's the immediate threat."

Locust shook his head.

"We don't have much time until Harmon unleashes phantoms from all those locations. The Jovians provided that technology. With Daedala in our custody, they will have to bargain with us. Plus, she owes you. Owes me. Got something better to do?"

Acting the decoy would mean she'd have to face UGPD hunters again.

The best ones.

"After all her fancy speeches about understanding phantoms, I'd have thought *La Rèsistance* would support her."

The rebels gave her dark looks. Pierro blew smoke from his nostrils.

"That offworld floozy hasn't donated money to Martians or pledged Jovian aid to our cause. She hasn't done anything but rile the mobs in every city she visits. That is not a coincidence."

"Obfuscation," Locust said. "She has the UG and our people distracted while she intends to steal what our ... ancestors built."

She frowned at Locust's meaningful glance. He was going to allow these people to continue believing that the phantoms were their ancestors, their relatives. But there was nothing to gain from telling them the truth. Strange, but she accepted Meleager's claims. It explained so much, but raised even more questions.

"Right-o, then. Now that we've decided, tell me how you're storming that dust flat atop jolly old Tharsis."

"Two teams," Locust said. "One climbing the eastern face, the other creating a diversion at the spaceport near the bottom of the mountain."

"It sounds too dodgy."

Pierro smirked.

"Like you said—they are pacifists."

Locust blew smoke above his head.

"Many people will die if we do nothing. This is our best choice."

"You need me because of my Jovian nanites. You hope Daedala still trusts me."

"Yes," Locust said.

Roxie cleared her throat. "If we have to kill her ...?"

"Then do it," he said.

"I'm not your bloody mercenary. I'm not a hunter anymore."

Locust crossed his arms.

"We have saved your life. Fed you, clothed you."

"Treated you." Pierro offered her a medical kit.

Roxie opened it: flesh putty, morphine, wound coagulant, nutrient bandages—everything a girl needed on a rainy day.

"I won't trade one master for another."

"Then serve yourself," Locust said. "They transformed you. Pay them back."

They stared at each other as the carryall bumped over a series of small craters. The other rebels waited in silence. Few viewed her with contempt now—they regarded her with hope. Street Angel, indeed. Dirty Cool would be laughing right now.

Thinking of him recalled memories of Doggie Boy, Amai Shi, and Legs. Laughing, drinking, doping. Trying to escape the hell their crimes had earned them.

And all this time, being used by Daedala and Harmon as lab rats.

"Leave Daedala to me, then," she said.

The carryall took them westward to Kasei Valles. With her gravboots busted, Roxie felt lighter. The typical nausea let her be as she tended her wounds. The flesh putty in her shoulder would have to be removed by a surgeon but at least it held. Her bruises were numbed by a light morphine dose, and the wound coagulant made all her scrapes scab over in seconds.

Along the way she spotted kill bot wreckage and trash piles where cities dumped unusable garbage. The refuse stretched for kilometers. A few rusted starship hulls creaked in the wind. Two abandoned Psycoids stumbled through the mess until a rebel shot magdarts through their heads. None laughed as the reanimated corpses fell.

Pierro nudged her.

"You don't find it pretty, what your people have done to our world?"

"You still going to whine and point fingers if your revolution wins?"

The other rebels chuckled while she and Pierro shared a grudging smile.

As the hours went by, Pierro whistled *La Marseillaise* while the others relaxed. The notes eased Roxie's tension. Combined with the morphine, it lulled her into a nap.

When she awoke, a full canteen and another megafood carton sat beside her.

She was grateful—but these people weren't her family. As soon as she couldn't benefit their cause, they'd leave her out here like so much rubbish.

They all watched as flames spread over another mesa north of them. Given the distance, it had to be Burners. In her former life Roxie would have been eager to blast them. Spend the creds on drinks, Cinn, maybe a good shag with some hot guy.

All of that was gone.

Legs wasn't here to offer a Cinn freebie or a pep talk, Doggie Boy couldn't make her laugh with a dumb joke. Amai Shi would never again inspire with her blade skills.

It was up to her to break free from Mars. For herself, and their memory.

But nothing could be the same for Roxie, even if she escaped offworld. Cinn had transformed her. Kill bots might be following her even now. Sensing her EM signature.

Too bad she wasn't a real ghost.

Night stole over the red landscape, turning it a rotten crimson. Though the cyclers maintained a decent atmosphere, enough dust remained in it to reflect sunlight a few hours after sunset.

Roxie wished she could have seen the planet's pre-colonial, dusty blue twilights.

Deimos made a flyby as the carryall stopped at a village beside Kasei Valles. The buildings were connected by corrugated passages and old starship modules. Some still bore faded insignia from when they'd left Earth. An ancient biosphere dome housed their hydroponics. Crusted solar panels still powered the settlement. Dogs yipped and panted, accustomed to the rebels' scent.

Outside the village, angular shapes beneath sand-covered tarps indicated hidden vehicles. With the planet's wind patterns constantly reshaping dunes in these wastes, SATSCAN never truly identified such transient anomalies.

Locust's band was greeted by dozens of excited natives. Hugs, kisses, and jokes were shared—though no one approached Roxie. People whispered behind her back or made gestures for the Rites. One little boy linked his hands and flapped them like wings at her until his mother shooed him away.

Ange de la Mort. She was a harbinger of change to them. Doom for others.

The people dressed in smocks or coveralls; handmade cotton or denim dyed red and orange. Women wore knitted scarves sewn with elaborate Flame symbols or Fleurant portraits. Unlike offworlders who'd lived on Mars for years, the natives aged well under the low gravity. The elderly had few wrinkles and Roxie never spotted a cane.

Three children followed her around, whispering about ghosts and sand banshees. They pointed at her revolver, giggled at her blood-caked clothes. Such young faces, frightened yet awed. Going around and around her.

Roxie finally stopped and glared at them.

"Look, just sod—"

Everything glowed red in her vision for a second, and she stumbled to her knees. The children's faces changed to those she'd shot on *Jubilee.* Unable to breathe, Roxie couldn't look away. The next moment, they were Martians again, gaping at her.

Trembling, she reached out to them.

"Oh, loves… I'm didn't mean…"

The children turned and ran deeper into the village.

As she stomped back up the carryall's ramp, Locust touched her good shoulder.

"Wait."

"They all think I'm some fucking monster," she whispered.

"Fear and adulation go hand in hand."

Roxie shrugged him off. "Where's the surgeon?"

"She will arrive in the morning, from Caseo."

"I can't sleep in this village. I was a hunter, it's too bloody weird."

"Come with me."

She followed him from the village into a crater no more than two meters deep, ten meters wide. Soft sand cushioned their steps, then rumps, as she sat beside him.

Out there with no light pollution, the stars shone with unchallenged luminance. Roxie traced a few constellations like she did in childhood. All those field trips to Luna's major craters came to mind and she smiled. Jumping around in low-G, her first kiss while floating from an ejecta cliff around Kepler Crater…

"You should smile like that more often," Locust said.

"I haven't had reason to."

"If we survive this… Mars will be different. You will be different."

Roxie looked him over, lit by Deimos's quaint light. She'd heard that Luna could make a night on Earth seem like day, before the Tellurics covered everything in carbon clouds. Viewed from a different position, Locust might be different.

"Why are we out here talking alone?"

"I need to know what you want. If we succeed."

She stared at the stars again.

"If I could leave Mars… I'd apply to be a freighter pilot, muck about between Titan and Enceladus. But no matter what happens, the UG won't employ me to shovel shite after what I've done."

Locust scooted closer.

"What if Mars stabilized?"

Roxie wet her lips.

"It won't, but okay, I'll pretend. I'd still want to leave."

"The other leaders of *La Rèsistance* want different things. Even with the UG gone, I'll need someone I can trust. Someone who understands Mars."

"Thanks for the nomination, but I don't know what I'll want if that happens."

"I know what you need."

A retort died in her throat. She needed to know what she was now.

If she could still enjoy life.

"Do you?" Roxie touched his thigh.

He traced a finger down her cheek.

"You are not a monster. You are—"

"Just shut up."

She manipulated his zipper.

Locust nibbled her earlobe. "So is this a pact?"

Her fingers dug into his open zipper.

"This doesn't guarantee you anything, love."

She tugged down her pants and underwear. He lifted her into his lap.

While Deimos disappeared and Phobos lighted the horizon, she grinded down on him. Harder and faster, bare thighs slapping against his, her rump pinched in his grasp.

Glowing energy waves swiped over the landscape in her sight. Spicy sweetness rose in her mouth as wind and electrical currents writhed like ethereal snakes before her.

But fucking him didn't excite her.

Teeth gritted, she sucked in through her nose. Her fingers dug into his arms while she fucked him harder. Locust gasped, his hardness filling her—yet still not satisfying.

As she rode in an unrelenting rhythm, Roxie gazed at the stars. Trying to reach for something that Mars, Locust, and vengeance could never give. While he grunted and moaned beneath her, bright spots filled her sight as she scanned the night sky. Once again the stars took on different shades. The arm of their galaxy glowed with distant life.

Locust could never take her that far.

She trembled as her vision filled with whirling colors. Phobos emitted waves of grays, blues, and browns, while Locust radiated red and orange, like the bonfire growing between her legs. A moan forced her mouth open.

He thrust up into her as she faced him nose to nose.

"What do you want?"

Orgasm eluded her despite how wet she got, how great his cock felt. Fear bubbled in her chest. The sky flared, filling her retinas with a million new colors.

She felt everything but what she wanted to feel.

Locust frowned.

"Goddamn it, what's wrong?"

Passion waned as her vision returned to normal.

The stars were just plain dots on black cardboard.

Roxie shoved him away before his ejaculate spilled over her. Grunting deep, Locust finished himself off in the sand.

"The fuck was that?"

She jerked her underwear and pants back up.

"We got what we needed, love."

He stomped over to her.

"What we needed? Bullshit. You can't use me like this—"

She pushed him back.

"It's done, right? Now lay the fuck off."

"You teasing bitch. You cannot get pregnant—"

In a burst of energy, Roxie flung him meters from the crater. He skidded onto his bare ass in the coarse soil. Her muscles came alive as her senses detected his heartbeat.

He gaped at her in a mixture of fear and wonder.

"Does that make me less? That I don't want your shite splattered all up into my useless fucking womb? I'm not your bloody repository. Not for your seed, and definitely not your fucking power play."

Locust's face pinched in hurt.

"Everything isn't about power."

"It is when everybody wants me."

"That's your problem, *Ange de la Mort*. You don't want anybody or anything except those fucking orange pills." He stalked back to the village.

She'd gotten her answer. For every new sensation gifted by Cinn, she'd lost one.

Roxie gazed at the stars until the wind dried her tears.

CHAPTER 21

Wind scoured over the bulbous summit of Tharsis Tholus as Roxie leaned back into the crevice. Despite her helmet's aural dampeners, the tempest bawled out all sound. She winced as lightning flashed in distant thunderheads. Each brilliant-blue, jagged finger made her skin pulse.

She'd never felt like that before a storm.

Locust had claimed they'd not have to wait long out here. He would fool around until the rust wind came back, then her team would really be in for it.

They'd barely spoken since the night in the crater, and the next morning, the surgeon had spent hours mending her shoulder. After a day's rest, she'd joined Locust and his two strike teams en route to Tharsis. The rest of Mars remained rife with civil disobedience, and Daedala kept giving speeches, inspiring the natives.

But Roxie still had questions. Daedala better have the answers.

Pierro and three more rebels waited in another cleft, wearing similar suits. Pressurized and equipped with powerful g-ballasts, the windsuits gave off no electronic signature. Thick rappel cords kept them from being blown off the extinct volcano.

Nine kilometers in height, Tharsis Tholus wasn't Roxie's choice for a vacation. The caldera was covered in ancient ash, making each step slippery. Her team had dealt with it since ascending from a sentry gravjet pad some five kilometers up the mountain.

Below, the plain stretched for dozens of kilometers, with Ascraeus Mons towering southwest of her position just below the caldera. At a massive fifteen kilometers in height, its peak disappeared into the lower clouds. Further south, Valles Marineris was hidden by a dust storm.

Dominating her view, though, was *Crimson Aegis*. Its humongous shadow draped the ground. The UG's fear of Daedala must be growing daily.

Pierro motioned and pointed upward.

She tossed a grapple over the landing pad lip a few meters above. After it caught and hung, she punching the button on her belt. The grapple's motor pulled her up.

A few gravjets flew around the volcano, thrusting a particle-filled breeze against Roxie. The force bumped her into the mountainside but the grappling motor kept lifting her. Since their raiding party maintained radio silence, she couldn't tell them that the aircraft was most likely Spotter Control.

SATSCAN had detected her, just like Locust planned.

The grappling hook's motor stopped as her helmet brushed the landing pad's lip. Dirt and pebbles slid onto her comrades and she grimaced.

Pierro gave her the middle finger.

Roxie pulled herself over the lip and rolled onto the landing pad.

Daedala's yacht, *Icarus*, waited.

A wind shear knocked Roxie over. Her elbows smacked into the pad but she crawled behind *Icarus*'s landing pylons. As the others climbed up, she drew her revolver.

No one on guard. No visible cameras or gunbots.

Her eyes narrowed in suspicion, but they had to go on.

While a rebel pilot hacked into *Icarus*'s entrance, Pierro pointed at a maintenance hatch built into the side of the volcano.

She hoped the floorplan Locust had acquired was correct.

Another ash-laden gust shoved Roxie into the side of *Icarus*. A dazzling fork of lighting struck the mountainside. Everything glowed in her vision for a few seconds afterward. Lights were brighter, ripples spread from her comrades' bodies, and wavy patterns played across the sky.

Pierro helped her up and cocked his head.

She nodded that she was okay.

Walking in a crouch under *Icarus*'s hull, Roxie made for the hatch. The same tingling sensation she'd sensed at Tithonium Chasma filled her body. It was the Jovian's defense system, scanning her for the correct nanites. She hoped Locust's diversion was working lower down the mountain. With the nanites connected to the Jovian computer system, Daedala would know someone had gained access.

At Roxie's approach, the hatch slid open.

They stood in a narrow hallway lit with sparse fixtures.

The silence disoriented her after leaving the roaring winds behind. She gave the hand signal to move forward and they crept through a maintenance room. Tool carts, engine couplings, and diagnostics terminals shadowed their advance.

Roxie viewed it all with an effervescent glimmer, as if everything gave off energy. Though her enhanced senses allowed her to lead them from the darkened chamber, her breath quickened. She hated not having control over her strange abilities.

In the next room, a skylight illuminated a wide circle on the floor. A chill crept up her back as she recognized the hieroglyphics inscribed on the walls. They were the same ones she'd seen in various pyramids. Now, her eyesight revealed something moving within them. Letters, numbers.

Pierro and the others removed their masks. Roxie did the same.

"How soon until your friend has *Icarus* ready?"

"Three minutes. With Daedala taken from here aboard her own ship, they won't suspect shit until we make the announcement."

"But if Locust has attacked, this place should be on total lockdown."

Pierro regarded her knowingly.

"Not if they think a phantom is coming. It's standard procedure to evacuate an area if SATSCAN detects one. It's the UGPD we'll have to worry about."

"I know the bloody rules. Doesn't mean they're playing by them."

Using the floorplan on Pierro's datapad, they hurried through red halls enameled with Flame iconography: fiery comets, eyes within a circle, and erupting volcanoes. They passed an empty barracks and numerous chapels. Still no one in sight.

A clack sounded ahead, followed by lowered voices.

Roxie held up a hand.

The others halted. She waited, finger easing over the revolver's trigger.

A voice echoed ahead.

"The Flame is salvation. The Flame burns away doubt, fear, and hatred."

She neared the corridor's exit and knelt behind an altar. A large circular chamber towered above her much like the Telluric cathedral. Columns carved with hieroglyphics rose to the ceiling. A flame burned within a pit in the center. Jovians dressed in white robes ringed it. Several handcuffed figures with sacks over their heads were led into the chamber by UG soldiers.

The flame danced in her sight with a thousand colors. Its energy expanded her senses, letting her detect everyone's heart rate, body temperature. Viewing them like she would a phantom, while on Cinn.

Daedala stood on a dais, dressed in sheer silken garments. Her red-blonde plaits were clasped with glass spheres, each containing a burning flame.

"The Covenant thanks you for your service. To secure what we have begun on this planet, our Second Earth, you have sworn to seal our secret as only a Covenant member can. With enemies at our doorstep, this must happen now."

Another Jovian dashed a tiny hammer against a gong, and a mellow tone reverberated in the chamber. The handcuffed people were nudged closer to the pit.

Daedala moved to the opposite side of it, the flames reflected in her amber gaze.

Pierro tapped Roxie's shoulder and held his datapad near her face. On it, a hacked SATSCAN feed displayed *Crimson Aegis* investigating explosions on Tharsis Tholus's northern slope. So Locust had bought them some time.

Even after what had happened between them … she hoped he made it.

"From the Flame we are born," Daedala said. "Through the Flame we pass, forging the elements within us into forms capable of surviving. Into the Flame we return, willingly. Without doubt, fear, or hatred, so that the next form created by the Flame will be even stronger."

The other Jovians chanted in unison.

"Until the cosmos is cleansed, and the stars shine with undying permanence."

As Roxie's grip tightened on the revolver, the identities of the handcuffed individuals were revealed.

Each one was a UGPD hunter. All gaped in Cinn-drenched stupefaction.

The other Jovians chanted in low voices. It was a Passing Ritual; a Covenant funeral. But these weren't old Jovians about to die.

Pierro tapped her again. She gave a single shake of the head. No, they had to wait.

Daedala raised her arms.

"It is time for you to enter the next phase. Present them to the Flame."

The first hunter was thrust into the pit.

Flames jetted upward, lighting the room in hellish orange hues. The hunter's raw shriek was a mixture of joy and agony. He laughed until the fire reduced him to ashes. The stench of broiled meat and burnt copper forced Roxie to cover her mouth.

Within the flame, she glimpsed an explosion of energy.

Daedala's smile waned as she gestured for the next hunter to follow suit. It was Mandrake, one of the newer hunters. He trembled as piss dampened his pant legs.

"Will I see them, will I see—?"

A Jovian shoved Mandrake into the pit with the same result as before. He screamed, thrashing as flesh sloughed off his scorched bones. His eyeballs melted form their sockets, skeletal fingers clawed at the air, but still he screamed.

Roxie viewed it all with gut-churning clarity, as if she witnessed every cell get ripped apart and claimed by the fire. The energy inside Mandrake's corpse burst through the air, but given everyone's reactions, she knew only she could see it.

Grim-faced, Daedala motioned for the third hunter.

"Surely one of you has passed the trials?"

Roxie stood and aimed at Daedala.

"Move and you die. Nobody will bother burning your corpses afterwards."

The Jovians remained in place, though their chanting ceased. The hunters waited in line before the pit, staring eagerly at the fire.

Daedala smiled with genuine happiness.

"I am very glad to see that the United Government has been unsuccessful regarding your capture."

Roxie stepped into the chamber, unnerved at the chilly air despite the flaming pit.

"You've been successful too, love. Now you can summon the ancients and ask for their secret. All while toppling the sodding UG."

Pierro and the other two rebels flanked her, aiming their weapons at the Jovians. For all the tension in her chest, the Jovians just smiled at her.

Daedala's eyebrows rose.

"You have been doing more than simply fleeing the authorities."

"Only after I gained access to that little complex. After you had Locust dust me with these bloody nanites."

Daedala came closer, ignoring Roxie's comrades.

"And what have you seen out there? The past, or the future?"

The gun wavered in Roxie's grasp. "No bloody clue what you're talking about."

"The Cinn has saturated your system. Why else would I have chosen you to help me? Why else would these pretenders have chosen you?"

She stepped closer. The Draco's barrel was centimeters from Daedala's forehead.

"Enlighten me."

"Despite your abuse of it, Cinnamoxidil hasn't destroyed you. It has enhanced you. And you want to know why."

Pierro pressed his pistol into Daedala's side.

"What does the UG want? Why are you working with them?"

"We are all of the Flame. Your tone implies that I have betrayed someone, or some principle. Tell me, what have you betrayed to get here?"

Roxie snorted.

"You all want it for yourselves. Whoever gets it, rules the Solar System."

Daedala frowned.

"Then you have learned nothing. The ancients merged with the cosmos itself! That knowledge was lost in all those pointless wars. Now that it has resurfaced, the very ones who tried to eradicate the ancients have returned to claim Mars as their own. The Caravans, the United Government—"

Pierro pressed the gun harder into Daedala's side.

"It belongs to us Martians. Not you."

Daedala regarded Pierro as a sand gnat.

"You are no different than the rest. You will use it to destroy and dominate."

"Cut the shite," Roxie said. "Why did you ally with the UG? Or is it Harmon? He allowed me to be your bodyguard at Chasma City so I could spy on you."

"Yes, you were a tool. Yet the Flame has forged you into something greater."

"Into what? A better tool?"

"That is up to you."

Roxie nodded to Pierro. "Put the cuffs on her. We're getting the fuck out of here."

A bullet whizzed past her face and ripped into Pierro's side.

She ducked and whirled around as UG troops poured into the chamber. They fired with precision, killing the other two rebels with head shots.

Grunting, Pierro rolled back and fired at the nearest blue uniform.

Roxie's first shot pierced a soldier's layered vest with a heavier EM round. She fired again, smashing apart the next soldier's helmet in a cloud of visor shards and blood.

Daedala and the Jovians remained in place. They'd been waiting for her all along.

"Run!" Pierro shouted as a smoke canister rolled from his hand.

Dense white smoke filled the chamber and the soldiers ceased firing. Seeing everything in glowing outlines, Roxie dragged Pierro back to the corridor they'd exited. The pit glowed like a beacon, pulsing with rippling waves.

"*Icarus*," Pierro breathed before a bullet slammed into his gut. He cried out and squeezed off shots into the smoke. She pulled him down the corridor.

"Come on, those undusted blokes can't beat us."

"You're our … best hope … get the hell out of here, leave me."

"Not going to happen, love."

"Offworld women."

Pierro's laugh was cut short as a shot clipped off his lower jaw. He died.

She shuddered, squeezed his hand, and sped through the compound.

Heavy footsteps followed.

After finally reaching the maintenance room, she flung open the dock hatch. She ducked and rolled left as two soldiers near *Icarus* turned around. One managed to get off a shot before she blasted them both from the platform. She ran for *Icarus*'s airlock.

The rebel who'd been hacking into the ship lay in his own blood.

A glowing form moved from behind an outcropping near the landing pad's edge.

She ducked under *Icarus* as a figure with a half-skeletal face leaned out and fired.

Energy fired in Roxie's limbs, granting her the split-second she needed.

The shot only grazed her stomach, tearing her windsuit and shearing a fiery line over her skin. She struck the ground, rolled right, and fired.

Her round blew apart the outcropping, but the figure leapt away and rained bullets over the pad. She scooted behind a pylon, clutching her stomach.

Styra's voice sent waves of fury through Roxie's body.

"So you can see me everywhere now. That makes this little raid even more fucking stupid."

As Roxie drew her magknife and cocked the revolver, thoughts raced through her mind. No one knew about this raid except for…

Locust had betrayed her. Led her right up here.

As she took a breath, a deep hum warbled through the air. Wind gusts tossed ash and pebbles. The landing pad shook from the approach of something massive.

Crimson Aegis hovered less than two hundred meters from the volcano.

Roxie edged to the other side of the pylon.

"Know what's really fucking stupid?"

Styra shot the opposite side of the pylon.

"Thinking you can win?"

She threw the magblade across the pad. No sooner had it clanged onto the pavement, than Styra blasted it apart. The next second she leaned out and fired just as Styra saw her. The bullet struck Styra's left knee as she dodged.

Roxie fired again.

Sparks gushed from Styra's damaged leg but she rolled off the pad. Gripping the lip in one hand.

She sighted down the barrel at Styra.

"Now, you piece of fuck knock-off—"

A crackling discharge arced over Roxie's body.

Every muscle clamped up, relaxed, clamped tighter, then spasmed. She dropped the revolver and collapsed. Writhing on the landing pad, she couldn't even cry out as electricity tore through her. She jerked and spasmed for several more agonizing seconds before lying still. Saliva pooled from her mouth onto the pad.

Two large boots clomped before her face. A nullifier barrel prodded her stomach. The stink of cig smoke crept up her nostrils.

"Game's over, Street Angel," Dirty Cool said. "This was your last fuckup."

Still numb from the nullifier shot, Roxie glowered at Daedala as Styra and Dirty Cool hauled her back into the chamber. The fire pit was surrounded by ash piles. Pierro and the other rebel corpses were arranged in a line nearby.

"These other hunters failed the test," Daedala said. "Will you?"

"She's too fucked to be of any use," Styra said. "Let's end this bullshit before—"

"It's Harmon's orders," Dirty Cool said. "We both had our chance at this."

Daedala glided off the dais and cupped Roxie's chin.

"This is not how I wanted this to happen. If you had not went after those alleged assassins at Chasma City, I would have already shown all this to you. But now, you trust no one. I cannot blame you."

Feeling returned to Roxie's lips. "Sod … off …"

Styra wrenched Roxie's arm until her shoulder cracked. "Listen to her."

"Like you did?"

With an iron stare, Daedala pried Roxie from their grasp and led her to the pit.

"You are not the first we've tested, this is true. But you can be the first of your kind. Look into the flames."

"You've killed …" Roxie worked her numb jaw. "So many …"

"Many more will die unless we learn the Leonid's secrets. I know you can see what the hieroglyphics in this chamber contain. These are knowledge stores left behind by the Leonid cult, the progenitors of our religion."

As Daedala's soft yet unyielding hands forced Roxie to look, she discerned movement within the symbols like before. Upon first glance they'd appeared as squiggles, like nanites in a pulse cloth. Now she caught differences in their hues, alternating flares in their glowing outlines. Bit by bit, she made out mathematical formulas within them. Notations beyond her ken.

"My … body?"

"It hasn't been your own since you first took the sacrament. With every month that passed, it conquered your cells, invaded your receptors, and heightened your senses. That is why it feels so euphoric in the early stages. That is Cinn, shedding the sensations you don't require, for those you do."

An angry sob shook Roxie.

Daedala caressed her bruised, dirty cheek.

"Only those attuned with the cosmos can know what the Leonids left behind. And now, after years of failed test subjects, the UGPD has finally produced a success."

"But you've … fucking killed!"

Daedala yanked Roxie around to face her.

"You want it to stop? You want the deaths of your friends to mean something? Then eat this block of Cinn. Enter Phase Three … and walk through these flames."

A Jovian acolyte held up a solid orange block of Cinn.

It was the size of thirty tabs.

Roxie licked her lips, then hated herself for it. The drug had taken so much from her, robbed her of sensations, stolen any future she'd had. All she could see were the ghostly outlines of reality, of those she'd loved—but nothing more. Like watching the sun rise but never beholding its full glory, or feeling its life-giving warmth.

Daedala's breath brushed Roxie's neck.

"I know you want it. If you wish to be complete….you must do this."

"You're just using me!" Roxie cried.

Daedala nodded, and Styra forced Roxie to her knees.

"You'll soon be free of such petty selfishness."

The acolyte gave Daedala the Cinn block. Two more pried Roxie's mouth open. She trembled as the flames in the pit rose, washing over her in furious orange hues.

"From the Flame you were born. Through the Flame you pass, forging the elements within you into perfection. Without doubt, fear, or hatred, so that your next form will be even stronger."

As the Cinn entered her mouth, Roxie gagged. A hand grasped her throat while another yanked her head back by the hair. Smiling with gentility, Daedala knelt and pushed the rest past Roxie's lips. The spicy sweet flavor stung her gums, burned her esophagus. The acolytes made her swallow, then shoved her to the floor.

Daedala rose.

"The strongest substances always come from adversity. From super-heated meteors to the planet's molten core far below us. And you, Roxie, from all this pain, from your wasted life, to a destiny of power and light."

Shaking on the stones before the pit, Roxie tried to make herself vomit. Tried to crawl away, resist the surging vigor within her. It spread through her veins like scalding water. She wailed, then shrieked as the sensation amplified to cataclysmic agony.

It felt as if her fingers and toes melted off, each tooth pooled to magma in her mouth, and every color seared her retinas like red pokers.

There wasn't a shred of ecstasy anymore. No orgasm, no joy.

Her heart stopped.

Cinn plowed into Roxie's brain and gnawed into her mind. In synergy with her very cells, it restarted her heart and other organs. She glanced down at her arms and legs, saw the violet magnificence coursing under her skin like radiant highways.

"Do it," Daedala said.

Styra kicked Roxie into the fire pit.

There was no pain. Only blinding majesty. Tossing in the cinders, among the fiery tongues, Roxie glimpsed faces in the hieroglyphics. Telling her to stop. Begging her.

Even as the windsuit slid from her body in ashes, she stood in the pit. The flames guttered out at her touch. Smoldering embers crunched under her bare feet.

She was naked, trembling—and unharmed.

The acolytes whispered to each other. Daedala's eyes widened. The soldiers backed away, weapons raised in shaking hands.

Everyone glowed now—but only when she wanted them to.

"Fuck," Dirty Cool mumbled.

"Take her," Daedala said. "Tell Harmon we can proceed."

A soldier shot Roxie with a nullifier again. The electrical charge burst over her skin but she merely wobbled and stared back at them. Energy dissipated from her body.

"Take her now!" Daedala cried.

Stunned by such energy output, Roxie couldn't move as Styra mashed a tranquilizer needle into her neck.

CHAPTER 22

Roxie squirmed as sand covered her body. Within seconds, it drifted up to her neck. The chilly Martian night made each grain a tiny dagger of ice, stabbing her flesh. She tried to breathe but mucus clogged her nose. Something traveled up her legs, then hopped onto her left arm. She managed to look down.

A sand rat gnawed on her arm, its teeth breaking the skin right above her veins.

"Fucker!"

She yanked the beast off. The sharp pain of teeth ripping from her skin made her blink and sit up.

Night gave way to day, but it was framed in angles, corners … under a ceiling.

Gasping, she blinked again.

The sand transformed into something smoother, warmer. Blankets. The sand rat in her grasp became an IV needle attached to a fat nutrient bag on a metal stand. Her arm bled where she'd pulled the needle out.

"Even asleep, you're a pain in my ass."

The voice was familiar.

She looked around. A figure gradually came into focus.

Dirty Cool rose from a chair and tapped a wall terminal.

"She's awake, fighting her IV again."

Roxie scanned her surroundings: a white-walled room crowded with medical cabinets, sink, and a sanitation bot. She lay on a bed with restraints around her ankles.

"I'm a pain in everyone's ass now."

Dirty Cool stood at the foot of her bed.

"Not for long."

"Where am I?"

"Aboard Crimson Aegis."

So she was aboard Harmon's carrier.

"Now you'll get what you always wanted, love. Ranked number one, an assload of creds, a ticket off this rock—oh, and a bullet in me."

Dirty Cool snorted. "Like you have any idea what I want."

"Legs tried to—"

"Amai Shi did too."

She glared back at him.

Dirty Cool leaned over her.

"You took care of her. Styra claims she had you, but I saw that shot. Chrome Cunt was almost dead on that volcano, if those boosted motherfuckers ever die."

"And you got me from behind. Way to take my mickey."

"That's because I'm not stupid. If you'd been smart, we could be arguing this bullshit back at *Fantôme Salon*, instead of here, like this."

The door opened.

Lorne Harmon entered, along with Styra and a Covenant acolyte.

"Pull up a seat, love, stay a while."

Harmon looked from her to the neophyte.

"You see? She is well-cared for. All of her wounds have been repaired, and her body fed. You can examine her for yourself."

The acolyte neared Roxie's bed, then glanced at Harmon.

"Daedala requested she be fed glucose bonded with Cinnamoxidil 9 extract. This IV bag is simple B vitamins."

Harmon swiped a hand. "She'll be more than adequate."

"For what? What the bloody hell—?"

Styra clamped a muzzle over Roxie's face. "She's fine."

The acolyte gave them dark looks. "Very well. I will inform Daedala."

"Outfit her, then bring her to the dock." Harmon and the acolyte left.

Styra flung the blankets away and ripped the restraints from Roxie's ankles.

"We will get you dressed. You must look presentable for your funeral."

Roxie grunted around the muzzle. Styra laughed and shook her by the collar.

Dirty Cool knocked Styra's hand away and Roxie landed back on the bed.

"You rough her up, we don't get paid."

"I rough you up, you don't see tomorrow," Styra said.

Dirty Cool's smile was brutal, and one Roxie had never seen.

"I shot off your real arm for that bullshit at Hellas years ago. This time I'll kill your ass."

Styra regarded him with amusement.

"I saved everyone from you that day. You were so overloaded on Cinn that you shot hunters and phantoms. But not me. I wasn't fucking afraid of what they'd made me."

"Never been afraid of shit," Dirty Cool said.

"Wear that mask all you want—but you're still a goddamn monster."

Styra slammed the door behind her.

Dirty Cool locked force cuffs around Roxie's wrists and ankles, then pulled off the muzzle. As she rubbed her face, he brought in a package and tossed it onto the bed.

"Put it on."

As she stood, the force cuffs prevented her hands or feet from moving too far, leaving no way to strike or grab something outside of the field. She barely slipped the synthskin jumpsuit over her underwear and bra. It tingled her flesh, one of the newer suits from the Caravans. It bonded with her form in sleek black lines.

"Posh me all up for an execution? How sweet."

"They don't want you dead. Yet."

Roxie fought to get the boots past the force cuffs around her ankles.

"Way to cheer me up. Didn't know you and Styra were old chums."

"She wanted Cinn to change her. Fuck, all she did was rob those Chinese vaults on Ceres, she didn't have to stay here. She was the closest to a Phase Three."

"So she had to stop you?"

He didn't reply for many moments, then stuck his face before hers.

"Cinn did fuck me up. But I was killing them all because I knew this was wrong."

"So you tried to take her out too, right?"

"I removed her arm. With a concussive."

Roxie smiled despite the situation. "No fucking way."

"She's one tough cunt."

"What about me? You know what I've had to go through, just to—"

Dirty Cool jerked her off the bed as she finished with the other boot.

"Nobody cares. If you're lucky, that Jovian bitch will kill you after all this."

Roxie eyed him. "What if she doesn't?"

"Then you'll scream for a long time."

As he escorted her through *Crimson Aegis*'s corridors, they passed platoons of soldiers. Dozens of other personnel, from medics, pilots, and drivers, gathering for the occasion. That's what it felt like to Roxie: a sporting event.

With everyone cheering for her death.

Like the carriers she had trained on at the academy, *Crimson Aegis* was built for war and nothing else. Cramped spaces, walls lined with computers and diagnostic vids, the stench of antiseptics and sour sweat—she could have been eighteen again, eager to see the Solar System.

Dirty Cool led her to a gravjet dock where a cadre of bounty hunters waited. She recognized a few. They all gave her cool looks and predatory smirks.

Next they entered a chamber filled with Covenant members. She tried to catch a glimpse of Daedala, but no luck. A few vidscreens, however, showed Roxie's face alongside graffiti reading *Ange de la Mort*. The news feeds showed it sprayed on destroyed UG tanks, written on city walls, even carved into dead soldiers' faces.

It was Locust. Using her face, even that stupid nickname, to fuel his revolution.

No wonder everyone scowled at her.

"Sucks to be you."

Dirty Cool yanked her by the elbow down another corridor where several elevators waited. They took one up to the bridge, which possessed large windows offering a panoramic view of Cydonia.

Roxie slowly inhaled as she examined the ancient structures: Façade Peak, Pyramid Three, Pyramid Eight, East Temple B. She'd hunted here more than any other location on Mars. Killed more phantoms here, lost more fellow hunters here than anywhere else. It was the gold mine of fossils and artifacts, with entry forbidden to natives and most offworlders. So many times she'd been on Cinn and viewed the intricate hieroglyphs along the pyramid walls, the old causeways now hidden beneath the sand, the humanoid phantoms that had once allowed her to escape.

Daedala entered the bridge from another door.

"Beautiful, isn't it? The greatest works of humanity were rendered therein, and now, we struggle to uncover them while killing one another."

"And they came all the way to Mars to pull it off," Roxie said.

Daedala strode over to her.

"The Tellurics left Earth in ashes after the old wars. They were victors to a dead planet. The ancient Leonids, loyal to the Flame, knew that Earth was beyond help. They had to find a different world where they could build a new society. One of pure energy."

Roxie rolled her eyes.

"So the phantoms you summoned and captured—the violence they do is more legit? Glad you cleared that shite up."

"They fight because they do not wish to relinquish their secret."

Lorne Harmon appeared with Styra and several UG scientists in tow.

Dirty Cool grabbed Roxie's arm, but Harmon waved him off.

"She cannot harm us with the inhibitor in her system. You are relieved until the operation begins."

Dirty Cool glanced at her and left the bridge.

"Now, you will grant us what we want," Harmon said. "You have been nursed back to full health. The Leonids do not take well to anyone less than perfect."

"Guess that means you'll have to stay up here, then," Roxie said.

"You must enter the lower vaults, beneath Façade Peak. The ones restricted to the highest security clearance."

"You will be given a schematic of the correct chambers to look for," Daedala said. "You will be aided by decades of Covenant research."

Roxie glanced from Harmon to Daedala and snorted.

"You bloody twats. Working together, hoping to share in the profits? All this time, hunters like me have fought this war for you. Died for you, all so you can live forever as blue light?"

Harmon gazed out the windows at the pyramids below.

"This transformation is reserved only for our greatest minds. The upper echelon of human development. By committing your crimes, sentencing yourself to a life of violence, you proved you are not among those worthy of what lies beneath these ruins."

"If I'm such a slag, why do you need me?"

Daedala's face drew back in the first hint of anger Roxie had seen from her.

"The phantoms think we want to use their knowledge for destruction—"

"You don't?" Roxie laughed until Styra grabbed her by the neck.

"Set her down."

Daedala's amber gaze bore into Styra.

Nostrils flaring, Styra finally let go and stalked to the other side of the bridge.

Daedala continued.

"The Leonids' knowledge is all that can save us now. Earth has been lost. The Caravans will never return there. Mars will soon be overpopulated. The Outer Systems do not have the space or resources to house everyone. Humanity must evolve itself—just like the ancients did."

"None of that shite will help me find what you're looking for," Roxie said.

Harmon swiped a holoboard in the middle of the bridge. A hologram appeared, showing people in leonine headdresses, makeup, and faux feline pelts.

"The ancients were not without their superstitions. They recreated the old mythologies of Earth. They even played up to pre-colonial fantasies, constructing pyramids here at Cydonia. Like any other cult, this one fed off of its members to power the ruling elite."

The hologram shimmered into a floor plan of Façade Peak. Harmon continued.

"It has taken the UGPD, with Covenant aid, nearly twenty years to map the target location. The lower chambers are accessible only to those who can see into the electromagnetic spectrum. Hieroglyphs that glow green can be manipulated to open passageways and access vaults."

Roxie wondered how many had died to discover that much.

"Manipulate how?"

Harmon and Daedala shared a look.

"You made me like this. Now tell me."

"Cinnamoxidil augmented the energy receptors on your cells," Harmon said. "You only need to touch the hieroglyphs to activate them. The main chamber, we believe, is marked with these hieroglyphs."

The holoboard displayed the same symbol the phantom had traced in the sand at Tithonium Chasma: rounded, with a cross on one end and a spiral at the other.

Roxie tried gauging their reactions. Always in the eyes.

"So why trap phantoms in those underground complexes?"

"The more of them trapped up here," Harmon said, "the fewer down there."

"The most powerful are buried below," Daedala said. "Sealed away with the technological process of changing flesh into energy; biological consciousness into a persona of light."

"Like the data inside the light streams?" Roxie asked.

Daedala looked pleased that she remembered.

"Yes. But also a soul."

"What sodding rubbish."

Daedala smiled.

"Of course it is. The soul never existed before. It was but mere legend, a comfort to those about to die, a child-like belief in the afterlife. But the Leonids achieved it. Life encased in pure light."

"Bollocks. Hundreds of phantoms have been destroyed over the years. Long before the UG came to Mars and sat on everyone's faces."

Harmon deactivated the hologram.

"That does pose a problem. There must be a dwelling beneath the surface. Or they recruit new members from the local population, though census data doesn't reflect that."

"What's in this for me? Do it or die, that the contract?"

Daedala shook her head.

"Your name will be cleared and restitution offered, should you succeed. You'll finally have your forgiveness."

Locust kept betraying her. He was the only one she'd told about that.

Harmon's face was impassive, his blue eyes calculating. Daedala wore a sincere but firm expression. Styra scowled.

"What happens to the rest of Mars, the other systems?" Roxie asked.

"What do you care?" Harmon asked.

"They must never know," Daedala said. "For the survival of our species, and to ensure a safe transition into our next evolutionary phase—the common people cannot partake of the Leonid's gift."

Roxie's heart sped up.

"You sick fucks. You'll continue as normal, won't you? Let them kill each other, starve and rot while the chosen few live like, what? Gods?"

Daedala looked at the floor, then leveled her gaze on Roxie.

"These people must die out for humanity to progress. The violent, the stupid, the disabled, the diseased, the mutated—they cannot be allowed to taint what is coming. They must not be allowed to render Mars as their ancestors rendered Earth."

"Is this what the UG wants?" Roxie asked.

"The UG wants territory, short-term profits," Harmon said. "I and my backers want a new era."

"I won't do it."

"You have no choice," Harmon said. "Where do you belong now?"

Before she could answer, Daedala took her hand. Her fine-boned fingers caressed her skin, then came to rest on the force cuff around her wrist.

"Cinnamoxidil has transformed you. You can see into the electromagnetic spectrum already, better than any Covenant elder. The phantoms recognize this. Your biology already resembles theirs. Who knows? In time, you might share in their glory, their discovery."

Roxie stared out the windows as *Crimson Aegis* hovered above Façade Peak. She could start over, change her name, alter her face through surgery. Get that pilot's license and fly all over the Solar System while they fought for temples and azure ghosts.

Out there it'd be just her and the stars.

"I do it my way. I want layered armor, Dracos, thermo grenades, some Cinn."

Harmon frowned.

"You are not going down there to shoot everything while getting yourself off."

"Then send that boosted bitch down there, love." Roxie jerked a thumb at Styra. "The phantoms will burn her to scrap before she gets a hundred meters down."

"She's a Phase Three now, Harmon," Daedala said. "The drug's euphoric effects are past."

Though Styra stomped around the bridge, Harmon regarded Roxie coldly.

"Fine. You will have everything you need."

"She'll run the first chance she gets," Styra said. "Then she's mine."

Harmon smiled.

"That is correct, Trent. All known exits will be sealed and guarded by our best hunters. If you attempt to escape, the bounty on your head will be reactivated."

Roxie shrugged. "Where do I sign?"

"Right here."

Harmon held up a thumbprint scanner. The same she'd used to sign every contract for years. It was the ultimate mercenary symbol, for it implied the signing away of one's rights to eliminate the rights of another. That's what they'd taught her in the academy.

That's why she'd sworn to safeguard the future…but she'd betrayed it.

As she raised her thumb to it, she noticed it wasn't the same model. The scan panel was larger, and numbers in the upper corner referenced radiation readings.

Harmon smiled again.

"In the event that you are even more different than you are now."

Roxie pressed her thumb onto the panel.

"Smart of you, love. You don't want me coming back as a ghost."

CHAPTER 23

The gravjet deposited Roxie atop Façade Peak and flew away.

Though attired in black synthskin, layered armor vest, and reinforced jacket, she missed her old duster. With a Draco holstered to each thigh, two magknives, and magdarts encircling her left wrist, she at least felt secure now. Four thermo grenades hung inside her jacket, along with a Cinn packet containing eight quadruple-strength tabs.

Equipped with the latest g-ballasts, she walked easily in her favorite style boots, which buckled over her knees. But no earbud to connect her with Spotter Control or *Crimson Aegis*. The entire operation was a secret. Given the planet-wide unrest, it looked normal for the huge carrier to defend the oldest and most enigmatic site on Mars.

Here and there she spotted a hunter or soldier, stationed at critical points where she might try to escape. She licked her lips, wishing she'd asked for a pack of cigs. It had been some time since she'd braved Façade Peak's subterranean levels.

As the inhibitor wore off—a triple detoxer shot—her eyesight saturated with color. Everything appeared more vibrant and focused. The soil was redder, the sky a little bluer. Unlike before, her brain didn't throb processing all the new colors.

Cydonia stretched out all around her in a conglomeration of hills, mesas, and valleys. A cycler operated in the far distance. She glimpsed green in the direction of Lunae Plain, but Cydonia had remained untouched since the Telluric invasion. Some believed aliens built the pyramids, and once, she had considered the possibility.

Now all those intriguing notions were crushed by the selfish reality that people had become gods at the expense of everyone else.

Roxie stared at the midday horizon, thinking of her friends.

How they'd died. Never knowing what they'd really died for.

She followed a path down from the top of Façade Peak. It spiraled around the summit until she reached an elevator used by archaeologists.

As she reached for the control panel, a slight rustle sounded on her left.

Roxie drew and aimed.

"Easy, sugar."

Legs's blonde wig tossed in the breeze. His tight red jumpsuit flared in her vision.

She gaped, then laughed.

"You're alive? SATSCAN will think you're a bloody fire, dressed like that."

Legs grinned.

"SATSCAN ain't got shit right now. Harmon and Daedala are probably holding hands, their ass cheeks clamped tight. Hoping you'll be Street Angel one more time."

His already had a hand on his gun.

Her joy withered away.

"You're working for those fuckers."

"I'm one of the hunters that's supposed to make sure you don't escape without finishing the mission, sweetie. But maybe—"

"Then I could just shoot you, right? Nobody would detect it."

Legs pulled out a cig.

"Honey, if you wanted me dead, then I'd be dead. Nice to see your reflexes ain't as fucked up as everything else you've came into contact with lately."

Roxie cocked the revolver.

"You helped me, I thought you were dead, and now you're here … fuck, why did you do it? How did you survive that explosion? Why keep working for them?"

"I escaped that carryall before it blew. No one in the UGPD knows I let you out."

"Then what the bloody hell are you on about?"

"I've been watching you. Warned you off from Aparajita's cache, heard you shacked up with those rebels, and here you are. You sure kept flying."

"You didn't come here to tell me that."

"The Jovians have been studying this lil' area for the last few months."

He puffed on the cig. At her frown, he dug out another one and flicked it to her.

Catching the cig, she shrugged.

"So? Good as place as any to burn a bunch of looney zealots."

"I heard there's a large Cinn stash on the lower levels."

"Not what I'm looking for, love."

He laughed.

"Think you'll be the last one they get addicted to that stuff? They've got plans, honey. You're just the beginning."

"I'm listening."

"We could help each other. After this, we'll both be set, be able to leave Mars."

Something about his smile, the way he looked at her, brought back memories.

Bad memories.

Roxie aimed at his head.

"Like you've helped me? Pushing Cinn on me every bloody time I walked into the *Salon*? You're their fucking recruiter, aren't you?"

Legs smirked. "C'mon, sugar, you know—"

She shoved him against the elevator door and put the revolver against his nose.

"Aren't you?"

His eyes took on a feral quality.

"You'd be dead now if it weren't for me! Told you once, Cinn has kept you alive. I kept you alive! What other chance did you have to survive the UGPD's program?"

"Doggie Boy and Amai Shi—"

"Are fucking dead!" he shouted in her face. "Is that whatcha wanna be?"

"Goddamn you …"

"Yeah. I am damned. Doesn't mean you gotta be."

She trembled with hurt, with rage.

"Why?"

He smiled sadly.

"Ain't never seen anyone like you. You never let 'em beat you, you never gave up. You never let this place destroy you like it has the rest of us. That's why I helped you. One of us has to make it out, make all this bullshit mean something."

"What if I can't?"

Gunfire erupted over Cydonia.

Shouts echoed across the valleys and mesas. Tiny flashes twinkled here and there among the ruins: muzzle blasts. Roxie's vision told her the distance and even the firearm model creating the flash.

"What the fuck?" Roxie stepped away from him.

"I suppose *La Rèsistance* decided to join the party. Everyone knows something big is sure going down."

"Then what do you want?"

He finished the cig and sighed.

"Hear all that shit? Whatcha think will happen after Harmon and Daedala get their lil' prize? Ordinary folks, people like you and me—we ain't got a chance against 'em. No one will see the ghosts coming to kill 'em, or scorch their children to fucking cinders."

A ground-level rocket sailed from behind a pyramid and struck a passing gravjet.

The craft careened into the side of Pyramid Three, blowing its top off in a shower of bricks and dust. Gunfire increased across Cydonia. Above, four gravjets darted from *Crimson Aegis* and strafed a mesa. Billowing flame clouds shot into the sky. A carryall filled with rebels blew apart.

As she stared at him, the whooshing sound of a fired coilgun and mechanical voices drifted into her ears.

Legs grinned.

"Necrostructs and Burners, too. Even the kill bots want in."

"You want that Cinn so people can see to fight back? Bollocks to that. Look at what it does to us! Who will you give it to? *La Rèsistance? The Titan Liberation Front?*"

"Thought you wouldn't be here to care?"

"Fine, then. We help each other get down there, but once I have what I need, I'm not carrying a load of Cinn out of there."

Roxie slammed the elevator button. The doors slid open and they entered.

He drew his double-barreled Draco as the doors slid shut.

"Cinn got us here in the first place. It'll get us back out."

She focused on the elevator display panel, counting down the levels as it lowered them into the mesa's interior. Cydonia's grainy air developed a cloying, earthy stench after a few moments. Operated by hydraulic motors, phantom radiation wouldn't short out the device.

"So how much are your friends paying you for this stash?"

"I'm giving it away for free, sweetie. Those people out there need it."

The elevator shuddered, then stopped. Its light flickered and finally winked out.

Roxie's skin prickled. A slight violet glow appeared around her and Legs.

"Phantoms are near."

Legs popped a Cinn tab into his mouth. "We do it the old way?"

She reached for the Cinn in her jacket, then hesitated.

"No. We do it my way."

The doors slid aside. A darkened hallway awaited them. Hieroglyphics marked the walls. A few lion-headed statues stood at attention.

Legs whistled.

"Fucking look at all that. Been awhile since I came down here."

Anthropomorphic designs glimmered on the walls. Humanoid figures with animal heads, a starship shaped like a fetus, comets darting through the void—and it all rippled with movement. The stones bore inscriptions that pulsed in time with her heartbeat.

Even when she'd needed Cinn to see such things, none of it had moved before.

"You going to be able to control yourself?" she asked.

"If you really are a Phase Three, then you can see more than I do. I've been a Phase Two for so long, the drug doesn't fuck me up now."

"Come on, then."

She forced herself to walk down the hallway. Excavated decades ago, the subterranean temple still retained uncollected artifacts. Jewelry, statues, busts of attractive people with feline features. There wasn't much dust, as if the excavators had just left with their brushes and particle cleaners.

Legs kicked aside a drinking vessel.

"Lovely lil' trinkets. This is all the fossil prospectors find. Pisses Lorne Harmon off every time."

"Quiet," she whispered.

"They already know you're down here."

Roxie ducked behind a statue as a bluish form appeared six meters down the hallway. It shimmered and overlapped itself in pulsing waves.

"Yeah, come to daddy."

Legs fired. The blazing form jerked away and vanished.

She wanted to reprimand him, but she needed him. Regardless of what those on *Crimson Aegis* said, the phantoms wouldn't just let her walk in and take their secrets.

"You finished?"

Roxie pulled out the plasti map schematic Daedala had given her. Her enhanced sight made out a cross-section of their current level. The path indicated they should keep following the hallway, then find a room filled with golden statues.

"Just getting started, honey."

Legs spun the cylinder on his Draco and continued down the hallway.

She trailed after, stuffing the map into her jacket.

The hallway reached an intersection. Braziers glowed with electrical flames, much like Daedala's fire pit. They cast everything in green, suffuse gloom. The stones beneath her feet rippled with hieroglyphics. Letters, polyhedrons, numbers—and within these were still more characters, singled out by her precise vision.

It was as if she viewed them through a microscope.

"How am I supposed to record—?"

Looking from the moving shapes to her gloved hand, Roxie sucked in a breath.

That was the true purpose of the nanites in her body. Organic, powered by her innate electricity, immune to EM, they were storing all the data she experienced.

The way forward was dim, with one brazier turned over. A passage on their left was cramped and dark. She consulted the map and put it away.

Legs lit a cig.

"Which way?"

Scowling at the floor, Roxie glimpsed a sphere among the symbols. Then a cross and a spiral. She knelt and removed her glove. As her fingers brushed the hieroglyphics inset into the stones, energy vibrated along her flesh. Violet electrical arcs coursed from her fingers to the symbols as if she were a conductor.

She swiped a finger. The symbols morphed into an alternate combination.

"Whatcha doing there? I feel all tingly."

"You can't see the little fizzles coming from my hands?"

He blew smoke over her. "Welcome to Phase Three, sweetie."

Roxie tugged her other glove off with her teeth. Using both hands, her fingers manipulated the symbols until she created the one from Harmon's holoboard. The arcs sizzled and popped, but obeyed her like extensions of her will.

Holding the symbol with the arcs, she lifted it from the hieroglyphic.

"Where?"

The symbol darted into the left passage.

"Okay, I saw that," he said.

"Eat another tab and cover me. Don't need you fannying about in the dark."

They entered the left passage. The corridor's stone walls were cracked the first few meters, then it became a tunnel of solid earth and sediment stones. Small sections had been cut from the wall. She ran a hand over the depressions and nodded.

"Those prospector blokes tried going this way and gave up."

Legs chewed, swallowed, then grunted with satisfaction.

"Yeah, I remember."

Silence stretched between them.

"How many of them did you bring down here?"

"Too many. You're better than the rest, I'll grant you that."

Roxie neared another brazier, flickering with cyan light.

"How many reached Phase Three?"

"You've been on their radar for a while now. They selected you after you saved that Jovian priestess out there on Syrtis. You know that was staged, right?"

Sweat trickled down her brow.

"There isn't a Cinn stash down here, is there?"

Legs cocked his revolver.

"There will be for me, once I get back. I don't want a fucking pardon like that dumbass Dirty Cool. Saving his creds until he returns to his daughter on the Caravans."

Roxie's blood chilled. So Dirty Cool had a daughter. No wonder he hated her for killing those children on *Jubilee.*

Not as much as she hated herself for it.

"So they just need my body returned. As long as the nanites in me record the information—they need me to unlock this shite, but can't control me. Can they?"

Legs blew smoke from his nose.

"Yeah, they're fucked up like that."

She slowly swung around, hand near her revolver.

"So why tell me … love?"

He was already aiming at her.

"Didn't need to tell you. You figured it out, like I knew you would. They don't know you like I do, sugar. Easy now. This ain't gotta be ugly."

She looked at his gun, then at him.

"Then what will it be?"

"I told you. We can both come out on top. Whatever you find down here will even the score. Ain't nothing can stop you then. Not UGPD, not me, not the damn Jovians."

"You're not loyal to anyone or anything. You're a vulture."

"Ain't you got it yet? This is how we live. We fuck with 'em, we lie, we cheat, and we steal. We even kill, sugar. Whatever it takes."

His attitude reminded her of Harmon and Daedala. The ends justified the means to all of them. Not matter how many suffered. No matter how many died.

From the intersection they'd just left, something banged against the wall.

Legs smiled. "Here they come—"

Roxie slapped aside his gun and pushed the brazier onto him.

Green flame burned through his jumpsuit. Screaming, he fired. The Draco's whizzing shot sailed into the intersection. She ran down the passage. Discerning every curve, stone, and corner with her eyesight, she easily outdistanced him.

Somewhere in a distant hallway, Legs smacked at his burning suit and gasped.

"Are you fucking crazy? We can both get what we want!"

Roxie hurried on, drawing one of her revolvers. Around the corner her sight was filled with electromagnetic waves pulsating along the walls.

"Street Angel!"

His shout echoed through the subterranean complex. She visualized it as an angry red wave rebounding off of the stone.

They wanted her to find the Leonids' secrets and then die.

Façade Peak was meant to be her tomb, then.

She dug out the Cinn block given to her aboard *Crimson Aegis*. Phase Three or not, that much Cinn would send her mind into the stratosphere.

This time the Cinn didn't even have a flavor. She made herself chew it. Slight burning sensations traveled through her limbs, but she didn't smile. Her crotch didn't warm with orgasmic heat. Quivering, she took another bite. It tasted worse.

She crushed and snorted it off her trembling fingers—but the usual laughter and joy refused to surface in her brain.

Cinn had really abandoned her. Her one true friend, the one who'd lifted her above the darkness, erased her guilt, cleansed her of responsibility.

Roxie squeezed her eyes shut and pressed the revolver barrel to her right temple.

This was best. Any further, and she was giving Harmon and Daedala what they wanted. Everything had been predetermined. Her finger eased over the trigger.

Through her closed eyelids, her breath appeared as a faint mauve cloud. The tunnels hummed around her. Flaring green symbols wriggled across the walls.

Arcs jumped off her skin now, interacting with the symbols. Transforming each one into the round character with a cross and spiral.

She lowered the revolver.

An intersection opened before her. Two blue forms edged closer.

"No. Please…"

Two phantom boys in old-fashioned jumpsuits studied her with cerulean eyes.

"Are you mocking me?" she cried. "You know I can't bloody take this, I can't bring them back…"

The boys didn't move.

Her fingers numbed on the revolver. Tears flowed down her face. She pressed the small of her nose and shuddered. The boys glowed brighter, and she shut her eyes.

"Just do it," she whispered. "I deserve it."

Moments passed. Nothing happened.

She opened her eyes. The boys watched her with timeless patience.

"But I'm not the best of humanity. My life is just a series of cock-ups. I'm a murderer, a doper, a boozer…why me?"

Both boys pointed at the newly-revealed intersection.

Roxie holstered the revolver and straightened.

"Okay, then. Show me what you want me to see. I'm ready."

Chapter 24

The boys entered the rock-strewn intersection. Trembling so much the grenades in her jacket shook, Roxie followed. Her sight came alive with new electromagnetic waves. She spied old carvings beneath the walls' dirt-caked surfaces, colored tiles underfoot, and a rolling script alongside the hieroglyphics she hadn't seen before.

The phantoms led her into a hallway with a higher ceiling. Lining it were alcoves similar to those the Jovians had created. Most were broken, with cracked transparent shields, busted frames. The Jovians must have modeled their own alcoves on them.

She increased her pace as the boys entered a circular chamber. Huge stones had fallen from the ceiling, smashing half of the chamber, but the rest took her breath.

Tall sarcophagi fashioned from seamless gray metal stood along the walls. Each was marked with the cross and spiral symbol.

Inside each sarcophagi was a pulsating blue form. Transparent canals ran from the sarcophagi to the center of the room, where a perfect sphere, eight meters in diameter, glowed with azure brilliance. The cave-in had just missed it, as if someone tried to destroy it but failed.

Roxie glimpsed an endless collection of faces within the sphere.

Visages of men, women, and children, in a staggering range of ethnicities. Some possessed bestial features, such as the lion-headed people. She also spotted one with lizard's scales, and a woman with feathers instead of hair. The faces came and went, swirling inside the sphere.

Staggering backward, Roxie finally took a breath. If she spent a lifetime down here, she'd not be able to count all of those faces.

The boys melded into a sarcophagi and vanished in a bright blue flash. Moments later, she glimpsed their faces among those within the sphere.

A large sarcophagi opened, releasing another shapeless azure form.

Energy sizzled through the air and encircled Roxie in a field of blue lightning. The chamber thrummed with depthless power as arcs sparked from her body and zipped into the symbols. The static charges popped into characters, floating around her.

Roxie forced herself not to run.

The form coalesced into a tall lion-headed woman in fluttering robes. She examined Roxie with searing blue eyes as the air hissed with energy. The phantom had to be a Class A, the most powerful and dangerous entity on Mars.

The phantom held up a hand, and the appendage morphed into a pyramid. It flashed with a dizzying array of blue shades, far more than the human eye could discern.

A million shades of cerulean scorched into her brain, each implanted with endless scripts like flattened DNA. Not entwined in a double helix, but crashing in a nonstop stream of overpowering ciphers. Though her eyes resolved each one as visible light, she'd no idea what the scripts meant. Letters and numbers flashed by so quickly in the beams that she moaned.

"What are you trying to tell me, love?"

The pyramid flashed the sequence again, but brighter.

"I don't understand—"

The phantom knelt and touched her face.

Roxie cried out, waiting for her cheeks to erupt in flame, or her bones to liquefy. Expecting the horrible pain to kill her as the phantom's merciless radiation broke her down one atom at a time.

It caressed her.

She took a deep breath as the phantom flashed different shades of blue, its feline face centimeters from hers. Its eyes, like twin blue dwarf suns, examined her with genuine curiosity. The sensations brought by its touch elevated her nerves to levels of pleasure, contentment, and joy she'd never dreamed of. Instead of drugging her, or inhibiting her thoughts, the phantom's touch invigorated her mind, letting her feel all of these things at once while letting her glimpse beyond the colors.

Beyond the centuries separating them.

The Leonids had sought escape from Earth's pain. Reviving traditions of heroes to sooth the colonists' shattered, collective psyche. Then, as Mars was tamed, breaking down the human body, one atom at a time. Instead of destroying it, the Leonids rebuilt it as something else.

Roxie shook as the colors revealed their secret to her unique eyes. Trillions of data chunks lay therein, in a substance that could never be destroyed, altered, or ignored.

The very light of the stars. Timeless, stretching over the cosmos.

Overwhelmed, she shuddered.

The phantoms were far more than an evolved humanity. They were a higher stage of life, encased in scintillating light across all spectrums.

"How?" she managed through numb lips.

The phantom stood back and produced a humanoid figurine from one of the sarcophagi. The figurine transformed from flesh to light, then back again. Hieroglyphics appeared on the figurine, which morphed into numbers, formulas. They weren't mere decoration or stuffy religious bollocks.

They were instructions.

"Why?" Roxie asked, her voice slurred by the energy flowing through her.

The phantom lifted the figurine. Its head opened up, a brain spun from its cranium, and a thousand light beams pierced it. The figurine reappeared in the sarcophagus, but was azure and shimmering—no longer a physical entity.

"Information … to energy? You're not really alive?"

The phantom throbbed, then flashed thousands of different hues. Its light became jagged, thrusting, harsh.

"I get it, I get it. You're alive. Just in a different way."

A way that Daedala and Harmon coveted. Did they even realize what immortality would mean? These were creatures of energy, yes, and possibly emotion... but they were not human. They were archived people, personas scribed into light and radiation.

No wonder there were so many of them—she doubted the phantoms really died. They simply returned here and built a new body, using the sphere as a database and the sarcophagi as wombs.

Roxie pointed upward.

"They want to be like you. They want to steal it."

The phantom rose to its full height while the sphere swirled faster.

"Maybe you could take me, if it always feels like that in there. I don't want to go back. Do you understand? There's nothing up there for me."

The phantom took up the figurine and made an azure copy of it in its other hand. The physical one took on Roxie's features. Smiling, healthy. The phantom figurine morphed into her appearance. No smile. Jagged features with robotic movements. A facsimile. Incapable of emotion, though able to stimulate a biological brain.

Just like Cinn.

Roxie's eyes widened.

"You're meant to interact with us. Teach us. Right, love? You were the bloody answer... and the Tellurics tried to destroy you for it. The Jovians tried to steal it, didn't they? That's why you don't allow anyone down here anymore."

The phantom pulsed light and dark. The faces in the sphere looked on her with tragic sadness. There wasn't any happiness in this immortality.

Just a record, like a datafile.

"Then why care if they find your secret?"

Sapphire-like comets leapt from the phantom's hand and soared into a representation of the Solar System and beyond.

"I don't get it. Are you leaving soon?"

The sphere darkened. Landmasses arose from the navy blue murk. She recognized them as Earth's continents. Rather than the green-brown regions she remembered from old vids, the land was brown-gray, faded. A graveyard.

"You don't want to create such a place again. But those buggers will take your secret eventually."

The phantom flared up, but she stood, not backing down.

"You know they will!"

"I know it too, honey."

She whirled around just as Legs fired both Draco barrels.

EM rounds cruised through the air like throbbing missiles in her vison until both struck the large phantom. It shimmered and staggered backward.

"You filth!" she screamed.

"Thought I taught you to shoot first, and not give a fuck 'bout questions later."

He fired again, destroying one of the phantom boys in a cloud of blue sparks.

As Legs cocked the pistol and phantoms poured from the sarcophagi, Roxie raced over, grabbed the figurine, and ran for the hallway.

Phantoms drifted from the hieroglyphics on the walls, they appeared from the ceiling, one even dropped so close that she had to duck as it swung at her. There was no way she could make it, not even with Legs back there ruining everything.

This was the only way. To keep Daedala, Harmon, and anyone else from gaining this knowledge—it was the only way.

She would stir up every phantom in Cydonia if she had to.

Fleeing down the previous passage, she could still hear Legs's laughter, and the crackle of the phantoms reciprocating his violence. As she skidded into the intersection, phantoms barred her path to the elevator. Two more crept from a wall crevice.

Figurine in left hand, revolver in her right, Roxie fled into the darkness.

Her vision revealed walls, floor, ceiling, broken statues, rubble piles. Everything was outlined as if traced with a light pen. She bumped into a wall, tripped over a fallen stone, then scrabbled back to her feet. Gasping in the complex's thin air, she pressed on.

Gunshot echoes receded behind her.

In the next corridor she stepped over charred skeletons. Her boots crunched them into dust as she ran. The corridor opened into a wide square chamber containing burnt equipment and more skeletons. Some of them wore UG uniforms. They had been at it a long time, feeling around in the dark, getting people killed for a selfish dream.

She ran up a ramp and jumped over fallen stonework.

A bullet whizzed through the air.

"Street Angel?"

His footsteps resounded meters behind her.

Roxie climbed over the crisped garbage until she reached a third ramp. Fleeing up it, she flinched as rock shards blew across her shoulder.

"The next one will go right up that cute lil' ass of yours, honey."

She stopped and turned.

"You fucking bastard."

Legs, his wig singed off, his jumpsuit ripped, leveled his gun at her.

"You got what we needed. Now hold still, I'll make it look good. A shot in the shoulder, maybe the thigh. Gotta make 'em believe us before we turn the tables."

Roxie held the figurine over the side of the ramp.

Unfathomable darkness waited below.

He glowered.

"So you wanna make this ugly after all."

"Kill me and the phantoms will never let you leave this place."

"I've enough bullets and Cinn." He walked closer. "Don't test me."

"Are you so bloody desperate? Stop being their fucking slave!"

He laughed. "Slave? We'll be their masters after this."

"That's not what Mars needs. It's not what I need."

Legs's eye twitched.

"I mean it. Let's go."

"No, love. You'll have to kill me."

"Fuck this. You see some ghost kids and get all noble? The Leonids enslaved people, too. Think they got all blue and shiny without exploiting someone?"

"You said all this bullshit needs to mean something."

"How many times did I give you Cinn when you felt so bad you wanted to die? All those times you needed to forget the pain of all the shit you've done?"

Her heart squeezed into an iron ball.

"Not as many times as I hated you for it."

Legs's dark gaze filled with sorrow.

A pulse grew in volume throughout the complex. Rustling noises disturbed the terminal silence in the chambers around them. She glimpsed electrical currents stabbing through the air in blues, purples, greens.

Legs smirked. His eyes narrowed.

Roxie frowned.

His gaze widened.

They both fired.

Her bullet struck Legs's gut, but his shot destroyed a phantom right behind her.

As he collapsed to his knees, Legs chuckled. The blood on his lips glowed bright red in her vision.

"You still think it's the eyes, sweetie."

"No," was all she could say.

"I don't blame you. I taught you too well."

"I thought you…"

He smiled, then winced as he clutched his gut.

"I was bluffing. Ain't gonna shoot my angel. Now get outta here."

Three phantoms inched across the ramp. More were coming from all directions.

"I can't leave you, I shot you, I—"

"Saved me. You finally saved me."

Legs grinned at her, then fired until all three phantoms were sparkling blue clouds. Their dissipating forms dusted short-lived embers on his jumpsuit.

More phantoms surged into the chamber.

Yelling, Legs kept firing.

Tears ran down her face as she fled.

Legs's screams echoed throughout the complex, pounding her eardrums as she slid down a huge rubble pile. Tumbling end over end, she finally landed in another brazier-filled hallway.

The pulse continued. It was an emitter.

Dabbing blood from her forehead, Roxie leaned against the wall. The pulse filled the entire complex, and now she understood why the phantoms were attracted to it. It was a nonstop beacon, challenging them. The colors of the pulse's energy wave hammered at her eyes, a siren's call demanding that she find its source and destroy it.

Roxie took a deep breath and ran back into the intersection. Energy roiled off the walls and floor in angry red waves. Phantoms crashed through the connecting passages.

A low rumble traveled down into the complex from above. Dirt and pebbles slid from the ceiling. Energized by the power all around her, she sped through the passages just ahead of angry blue forms.

A crackle filled the air. Her skin tingled. The figurine in her grasp throbbed.

Her breathing sped up, lungs barely keeping up with demand. Her scrapes and bruises numbed as if those parts of her body were gone.

The elevator was only a few meters away.

As she neared it, she noticed the electrical control panel was dead.

Heart beating faster, she flipped open the hydraulic control and pressed the lever.

A popping sound echoed behind her.

Roxie turned and fired.

A phantom man vanished into blue particles. Three more drifted from the other hallways. She ripped a thermo grenade from her jacket and tossed it. The explosion nearly blinded her, but phantoms fled the intersection, save for two of them.

She pressed the other lever.

The elevator shot up at emergency speed as the phantoms charged the cage. She fired twice, taking out one, but the second ripped off the elevator doors and incinerated the ceiling. She covered her head as the elevator left the phantom behind, though embers and heated slag rained over the cage. The rush of air as the cage ascended cooled them, but she patted out a few burning through her synthskin.

In her enhanced vision, each resembled a tiny little hell trying to consume her.

Arcs spread from the figurine to her fingers and healed the graze on her side.

She slumped and stared at her hand.

"What the fuck?"

Roxie examined her cuts, bruises. All were gone, though her synthskin was pocked with smoking holes. The figurine withered. New energy thrummed in her veins.

A deep, cold terror seized her. She really wasn't human anymore.

She lay her head against the cage as the elevator neared the top. With the figurine stuffed into her belt, she raised her fully loaded Draco. It no longer gave her confidence.

The tears came again.

"Legs, you stupid … ah, damn it … goodbye, love."

The cage jostled as it screeched to a halt near the top. The outer door slid open.

Afternoon sun revealed two soldiers with frack rifles.

As they turned, Roxie shot both in the head.

Brains and blood pooled down into the cage as she stepped out. She grabbed a frack rifle and gazed up at *Crimson Aegis*. All around her, blue forms, explosions, gunfire, and gravjets circled Façade Peak in a maelstrom of destruction.

She could see the path of every bullet and missile, sense the life energy seeping from wounded soldiers and rebels, visualize the heat fading from dying bodies.

Felt a prickle on her skin with every phantom destroyed.

She touched the figurine.

Whatever the phantom had tried to offer, it was all inside of her now.

CHAPTER 25

As Roxie neared the gravjet that had brought her, a bullet ripped into the attendant's chest. He collapsed off the ramp into the dirt. She ducked and wheeled the frack rifle around, but a second shot pierced the cockpit window and split the pilot's head open. The woman slumped over the controls.

Locust crept from behind an outcropping, rifle aimed at her. "Don't."

Other rebels appeared, armed with SMGs, shotguns, and pistols. Their dun camo fatigues were dusty and ripped.

Despite the anger she held toward Locust, Roxie remained calm. She wouldn't give him the pleasure of any emotional investment from her.

"I need to get on that carrier, love."

"To give them what they want? No. Hand it over."

Roxie kept the rifle aimed in his direction. An explosion rocked the ground as gravjets strafed insurgents behind Pyramid Seven. The rebels shared apprehensive looks.

He smiled.

"They would not blast this place apart unless you have what they wanted."

She carefully slid the figurine from her belt.

The rebels aimed at her. Even Locust raised his rifle higher.

"You look like shit. How much trouble was it worth?"

"More than I'm willing to take from you." Roxie rolled the figurine to him.

"Here. My contribution to your *Glorieuse Révolution*."

His eyes narrowed. "What is the price?"

"Legs already made the down payment." She nodded at the battle around them. "Looks like you've got the rest of the balance."

"You bitch."

"No, I'm *Ange de la Mort*, remember? You needed me all along to unlock this place. You expected Legs to help you. But he wasn't as greedy as you thought."

"Legs was going to give us the Cinn we need to win this war! The UG will slaughter those who are blind to the phantoms—"

"You'll always be fucking blind." She backed up the gravjet ramp.

"I could kill you."

Roxie shrugged. "You could."

The ground quaked as a temple imploded half a kilometer away. Centuries-old walls caved in amid fiery clouds. Black smoke mushroomed into the sky.

She looked from it to Locust and arched an eyebrow.

"People are dying while you waste time."

Locust nudged the figurine with his boot, his eyes never leaving her.

"How do I know this is what my people need?"

Roxie laughed.

"You fuckwad. You really think I'd haul that all the way up here, just to make you believe me? I'm not as trusting as Pierro."

The rebels glanced at each other with uncertainty. Locust's jaw hardened.

"He bravely sacrificed himself."

"Doesn't matter now," she said. "I'm off."

"Not without the Cinn Legs promised us."

On a hunch, Roxie reached inside the gravjet's door and pulled the manual cargo release. A compartment opened on its underside, dumping four octagonal crates.

The *coup de grâce* in Legs's little plan.

While the rebels examined the crates, she backed all the way into the gravjet.

Locust lowered the rifle and smirked. "Did you find forgiveness?"

"No. I earned it."

Any moment she expected a bullet in the back, but she managed to close the ramp, enter the cockpit, push the dead pilot aside, and sit down before Locust noticed the thermo grenade she'd attached to the figurine.

He leapt behind the outcropping as she activated the gravjet's engine.

"You fucking traitor!"

She ascended ten meters off the ground before the grenade exploded.

Rocks struck the gravjet's hull, followed by rebel bullets. A huge orange dust cloud rose from the busted crates. Enough Cinn to take her to heaven and back.

Roxie thumbed the throttle and blasted away from Façade Peak. Soon she gained altitude over the raging conflict. Wind nipped at her face through the cracked windshield.

For the first time in forever, she was free.

The console speaker crackled to life.

"*Hawkblood Three*, this is *Crimson Aegis*. You have Trent onboard?"

She pulled the headset off the dead pilot and activated the mic.

"*Aegis*, this is *Hawkblood Three*. Trent here. Crew's dead, but I'm good. Approaching your position now."

Seconds ticked by as she circled Cydonia. Tanks burned near the northern perimeter. Gunfire flashed with horrible regularity around Pyramid Five. Pyramids Two and Four burned from within. All the excavation work and deaths, all the hunts she'd undertaken here—all for nothing.

The headset speaker beeped.

"This is Harmon. Fly into the aft docking bay. We eagerly await your arrival."

Roxie scrolled over the gravjet's console, checking fuel, armaments, and distance from *Crimson Aegis*. Upon reviewing the onboard missile inventory, she smiled.

Veering to port, she flew in a long arc toward the carrier. She studied its battery placement, and which guns were firing on the rebels below. The carrier's defenses wouldn't ignore her for long. Already two other gravjets had broken off from strafing and now followed her as escort. Harmon was leaving nothing to chance.

Neither was she.

Crimson Aegis grew larger through the windshield. Roxie eyed the docking bay. It opened on either side of the carrier: a straight shot through.

"Trent?" Harmon called from the headset.

She punched the accelerator.

Both gravjets matched her speed. The engine thrummed and air streaked through the damaged windshield, making her squint.

Even with her eyes closed, she could still sense the carrier's energy signature. Just inside the docking pay, powering its massive gravity jets.

"Trent, what are you doing?" Harmon asked.

She sped into the docking bay without slowing. The two gravjets followed until one tried to veer away. It smashed into the side of *Crimson Aegis*, igniting a fireball that engulfed half the bay. Bulkheads and maintenance personnel were cremated.

She jettisoned the gravjet's extra fuel stores straight into the angry fireball.

The explosion billowed and expanded to consume the carrier's gravity generators.

"Trent!" Harmon screamed.

The other gravjet followed Roxie out the other side, but she dove and raced alongside the carrier's underbelly. She locked missiles onto its gravthrusters, fired, and rolled starboard. She cleared *Crimson Aegis* as the missiles struck home.

Concussive blasts rocked the air, then a ripping creak shredded all sound. Heat from the fireballs blackened the windshield. Every alarm sounded and shorted out.

Roxie tugged the manuals but the aircraft lost all power.

The other gravjet zoomed after her, its rotary cannon ripping apart her craft's wings. The high-caliber rounds punctured jagged gaps in the cockpit. Her gravjet spun.

Air slapped at her face. Flying glass shards sliced her right arm. Trying to time her spin, Roxie jerked the ejection handle.

The cockpit blew away from the fuselage as the gravjet exploded.

Air whistled past Roxie as the pilot's seat spiraled up into the sky, then jerked as a parachute sprouted from it. The seat swayed as the parachute slowed her decent. Her stomach tossed with nausea but the old academy training came back.

She refused to blackout.

As she floated back down to Cydonia, safety boats ejected from *Crimson Aegis* right before it slammed into the surface of Mars. It drifted over Pyramid Six, knocking it to debris, plowed through Pyramid Seven, leaving it a dusty ash cloud, before finally crashing nose-first into Façade Peak. The carrier ripped through earth and rock as it buckled up onto the ancient mesa before its gravthrusters all exploded.

The detonation blew Roxie's parachute so hard, it ripped one of the tethers. Her rifle and grenades were blown off of her. She gripped her seat straps as she dipped face-down toward the ground. The noise of the carrier's death numbed her ears, bashing out all other sound, leveling Cydonia with unspeakable destruction.

Bricks, stones, bodies, bulkheads, and kilotons of sand flew into the sky. Another explosion pierced the reddish haze as the carrier finally tumbled down what remained of Façade Peak. The titanic boom of it striking the ground created another sonic shockwave and even greater dust cloud.

The energy released made every dust speck glow in Roxie's sight. Rippling wells of power cascaded over Cydonia. They buffeted her senses, setting her psyche aglow with a spectrum of devastation.

Roxie grabbed a filter mask from the pilot's seat and tugged it on as the dust cloud enfiladed her. Hundreds of particles lanced her parachute and she drifted faster toward Pyramid Eight. A breeze whipped up from the valley below churned the dust as well as her tattered parachute, sending her in the direction of Bamberg Crater, several kilometers away.

Cydonia was a shambles. Gravjets buzzed back and forth over it, tanks rumbled along the southern perimeter, and a few rebel carryalls sped eastward for Arabia Terra.

Roxie tensed as the seat dipped into the bulging dust cloud. She had no way of knowing how close she was to the ground. Curling into a ball, she decided it was best—

The seat struck a cliff then tumbled into a ravine.

She remained balled-up as the parachute caught on the cliff, yanked her back ten meters into the air, then ripped free of the seat. Once again she dropped. The seat became a throne of death as it thudded against the ravine, skidded down an embankment, then rolled across the ravine floor, bouncing her body against rocks.

As the seat finally came to a stop, Roxie vomited blood into her mask.

With a shaking hand, she ripped off the mask and sucked in dirty air. The grit scoured her throat. She coughed in stuttering heaves.

Dangling from the remaining seat restraints, Roxie groaned. She hurt all over.

A low roar died in the distance and she lay there for a while, trying to catch her breath. Swinging back and forth made her want to close her eyes…

A whirring noise traveled on the air.

Roxie opened her eyes. The sun had changed position, now casting the ravine bottom in dim light. She needed to get up, keep moving.

The noise grew louder. Roxie unbuckled the restraints while bracing her knees on the ground. As the straps slid away, she fell face-first into the dirt.

She drew one of her revolvers, made sure it still cycled, then reloaded the cylinder. The other revolver was gone, and one of her cartridge pouches had come loose in her descent. She removed the jacket, now shredded and burnt.

A gravjet flew over. Its searchlight scanned the other end of the ravine, less than a hundred meters away.

Roxie crawled from under the seat and clambered up the embankment. By the time the gravjet made a return sweep, she'd hidden behind rocks near the ravine's edge.

They would still spot her seat and parachute.

She continued on.

A second hum came and went, and she ducked back behind the rocks. Harmon and Daedala still wanted her, thinking the information in her nanites would make all their fantasies come true. She checked the cylinder again, then slammed it shut.

She'd done all she could do. Façade Peak was a cairn of lost ambition, Legs's deal with Locust had been foiled, maybe Harmon and Daedala had died on that carrier…but as she gazed at the landscape, she recalled her old academy oaths.

Protect and serve all citizens of the United Government. Maintain law and order. Safeguard the future of humanity as it colonized the stars.

Sand slid down the cliff above her.

Roxie ducked as a shot pinged off the tumulus where she'd been crouching. She scrambled around an outcropping, then ran up a small hill ringed with boulders. In a nearby crater she spotted a hunter creeping over the sand. As she raised her gun, a scuffle of boots made her duck. A second shot whizzed over her head.

The hunter in the crater looked up just as she planted a bullet into his gut.

Turning, she spotted a SATSCAN station atop a nearby mesa.

Safeguard the future of humanity.

Roxie hurried along the ravine's edge. The hunter she'd shot in the crater called out, still alive. That was even better. Anything to distract the others out there.

With each passing minute, her eyesight revealed more heat signatures all around. Not all glowed violet, like most humans, or blue, like the phantoms. Many glowed yellow—kill bots, judging from the regulated energy output.

The hunter keep screaming. Roxie neared the foot of the mesa. As she hurried up a dirt track, a shot rang out. The hunter fell silent. She hurried on.

With that many phantoms still around Cydonia, even more necrostructs and Burners wouldn't be far behind. The UG had a huge mess on its hands, thanks to her.

She intended to make it stick.

A different hum built up through the air. She paused and swallowed. Blunt energy waves pulsed in her sight.

It was an emitter.

Only someone who wanted her dead at all costs would set one off with so many phantoms around.

Roxie ran faster, though she limped by the time she reached the mesa's first terrace. Cut into the rock by colonial engineers, it offered a grueling climb to the summit. The SATSCAN station waited on the third terrace.

A whirring shot sounded on her right, near the ravine. A puffing noise followed.

Her skin prickled. Someone had bagged a phantom.

Another shot, behind her this time.

Roxie skidded against the side of the mesa. She shook all over, fatigue setting in. After scanning the landscape, she ran for the third terrace.

The air chilled her skin as the sun neared the horizon. Sirens blared over Cydonia far away. Gravjets and a second carrier flew from the south, probably from New Paris.

Whoever was following her had gotten here fast, and not on foot.

She scrambled onto the third terrace and gazed around. A gravjet, a hoverbike, there had to be something. She sucked in breaths faster, the gun shaking in her grasp.

A glint of metal caught her eye right before a shot zipped past her shoulder.

Roxie hit the dirt. Swiping the revolver left to right, she spotted nothing.

They were toying with her. Tracking her down like a beast.

"Street Angel…"

The voice reverberated up the ravine, rebounding from mesa to mesa.

Roxie scanned about, blinking sweat from her eyes.

"Street Angel?"

She ducked and rolled as a third shot zinged over her head. She kicked a large stone off the terrace, then fled up the wide ramp straight for the SATSCAN station.

Wolves howled a few hundred meters to the north.

She jerked around.

Glowing forms moved in her vision but they were all too far away.

A shape moved from behind the station. Roxie twitched and fired.

A bounty hunter clutched his chest and aimed at her. Gritting her teeth, she mashed the trigger. The bullet ripped his jaw and ear off. He stumbled off the mesa. Down he went, a wingless bird daring to fly in her shrinking world.

The emitter hummed again.

Spots rose in her eyesight and Roxie blinked. So many shapes out there, plodding toward her position. Violet, blue, yellow. Tracking her with Cinn-enhanced eyes, internal sensors, or SATSCAN.

The electromagnetic spectrum teased her with ghosts, people she had known … people she had killed. The real ghosts of Mars rose up and laughed at her, their voices echoing across the landscape.

Roxie tuned in circles, panting, grunting. Finally she closed her eyes.

"Come and get me."

A sparkling blue shape rose from the terrace. Another drifted around the station.

Roxie blasted one, but the second flung a boulder at her. She dropped onto her stomach, feeling the wind off the missile pass over her. It struck the terrace wall, showering her with rock slivers and dust. She rolled aside and fired.

The phantom disappeared in a burst of cerulean flame.

Her vision drifted into the alternate world surrounding them, one where the ancients had retreated, where she could be anyone she wanted to be.

She approached the station. Colors swirled in her eyesight. The door slid open.

The tips of her fingers glowed blue.

CHAPTER 26

Inside the station Roxie passed holo cubicles, their occupants having evacuated before the Cydonia operation. Vidscreens played press reports of terrorist bombings outside New Paris, an uprising in Ilios, and a pitched battle in Scraptown.

Every incident was blamed on *La Rèsistance*, with footage of dead UG soldiers and burning trams to convict them in the media's eye.

Her face popped up again and again as a person of interest, a terrorist leader—even an addict driven mad by Cinn. They didn't bother using her real name.

Just *Ange de la Mort*, as if that explained everything.

The station rumbled as the battle came closer. She found a functional holoboard. After a few swipes, she locked the station down. It might buy her enough time.

She swiped the holoboard again, seeking the station's communications interface. The satellite array was shut down. She swiped, pinched, tapped. Still shut down.

Someone had done it manually. There'd be no uplink with off-world networks. Just using the Martian network wasn't enough—the UG censored it, and anything she sent out would be stopped.

"Fuck."

She walked through a tight corridor into the satellite array chamber. Maybe she could get it to work with some tinkering. With phantoms coming up the mesa, she had little time before the station's 'tronics shorted out.

Bullets pounded the outside walls.

She leaned against a wall and shuddered.

Surrounded. Down to one pistol. Not many bullets left. No friends or allies.

She had no right to hope for anything.

An explosion struck the mesa. The station shook.

A panel fell from the wall and the vidscreens displayed warnings. Red and orange caution lights throbbed in her sight. The information in the wavelengths told her the station was on fire, that necrostructs had surrounded it.

Data transmitted through light, like Daedala had said.

Maybe she really was becoming one of them.

She hurried to the control bank where a railing overlooked the massive cylinder that moved the satellite dish above. A light collection aperture was attached to an old-fashioned I/O port.

Swiping a nearby holoboard, Roxie configured the cylinder, then fixed the aperture on a dedicated channel. It was her only option.

She held up her hand. Each finger flared bright blue.

With no idea how to send the information that her nanites had collected, she thought about everything she'd seen beneath Façade Peak. The hieroglyphics, the sarcophagi chamber. The phantom that had interacted with her.

Arcs of light popped off her fingers and entered the aperture.

The effect made her cry out. She stood paralyzed by the energy coursing through her. The aperture became a hungry vessel, devouring everything she could give it.

Holding Doggie's Boy as he died. Saying she was sorry in Ami Shi's ear, even as her friend breathed her last. That grin from Legs before she finally ran.

She wanted to scream and curse. Wanted to tear it all down: Mars, the UG, everything. She and her friends had lost it all.

The energy drained from her and she staggered back, gasping.

The aperture's control bank beeped. It was done.

A whistling noise made the hairs on the back of her neck tingle.

Roxie sensed incoming energy at a murderous velocity. She jumped over the railing as something struck the ceiling.

A fireball whooshed throughout the station. The cubicles melted, the terminals exploded, and the vidscreens shattered. Roxie scurried beneath the aperture as flaming tongues stabbed at her. White-hot ruptures exploded inside of her. She couldn't move or scream, just watch as her skin glowed bright blue for an instant, then faded.

The flames burned out, no more than an incendiary blast. Sparks belched from mangled conduits, scorching the floor before smoldering to black nuggets. She sensed every tiny point of energy, how hot it was, when it would extinguish.

She turned as something clicked above her.

Daedala stood with several Jovians at the melted railing.

Dirty Cool trained his shotgun on Roxie.

"You won't shoot me. I'm the key to all your bloody plans."

"You could have anything at this juncture," Daedala said. "If you give me what I want. You could leave Mars, have a mansion on Ganymede."

"Like Legs?" Her veins quivered with fresh energy, gained from the blast.

"Is that what you really think?" Daedala asked. "Even if you survive this, you'll be hunted. Only the Covenant can protect you."

One of the Jovians whispered and pointed at the aperture.

Daedala's face hardened.

"So you refused to wait."

"It worked?"

One Jovian produced a datapad and showed the screen. A signal was traveling along the UG network. Unstoppable and filled with Leonid data.

A weight lifted from Roxie's chest.

"Then everyone knows."

"Do you really think people will use this for good?" Daedala asked.

"You won't."

Daedala knelt at the railing and extended a hand.

"You have no idea what you are capable of, or who you could harm. You must come with me. My ship is almost here."

A gunshot scattered a Jovian's brains over Daedala.

As the group turned, a second shot blew out another Jovian's throat. A third shot nicked off Dirty Cool's right ear and slammed into the Jovian behind him, crushing her chest in red spray. Squeezing off a fourth shot, Styra charged through the ruined station.

"Kill her!" Daedala shrieked.

As the Jovians returned fire, Styra leapt over a burning cubicle and fired again.

Wavelengths in Roxie's eyesight rippled, pulsed, flared. Telling her the best place to move, the weakest points to shoot. The only way to survive the cerulean horde marching down upon them.

Roxie somersaulted over the railing and fired. The round sheared off Styra's left arm at the elbow. Not breaking stride, Styra crushed a Jovian's skull with a single kick and blew the shotgun from Dirty Cool's grasp. She sprayed magdarts at Roxie, who barely dodged the miniature explosions. The force still shoved Roxie against the wall.

Two phantoms stalked through the station behind Styra. Leonid features, muscular bodies. From their glow and power output, Roxie knew they were Class Bs.

Styra smiled.

"You see them, don't you? So do I."

Dirty Cool rose and swung a magblade at Styra.

She kicked him across the station, then turned and shot both phantoms. As their bodies dissolved, Roxie's veins throbbed. Her sight swam with millions of shades the human eye was never meant to see.

Searching for a state of being humans killed to understand.

As Roxie stood and aimed, Styra held her pistol against Daedala's chest.

"Harmon and everyone on that goddamn carrier are dead. But I can still fix this."

"You're mad," Daedala said.

"Trent will never be loyal, never do what's best. Take me instead. I can still give you whatever Harmon promised. I can be the one!"

Ignoring Styra, Daedala regarded Roxie with awe.

"She is already … beyond our wildest expectations."

Roxie sensed a wall of azure energy just outside the station walls.

"You want to take my place? Be my guest, love."

Blue arcs spread from her body. Beckoning those outside.

"You wouldn't dare," Daedala breathed.

Phantoms tore down the station around them. They scorched any wounded Jovians and threw concrete chunks at Styra. Dust and rubble billowed into the night.

Roxie ran.

"Wait!" Daedala cried, following her.

Three phantoms chased after them.

The station collapsed as shots and explosions rang out. *Icarus* hovered thirty meters away, its ramp extended. Covenant members motioned for Daedala to hurry.

An empty containment alcove waited on the ramp behind them. Waited for her.

"We can change everything!" Daedala called. "Roxie, please!"

Icarus came closer while a fireball blew from the station's ruins. She didn't flinch as shrapnel flew past her. The phantoms now crackled around Daedala.

Roxie aimed the revolver.

"Tell me what you promised Locust."

"I promised him you would live."

Roxie sucked in a breath, gripped the revolver tighter.

"Why?"

Even as azure hands neared her throat, Daedala remained still.

"Because he knew this was the only way you would survive this planet. As a Phase Three Hybrid. And that only I could give that to you."

Shaking, Roxie cocked the hammer.

"Bollocks. Tell me, goddamn you!"

"From the first tab you ate … to the first phantom you saw … you already knew this was your only chance. Cinn made you thus. You became everyone's avenging angel."

Crying out, Roxie fired again and again.

The shots sped like angry comets into each phantom, their destruction creating a blue halo around Daedala. Behind her came more phantoms, necrostructs, and a Burner, all attracted to Roxie's energy signature. Her heart hammered like an organic emitter, summoning demons from the Martian night.

The Draco's hammer clicked. Roxie blinked.

Blue clouds faded amid smoking necrostructs. The Burner, its eye sensors shot off, staggered from the mesa and tumbled far below.

Two Jovians dragged Daedala up *Icarus*'s ramp while she flailed. "No! We need her!"

"The mesa is surrounded," one Jovian said. "We must go!"

Her eyes met Daedala's. An eternity passed as they studied each other.

"I made you!" Daedala finally cried. "You are mine!"

Roxie gave her the finger.

The ramp hatch shut. *Icarus* streaked into the sky.

Gravjets circled the area while another carrier hovered half a kilometer away. In her enhanced vision, she glimpsed blue outlines and shimmering figures everywhere.

A single heat signature approached. She reached for more bullets in her belt.

"Fucking look at me, Trent."

Roxie slowly turned.

Aiming her pistol, Styra smoldered from a hundred different burns. Most of her armor and skin were scorched away, revealing blackened metal underneath. One of her eyes was missing. Crisped intestine dangled from her eviscerated gut.

"You missed your ride, love."

Styra's laughter was stuttering and mechanical.

"They'll be back once I've killed you. I was meant for this, not you. I'm going—"

Her head exploded in a burst of metal. Her body whirred, then collapsed.

Roxie held her breath as four barrels pointed at her.

Despite his tattered body, Dirty Cool stood calmer than a kill bot.

"Drop it."

The distant whoosh of gravjets leaving the carrier drifted on the wind. Emergency sirens echoed over Cydonia. There was less gunfire, fewer explosions.

"I mean it," he said.

Roxie still held the revolver in one hand, bullets in the other.

"Me too."

Dirty Cool tugged off his mask. A bloody cut ran the length of his cheek.

"Quit being stupid. I will frag your ass."

"Why? Harmon is dead, you killed Styra, and that Jovian tart is speeding back to Io. What've you got to lose, love?"

"Because you're not taking all this away. You think you're saving all these dumbasses, but you're not."

Roxie hummed with latent power. Arcs popped off her skin.

"And you are?"

He stepped closer.

"My sentence is almost up. I'm about to get the fuck off this rock. You're not messing with that."

For the first time she noticed a flower embroidered on the red bandana around his neck. It was really a girl's handkerchief. She recalled what Legs had told her earlier.

"What's your daughter's name?"

Sweat rolled down his face despite the cold air.

"Drop the goddamned gun!"

"Think she'll be safe? *La Rèsistance* will still want Cinn, the phantoms will still attack, and the UG will likely declare war on the sodding Covenant."

The four barrels stopped a few centimeters from her chest.

"You don't know shit."

"They'll never let you go. They'll keep the wars going, keep summoning phantoms so hunters can kill them—until they make another version of me."

"Millions might die, now that everybody saw that crazy shit you uploaded back there. People will riot, knowing the ghosts was a UG lie. Knowing that Cinn can turn you into a … whatever the fuck are you now."

"You already know."

"The Caravans will never find a home. My daughter will never …"

His jaw clenched. Heavy breaths pushed out his chest.

"You think I should just take a Cinn tab and forget all this shite?"

Dirty Cool glared at her.

"That's all you've ever done. Why give a damn now?"

"I've still got to earn my forgiveness. For all my fuckups."

He pressed the shotgun barrels against her chest.

"Like *Jubilee*? Or Aparajita? We're all monsters here. Cinn isn't forgiven."

"Then collect you bounty. Spend the creds on your daughter."

Dirty Cool's eyes widened. Seconds ticked by until he jerked back.

"Fuck you."

One by one, Roxie loaded bullets back into her revolver. The sirens were drawing closer. Searchlights stabbed into nearby ravines and valleys.

"What the hell are you doing?" he asked.

"I'm going to save a many people as I can from what's coming. Phantoms, mercenaries, hunters, UG jarheads—whoever I have to shoot to keep Mars safe."

Dirty Cool stuck his finger in her face.

"You're not Street Angel. That was a bullshit name, a joke. You don't have wings to escape all this. Damn it, you listening? Tell me who the fuck you'll save!"

She thumbed the last round into the cylinder. Snapped it shut.

"Myself."

He aimed the shotgun again. "They'll send me after you."

Roxie turned and started to walk down the terrace.

"I know."

"Me, Moloch, and all those new motherfuckers in the UGPD. Claymore, Jolly Roger … won't be no hesitation then!"

A frigid breeze whipped at Roxie. Sand stirred little dust devils along the terrace. She took a few steps, then looked over her shoulder.

"Tell me her name, love."

Dirty Cool glowered at her.

"Felicity."

"I bet she's beautiful."

He stared up at the stars.

"She is."

Roxie smiled, then clambered down the path.

Shimmering cerulean demons roved through the night as shots continued to reverberate over the landscape. Dingoes yipped somewhere to the west. An orange blur stained the east as *Crimson Aegis* continued to burn. She shut her eyes against all the glowing outlines, the wavelengths exposed to her.

She wasn't human or a phantom. Neither was she anyone's angel.

At least the ghosts in her mind could sleep at last.

Gravjets hovered near the carrier, now less than a kilometer away.

They would be tracking her, come morning.

She would be ready.

About the Author

"*Only when facing the extremes of environment, physics, and reality, do my characters realize who they are. Then I realize who I am.*"

Tony Peak is an Active Member of SFWA and an Affiliate Member of HWA. He is represented by Ethan Ellenberg of the Ethan Ellenberg Literary Agency. His debut novel *Inherit the Stars* was published by Penguin Random House in November 2015. His interests include progressive thinking, transhumanism, and planetary exploration. Residing in southwest Virginia, he has a wonderful view of New River. Find out more at: www.tonypeak.net

About the Publisher

This book is published on behalf of the author by the Ethan Ellenberg Literary Agency.
https://ethanellenberg.com
Email: agent@ethanellenberg.com

www.ingramcontent.com/pod-product-compliance
Lightning Source LLC
Chambersburg PA
CBHW070630100726
47907CB00007B/1918